Summer Campaign

Summer Campaign

CARLA KELLY

SWEETWATER
BOOKS

AN IMPRINT OF CEDAR FORT, INC.
SPRINGVILLE, UTAH

BC
113

© 2012, 2015 Carla Kelly

ISBN 13: 978-1-4621-1225-8

Published by Sweetwater Books, an imprint of Cedar Fort, Inc.
2373 W. 700 S., Springville, UT, 84663
Distributed by Cedar Fort, Inc., www.cedarfort.com

LIBRARY OF CONGRESS CATALOGING-IN-PUBLICATION DATA

Kelly, Carla, author.
 Summer campaign / Carla Kelly.
    pages cm
 Miss Onyx Hamilton is on the verge of making what everyone agrees is a perfect marriage. The overwhelmingly respectable Andrew Littletree is so taken by her virtue and beauty that he's willing to overlook the scandal clouding her birth and her lack of family and funds. But then handsome, charming Major Jack Beresford comes galloping into Onyx's sheltered life. With his wealth and aristocratic blood, Onyx knows it's highly improbable that he would ever ask for her hand. Fortunately, the laws of probability have no effect on what Onyx is ready to give this supremely unsuitable gentleman. Her heart.
 ISBN 978-1-4621-1225-8 (mass market : alk. paper)
 1. England--Social life and customs--19th century--Fiction. 2. Man-woman relationships--Fiction. 3. Interpersonal attraction--Fiction. I. Title.
 PS3561.E3928S86 2015
 813'.54--dc23
                              2014033617

Previously published by Signet/New American Library in 1989.

Cover design by Angela D. Baxter
Cover design © 2012 by Lyle Mortimer
Edited and typeset by Melissa J. Caldwell

APR 15 2015

Printed in the United States of America

10 9 8 7 6 5 4 3 2 1

For my daughter Mary Ruth Huerta,
and in memory of Sheldon Lundberg

Prologue

"I . . . I . . . W-WANT TO GO HOME."
Major Jack Beresford looked around him and
pulled his cloak tighter. He raised his shoulders
and hunched his neck down, but still the rain crept down
his back and settled in a discouraging puddle where his
belt was gathered tight to hold up someone else's breeches.

A dead man's breeches. This remembrance was to
himself only, so he did not stutter, thinking the memory
instead of speaking it. The cloak was borrowed, the boots
his own, and thank heaven for that too, because no one
else had feet so big. The uniform jacket was loaned on the
promise that it be taken eventually to Curzon Street and
given to its owner's little brother for adoration until some
future date, when the rightful owner returned to claim it.

"I-I'm going . . . home." He spoke out loud again to
give reassurance to the fact.

Jack leaned against the ship's railing and braced himself against the pitch and yaw of the cross-channel packet
boat. He would have liked better weather, but this was
familiar weather, foggy and damp and totally different
from the dry scorch of Spanish summers.

1

As he watched the dimly outlined cliffs, the mist gradually rose until he could see them for what they were, white cliffs decorated with seabirds that swooped and bobbed on the breeze until the air was sharp with their raucous welcome. Tears started in his eyes, but he had not cried since Badajoz a year ago, and he knew the moment would pass.

"Lovely sight, don't you know?"

Jack recognized the voice of his colonel and moved over, even though the railing for the entire length of the ship had no other people bellying up to watch for England.

"Ye-yes, lovely sight, sir." Jack cleared his throat. "But . . . but I do not wish ever to see it again."

"How's this, man?" asked the other officer.

"S-s-simple, Lord Carlton. To see this again would mean I was approaching England again. Th-that would mean I had been away. And I do not mean to be away—not ever again. No."

The colonel nodded and was silent for a moment, then he turned to look at him, compelling Jack to face him. "And what have you planned?"

Jack shrugged and would have turned back to the railing, but the colonel put out his hand and held Jack's arm.

"I want to know, Beresford. I really want to know."

"Well . . ." Jack looked down at his feet. "Home . . . home to Adrian, of course. His last letter w-w-worried me."

The colonel let go of Jack and reached into his pocket, pulling out a cheroot. He glanced up at the major and grinned. "Blasted Spanish habit. Think Lady Carlton will take one whiff and make me repair to another bedroom?"

Jack grinned for the first time. "S-sir, how long have you been gone?"

"Four years, same as you."

"I th-think she w-won't."

The colonel laughed. He scratched a flame from the lucifer he held cupped against the wind, but the match puffed out. The colonel crammed the cheroot back in his pocket. "But seriously, my man, what plans have you made?"

Jack turned again toward the water and watched the cliffs. The sunlight was watery, but the gleam of white was enough to make him squint.

"J-just home."

The colonel smiled and put out his hand again. "Several of us are hiring a chaise and four and posting together to London. Come with us, boy. You know your aunt wants to see you."

"No. You . . . you know what would h-happen."

"Beresford, so what if the ladies want to gather around and pat your arm and cry a few tears and make you tell the story again and again!"

"No. I-I'm no hero. I led heroes, but I'm no hero."

The colonel sighed. "That's the devil of it, Jack. You are. And don't walk away from me! I'm still your colonel, until such time as you see fit to officially resign your commission."

"S-sorry, my lord."

The colonel smiled in apology for his outburst and touched Jack again. "Stubborn burro. Foolish, stiff-rumped, back-up, blasted nuisance burro! I'll miss you, Jack. Promise to visit us when next you come down to London."

"I . . . I will, sir."

Leave-taking at the Dover dock was easier than he had dreamed. A slap on the back, a handshake, a promise here and there to visit, to drop in at Watier's, to down a bowl together some Christmas. All his gear was in a borrowed duffel bag. It was new, bought since the bombardment, and contained only a hairbrush, razor and cup, and his one good uniform, saved from the artillery barrage that destroyed the village because he had sent the coat and pants ahead to Lisbon for alterations. He had a few souvenirs for Adrian and Emily, and that was all.

He shouldered the bag and would have left the wharf, but he chanced to look around once more and ended up helping the wounded come ashore, long after the other officers were gone. He left them finally with the able-bodied men, protected from the drizzle under a long wooden porch. From the looks of the stains on the wood planking, the porch had long been sheltering the wounded coming back from Boney's wars.

He didn't want to travel by night, so he hitched a ride into Dover and had the carter drop him off at lodgings that held more promise than those closer to the docks. It was a small matter to speak for room and board for one night and ask the way to the nearest stable.

And then there was nothing to do but sit on the bed and stare at the wall and wait for sleep to creep up on him when he wasn't looking.

He did not surrender willingly. Even as his body cried out for rest and his eyes burned into his brain, he fought sleep.

Major Beresford, late of His Majesty's Forty-fifth, knew that he would wake up screaming. He knew that before his eyes opened wide, or someone shook him out of it, he would be back at Badajoz, and he didn't want to be there, not now especially, now that he was back in England.

His own screams woke him, as he knew they would. He could almost hear his heart beating faster and faster. He hunted around for the bedclothes he had flung off in his frenzy to escape and wrapped them about him as he shivered and perspired at the same time.

When he went downstairs in the morning, he knew that he had wakened the entire inn. He could tell by the way the innkeeper looked everywhere but at him as he paid his shot and went into the taproom. As he drank his ale and dipped his bread in it, he could feel people staring at him.

The ostler already had the horse saddled and ready when he crossed the yard. He flipped the man a coin.

"Good-o, Major, and thank ye."

Beresford nodded and swung into the saddle, securing his little bundle behind him. He breathed deeply of the sea air. The sky was sea blue and there were birds. Not the scavenging birds that flew around the battlefields, waiting for opportunities of their own to thrust and parry; not even the seabirds of yesterday, but small birds, wrens and swallows. English birds.

Major Jack Beresford didn't know if he could get home fast enough.

Chapter 1

⁓

THE REVEREND MR. ANDREW Littletree had come to propose. Onyx Hamilton had known for several days that he would. During his last visit, she had simpered and postured as she sat with Amethyst's mending, uttering "Is that so?" or "Really, sir?" in her soft voice, as the conversation demanded.

Conversation was never very demanding with the vicar. He required only an audience. It mattered not that she listened. He knew with the instinct of the truly self-involved that she would hang on his every utterance. Anything less than her total attention would never have occurred to him.

Onyx had discovered ways to make his weekly mono-logues educational. Before she heard his gig in the front drive, and certainly before his "Miss Hamilton, oh, Miss Hamilton" summoned her into the Blue Parlor (the Yellow was for death and company of a more illustrious nature), she mentally extracted a volume from the library of her lively brain and opened the book behind her eyelids, where he could not see it.

One week her private topic might be the poems of

Ben Jonson (although Lady Daggett did not approve of poetry about dead children or popish ideas). As the vicar ranged on and on about his virtues and the defects of others, and as she nodded and smiled over her mending, she was mentally reviewing the pitiful death of Solomon Pavy, or thoughtfully considering the romantic implications of supping of Jove's nectar.

She knew when her attention would be required. Always before he made a statement demanding comment, the Reverend Mr. Andrew Littletree would clear his throat. Then Onyx Hamilton would lower her needle and thread in her lap, raise her fine eyes to his countenance, and await the pearl soon to issue forth from his lips.

But this week, she knew the visit would be different. Lady Daggett had hinted so last night over the whist table, where Onyx allowed herself to be beaten with prodigious regularity.

"Onyx, the time is ripe," Lady Daggett had said in a tone that carried throughout the room. "I am sure that the vicar will bring himself up to the mark this week." To add emphasis to predestination, Lady Daggett laid down her cards with a snap and sat back in triumph. Whether it was in pleasure over her excellent hand or in satisfaction that at last Onyx would be suitably engaged and out of the Daggetts' establishment, Onyx did not know.

"How is this so, Lady Daggett?" she had asked. Playing whist night after night bored her, but it was no worse than the boredom she suffered each Tuesday week after week during the vicar's prosing, improving visits.

"He has asked to speak to Sir Matthew. That can only mean one thing. Are you prepared with your answer?"

Onyx was prepared with her answer, but one last shred of stubbornness compelled her to silence.

"Oh, come now, Onyx!" said Lady Daggett, tossing aside whatever remained of her patience. "You knew it would be this way, especially when Sir Matthew adopted my daughter Amethyst and not you. Come now, and do as you are told!"

Onyx's resistance crumbled in the wake of Lady Daggett's wrath. She knew that she had to accept the reverend. It was not a fact that filled her with any enthusiasm, but she knew her duty. And now it was knocking at the front door.

Onyx put down her needlework and looked into the mirror, fluffing her brown hair absently and tucking the lace a little higher across her chest. Andrew Littletree had made it plain to her in his roundabout way that he did not approve at all of ample proportions, but there wasn't a great deal she could do about her figure. There it was.

"And what will it be today?" she asked herself. "What will I occupy my brain with?" Ben Jonson could never do justice to the occasion. It would have to be the properties of oxygen. That was it. Her twin brother Gerald's schoolbooks had found their way into her room two years ago, when they had been threatened with extinction, and she had learned French by reading poor, headless Lavoisier's treatise on the properties of oxygen. Yes, it would be oxygen. She would require deep drafts of oxygen to get through what promised to be a trying interview.

She waited until the front door opened and closed and the footsteps hurried up the stairs, followed by a scratching on her door.

"Yes?" she asked.

"Miss Hamilton, it is the vicar."

She opened the door on the maid, whose eyes were round as breakfast biscuits. "Miss, I cannot imagine what is the matter, but my lady has shown him into the Yellow Parlor! You had better come quickly!"

The Yellow Parlor. It was reserved for deaths and other auspicious moments, and as she descended the stairs, she knew that she didn't want to enter the room. Her last venture into the Yellow Parlor had been two years ago when Sir Matthew pulled her inside to tell her of Gerald's death. She didn't want to go there again. She could still remember Sir Matthew's fingers on her arm, and the way he shook her when she started to cry and had hissed at her, "Enough of that, you silly girl! Do you want to upset Lady Daggett? I won't have it! Gerald's dead, and that's it!"

So it was. She had not cried another public tear for Gerald. She had not dared.

Onyx paused outside the door. She twisted Gerald's ring on her finger, relying on the sparkle of ruby and tiny diamonds to cheer her. She held her hand up to the light, watched the glitter a moment, and then opened the door.

The Reverend Andrew Littletree stood with his back to the door, over by the little collection of Sevres vases that Sir Matthew prized so highly. He had picked one up and was looking at it intently, holding it to the light, turning it this way and that.

I wonder if he is pricing it, she thought and caught herself before she laughed out loud. It would never do for her future husband to know that she thought him silly. Without a word, she went back out the door, closed it silently, and then opened it again, making sure that she was louder this time. When she looked at the clergyman again, he was standing in front of the table, the vase back in its usual place, shivering just slightly from the encounter.

"Reverend Littletree, how nice to see you," she said in her quiet voice. "What is it that brings you here today instead of your usual Tuesday?"

The vicar smiled at her and then posed as he always did, one foot pointed in front of the other, one hand on his hip, the other clutching his coat front, as if he were on display before a congregation. "I had rather an important matter to discuss with your stepfather, or rather, Sir Matthew, my dear," he replied. "If indeed, I may call you 'my dear.'"

She made no comment but came farther into the

room, wishing herself anywhere but there. If she looked apprehensive, it did not show. The vicar was warming to his subject, and consequently, his thoughts were entirely self-directed.

"Of course," he continued, "once we become one, I will not call you by such a tender name. It would not be seemly in a clergyman, do you think?"

She had a thought on the matter, but he did not hesitate in his headlong prose long enough to reflect that questions required answers.

"Yes, we will reserve this moment as a matter between us, and it will never come up again," he continued. "Never." The sound of his voice resonating in the room must have pleased him, because he repeated "never" again, and then motioned for her to take a seat nearby. She sat and waited for him to clear his throat.

He did finally, after striking another pose. "Onyx . . . I may call you Onyx, mayn't I?" he asked. "Although I cannot imagine what Lady Daggett was thinking when she named you. I do believe I will call you . . . Mrs. Littletree . . . later. Yes, that would be appropriate, I think, and certainly less . . . pagan."

She stared at him in wonder. *If this is a proposal, how very odd*, she thought.

The vicar sighed heavily, as if he regretted what was to follow, as if the weight of marriage to her was already onerous. He came toward her quickly, and for one precarious moment, she thought he was going to drop at her feet. She knew that she would burst into laughter if he did, so she was relieved when he lowered himself carefully down beside her on the settee and possessed himself of her hands.

"Miss Hamilton, you know that in my position I must have a wife."

She said nothing. His hands were clammy, and he smelled faintly of wax candles.

"Lady Bagshott was reminding me of that fact only

last week." He inched closer to her, and Onyx resisted the urge to slide further away. "She says marriage is my duty. As the worthy example for my entire parish, Miss Hamilton, I must marry."

He cleared his throat again, and she closed her eyes. The reverend giggled. "You are a woman of such becoming modesty, Miss Hamilton! Such a virtue makes me able to overlook your decidedly unfortunate origins and your total lack of monetary expectations."

When Andrew Littletree said nothing else, Onyx opened her eyes. He was still there. No amount of wishing had changed that. When he still said nothing, but only continued clearing his throat, she said, "Sir, is there something in particular you wish to say to me?"

She recalled the vicar to himself. He divested himself of her hands and clutched the front of his black frock coat again, turning slightly so he was in silhouette against the morning sun. When he had arranged himself in what he must have considered a matrimonial tableau, he spoke.

"Miss Hamilton, will you make me the happiest man . . . and do yourself a great honor . . . by marrying me?"

She looked at him in silence, watching the way his Adam's apple bobbed up and down, noting the flecks of dandruff in his thinning hair and the raw little nicks where he had cut himself shaving that morning. *Every day*, she thought, *for the rest of my life, I will wake up and see that face on the other pillow.* The thought was daunting, and words failed her.

But he was speaking again, made bold by his initiative, and secure in the knowledge that both might and right were on his side, not to mention the Church, and probably God.

"My dear Miss Hamilton, Sir Matthew has already told me how grateful you will be for my offer, and he has given his full approval. What more could you ask?"

What more, indeed? "Very well, sir, I will marry you," she replied in a voice not like her own.

The vicar did not notice the strain in her voice. He captured one of her hands again, a hand now as cold as his own, and carried it to his lips. "Do not think I am overly bold, Miss Hamilton, if I seal this agreement with a kiss." He touched her hand to his lips, and she closed her eyes again and sighed.

He mistook the message. Quickly he lowered her hand to her lap. "Oh, my dear, I did not mean to make you overwrought! I feared it would be thus! I will remember to keep my affections within proper bounds, indeed I will!"

He was speaking louder now, and Onyx patted his hand, fearful that someone in the hallway outside would overhear this silliness. "Really, sir, do not be alarmed. I was merely . . . overcome with your generous proposal for a moment."

But the vicar was warming to his subject and would not be silenced. He wagged a warning finger at his betrothed. "Miss Hamilton, there can be no place for passion in marriage to a clergyman. You must remember yourself."

She swallowed. "I will, sir. I promise. It was merely the excitement of the occasion . . ."

He rose then and pulled her to her feet. "Very well, Miss Hamilton. Lady Bagshott tells me that ours should be an early marriage, one this summer, if possible. She feels that my parish will benefit by our good example, particularly during the fall harvest, when winnowers and reapers sometimes forget themselves in the haying fields."

Onyx could not follow his logic. Hers was a clear mind, a direct mind, one unacquainted with the twists and turns of a brain made foggy with overmuch contemplation on the Divine and too much deep breathing of incense.

"We will be married from Chalcott, of course." He

peered at her, as if to detect some disagreement, and saw none. "It is to be our home, thanks to the generosity of my patroness, Lady Bagshott, and her brother, your own dear Sir Matthew, who has been so condescending in this matter."

She waited for him to continue. He looked at her and smiled at what he saw, someone with a scrupulous mind, a pretty but not too pretty face, someone highly conformable and of gentle demeanor. In short, a woman who, with proper admonition, would do him credit.

He cleared his throat. "Miss Hamilton, I did not think it a wise idea to seal our engagement with a ring."

If Onyx was disappointed, she did not show it. She had only one goal in life right now, one aim that propelled her toward the door: to get away before she burst into tears, or laughter, whichever came first.

"Such a vulgar display as a ring is not the thing for the wife of a man of the cloth. Not the thing, indeed! I would not sully the beauty of your hands with something as frivolous as a bauble." The vicar looked with pointed displeasure at Gerald's colorful ring on her right hand.

She paid him no mind but continued on her stately way to the door. She was slightly ahead of him. He cleared his throat again, and the hairs rose on the back of her neck. *I could grow weary of that even before the wedding*, she thought as she composed her face into a smile and turned around.

He came to her quickly and took her hand again, holding it against his chest, where she could feel his heart leaping about like a rabbit in a trap. "My dear, before we must leave the comfort of this charming room and venture into the glare of your family's approbation, may I not . . . kiss you?"

Dutifully she leaned forward. His lips were wet on hers and seemed to have no life of their own. *I have just been kissed by a cod*, she thought. The notion was so diverting that only the greatest force of will kept her from laughter.

The vicar seemed satisfied. He wiped his lips, straightened his neckcloth, and opened the door with a flourish.

If Wellington's army and all his Spanish and Portuguese allies had been bivouacked in the hall, Onyx Hamilton could not have been more surprised by the sight that greeted her. Was it possible that the Daggett family employed so many servants? What could possibly have drawn most of them to the corridor that afternoon? Did the walls need scrubbing? Were the draperies out of adjustment? Was there a great need for the windows to be cleaned? That tiny crack by the casement replastered?

And there were Lady Daggett and Sir Matthew standing by the large windows that gave out onto the Bedford countryside. Certainly Onyx had spent many an afternoon curled up in the window seat looking across the fields toward the river, but Sir Matthew had never been inclined to pause there before this moment. Whatever Lady Daggett was showing him seemed to have his full attention. This, in itself, was odd. Nothing ever claimed Sir Matthew Daggett's full attention except his quarterly 'Change reports and the miseries of others.

The only person missing was Amethyst, and that oversight was soon remedied. Even as Onyx and the vicar stood in the doorway of the Yellow Parlor, she heard the front door slam and soon saw Amethyst Daggett hurrying up the stairs.

She was dressed in her riding habit and carried her crop. Everyone else was still intent on continuing the charade, but Amethyst took one look at Onyx and the vicar and threw herself into Onyx's arms.

"Oh, Onyx, I am so glad! Just think! Soon you will be Mrs. Littletree! What a marvelous thing, don't you think?"

Like the vicar, Amethyst did not mean a question to

be answered. Even as Onyx opened her mouth to reply, Amethyst whirled around and hurled herself at her stepfather. "Oh, Papa, am I to be maid of honor?"

As this was a more important question, Amethyst did pause for a reply, looking up at Sir Matthew, who was forced to end his little performance at the window and regard the happy couple over his adopted daughter's tangle of blonde hair.

"Congratulations to you both," he said. "Surely this is a great day for the family. The first wedding." His words were promising enough, but all animation died there. "As for you, puss, I think you will not be a maid of honor. This will be a rather simple wedding, as, I am sure you realize, propriety dictates."

Amethyst began to pout as she tinkered with the silver buttons on her stepfather's waistcoat. Tears welled up in her amethyst-colored eyes and slid along her long eyelashes, where they hung like dew.

Onyx looked away. She had watched Amethyst practice that spectacle in the privacy of her room until it was perfected to an art. Now would come the little sniff, then the catch in the throat.

Amethyst did not fail. Sir Matthew was blancmange in his stepdaughter's hands; he capitulated after the little sniff. "Now, now, puss, don't start in! Maybe Onyx can have one attendant at her wedding. Come on, my darling, and let me show you that little frippery I picked up for you in the city."

Amethyst sniffed back what emotion there might have been behind the tears that no longer threatened to fall and went down the stairs, arm-in-arm with her father. The servants melted back to their various posts throughout the house, and that left the happy couple with Lady Daggett. She came to them with arms outstretched. She kissed Onyx carefully on the cheek and twinkled her eyes at the vicar, who blushed and tugged at his collar.

"How happy I am for this moment, and such a surprise!"

Onyx scrupulously overlooked that little piece of fiction.

"Thank you, Mama . . . I mean, Lady Daggett."

"How this would have pleased my poor dear Reverend Hamilton," Lady Daggett continued, and then dismissed her first husband from her mind. Turning to the vicar, she continued: "Sir Matthew tells me that you have plans for Onyx this summer, even before the wedding."

"Oh, indeed, Lady Daggett. Sir Matthew has given me permission to spirit her away to Chalcott."

This was news to Onyx. "And what, sir, would be the purpose of that?" she asked.

"Miss Hamilton, it falls to you the happy pleasure of setting the vicarage to rights before our upcoming nuptials."

"Oh?"

He turned to Onyx and looked her in the eyes, perhaps for the first time since their tête-à-tête had begun in the Yellow Parlor. "Lady Chalcott has said she will spare no expense to renovate the vicarage, but, Miss Hamilton, it has fallen into sad repair since the death of Reverend Palmerston. What with that nasty bit of unpleasantness in Spain, it has been impossible to find anyone else until now."

"Should *you* not supervise this task?" she asked.

"Oh. I cannot! I am leaving immediately for Cambridge. Do you not recall that I am sitting for a series of lectures on homiletics?" He paused then and struck another pose, as if the mere mention of sermonizing moved his limbs of their own accord. "Lady Bagshott felt it would be a very improving thing."

"I cannot doubt that," Onyx murmured.

"She is so condescending," he went on, "so concerned with the welfare of others. She has even consented to allow you to take your meals with her for as long as the repairs of the vicarage take."

"How good of her," said Onyx rather grimly. "I am sure I do not know what to say."

He looked at her. "Yes, that is a problem you must learn to deal with, Miss Hamilton. Sometimes your conversation is so brief, I wonder if you are attending to all that goes on." He patted her hand. "You will learn, my dear, I am sure, how to be a proper wife for a vicar, to say and do what is expected of you." He struck another pose. "You, Onyx Hamilton, will be an example for the entire parish."

Some demon within goaded her on. "Such a responsibility, sir! I wonder that you should consider me capable of learning proper behavior."

The vicar was not well acquainted with sarcasm. "I shall teach you, my dear, as will Lady Bagshott, I am sure."

There was no tiny pause that Lady Daggett could not fill. "My dear sir, Onyx is a dutiful and conformable girl. She will be everything that you require. Won't you, dear?"

The look she gave Onyx was the equivalent of a swift kick under the table.

There ended the interview. With a bow to Lady Daggett and cod's lips on Onyx's cheek, the Reverend Andrew Littletree took himself off, descending the stairs with such majesty that Onyx was forced to turn her little laugh into a coughing fit.

Lady Daggett eyed her charge. "Onyx, you must learn to school your tongue and follow the admirable example of my daughter Amethyst, who is a delight to all who know her."

"Yes, Mama . . . I mean, Lady Daggett."

"It is high time you were no longer a millstone about Sir Matthew. I was beginning to despair."

Lady Daggett turned to follow the vicar down the stairs. She looked back at Onyx. "Reverend Littletree means for you to be off as soon as possible. Apparently there is much work to be done at the vicarage." She paused as if waiting for a comment. "Don't you have anything to say, Onyx?"

Onyx could feel the tears welling up behind her eyelids, feel the familiar pain in her chest that she had fought so hard to ignore for the past two years, but Onyx Hamilton was a stubborn person, as stubborn as her brother, Gerald, had been.

"No, Lady Daggett, I have nothing to say. Everyone has already said everything for me. If you'll excuse me now, I'll go pack."

By walking fast, she made it to her room before the tears started to fall.

Chapter 2

THE HORSE THAT TOOK MAJOR Beresford out of Dover wasn't much of a horse, but there was nothing else left in the stables. He knew the nag would get him as far as London, where they could part company, probably under mutual consent.

"I've eaten better horses than you," he said out loud to the beast as it sauntered along under leaden skies. "Cooked on a green stick over a fire. Raw during a siege."

Spring was late in coming this year. It was nearly June, but the hawthorn buds were just beginning to blossom. When he stopped to eat the bread and cheese the landlord had slapped together for him, he noticed lilies of the valley hiding along the fence row and smelled, but could not locate, lilacs in bloom somewhere.

What a change it was from hectare after hectare of olive trees that appeared dead even when they were alive, and windmills with tattered sails, exhausted from the effort of turning round and round. Here there were no denuded areas, no rubble and craters that were the autograph of an army with serious intentions. Here summer was struggling to come, and nothing more. It was enough.

As he rode farther and farther away from the coast, he felt that the weight of Spain should lift from his shoulders. For four years he had planned for this to happen, but it was not so. The tune he hummed was Spanish; he quit humming. He could not dismiss his thoughts so easily.

And so Major Jack Beresford remembered battles fought, horses eaten, friends dead. After being held captive a few hours by his memories, he no longer noticed the countryside. He was in Spain again.

By early afternoon of the next day, he arrived in London. Jack had never spent much time there; he had always been glad enough to leave the social schedule to Adrian and Emily. London was dingier and busier than he remembered, and again he felt the deep, almost overpowering longing to keep riding toward home until he either got there or dropped from the effort.

"But such an effort requires a better horse," he said, "or at least one that is a more adroit conversationalist, if we are to survive this journey in relative good humor."

Jack had to ask directions several times and rely on the reconnoitering skills he had honed in Beau Wellington's service, but before the tall buildings had completely buried the narrow streets in afternoon shadows, he found himself in front of Herkabee and Marsh, the family solicitors. A better horse demanded more money than the Spanish coins that jingled in his pockets.

The porter refused him admittance. Despite his irritation, Jack Beresford's whimsical humor overcame the moment. In his borrowed uniform, he knew what he looked like to the man: an out-of-work veteran scrounging around respectable establishments for something to eat. He had already noticed several such men in ragged uniforms on London's streets.

He rattled the coins in his pockets, but the porter just ignored him.

"I need to speak to Alistair Herkabee," Jack insisted.

"What you need, and I don't mind saying it, is a visit to the guard of the watch. Move along, now."

It seemed to be good advice but, under the circumstances, was less than adequate. The major probably would have been standing there until after closing hours if Alistair Herkabee himself had not suddenly appeared in the doorway to usher out a well-favored client. The solicitor looked at Major Beresford and then looked again. The slight smile on the solicitor's face grew and spread as the porter glanced from one man to the other in dismay.

Herkabee held out his hand to the major. "It would seem, sir, that you have returned from the wars at last."

Jack shook his hand. "I have. I'm n-not going back."

"Good. Come in, man, and let me know how I can serve you."

When he emerged from the building an hour later, the Spanish coin had been replaced by good English money, enough to get an amiable horse, new clothes, lodging for a year if he wanted it, and sufficient capital to "drop a bundle at White's like a proper gentleman again," according to Alistair Herkabee, "and get drunk as a lord."

As Major Jack Beresford's plans included only the first item on Herkabee's list, he murmured his appreciation again to the solicitor, who followed him out the door and onto the street. He mounted his hack and headed immediately for Tattersall's, which proved to be closed. Beresford yanked off his forage cap and slapped it against the door. As he turned and leaned against the door, hat in hand, someone dropped a coin in it. He looked up, amusement chasing away his anger, into the face of Marshall Tidwell, a former classmate at Harrow and, from the looks of his high collar, intricate tie, and pants a color reminiscent of an overdone biscuit, a Bond Street beau. He stared at the dandy, then he took the coin out and bit it.

"Sound money, sir," he growled, falling into his best North Country accent. Tidwell had no idea who he was. "Any m-more where that come from, gov?" He lurched away from the wall and the dandy leapt backward into the street, forgetting all dignity in his desire to get away, much to the delight of a carter sitting on a nearby wagon.

Beresford took another step toward him, and Tidwell readied himself for instant flight.

"Wait a minute, Tides, don't you know who I am?"

It was Tidwell's Harrow nickname. The dandy paused and turned his head slowly, not so much because he was afraid as because with his tight neckcloth a rapid movement would have strangled him. What Tidwell saw did nothing to encourage him: a soldier, rather tall, with brown eyes, brown skin that spoke of a foreign clime, and auburn hair much too long for the dictates of Dame Fashion. There must have been some expression in the soldier's eyes that brought back rowdy evenings, but not until Beresford smiled did Tidwell extend his hand.

"Jack! '*Cum Juno omnipotens . . .*'"

"'*Longum miserate dolorem*,'" Beresford concluded, grasping the dandy's kid-gloved hand. "And that's all the *Aeneid* I remember. H-Harrow was a l-long time ago."

"Dashed long time ago. I didn't recognize you."

"I didn't expect you to. Put any bears in a steeple lately?"

Tidwell laughed. "Did we do that?"

"I remember something about a bear. It may have been a boar."

They began to walk toward the city again. Tidwell motioned to his tiger to drive his curricle beside them as Beresford's horse trailed behind.

"Lord Paget has a set of prime goers on the block tomorrow. I toddled over for a look. Too late, it seems."

"I'm here for a horse. What time in the morning does Tatt's open?" Jack asked.

Tidwell looked at him in wide-eyed surprise. "You're

asking someone who never rises before noon? Spain must have dazzled your brain-box."

Jack smiled, but at the same time felt a flash of irritation that four years ago would have dumbfounded him. *Was I like Tides Tidwell once?* he asked himself as they sauntered along.

"I just want to get home," he said finally, when his temper cooled.

Tidwell stopped still. "You can't do that! Didn't I remember hearing the newsboys shouting something this time last year about the 'Hero of Badajoz?'" He took Beresford by the arm, careful not to get Spanish dust on his coat of palest blue superfine. "Look, man, come with me this evening! You'll make me the darling of Almack's. The toast of Watier's. Even my tailor may extend my credit."

"No, Tides," Jack said firmly. "I'm going home."

"Suit yourself then," Tides sniffed.

They parted company at the corner. "My regards to your brother and Emily," Tidwell said as he climbed into his curricle again and took the ribbons from his tiger. "By the by, we didn't see them in London during the Season, and a Season without Emily Beresford to brighten it is dull work indeed."

"I th-think Adrian is ill."

Tides waved his hand, "Well, man, tell him to stiffen up a bit! Tell you the truth, the Season was dashed flat this year. Adrian wasn't here with his cockroach races. You tell him from me that since he wasn't here, no one, absolutely no one, placed any wagers on Prinny's waistline or Caro Lamb's lovers. Or is it the other way round? Dashed if I know."

Jack watched Tidwell as the tiger climbed around to his perch behind. Again he felt that same shock. *Did we do things like that? I don't remember it*, he thought.

"Well, sir, if you won't make me London's most

popular host, can I at least offer you my rooms on Half Moon Street?"

Jack shook his head. "Thanks, but I'll lodge here tonight."

Tidwell looked around him. "If you do, keep your door double-locked and prop a chair under the knob." He leaned forward confidentially. "This is not a well-regulated neighborhood, Jack."

"I could tell you about caves I've slept in, Tides, and cannibals I've seen," said Jack, stepping back.

Tides jerked on the reins and his horses danced about. "Merciful heaven, man, what kind of a place is Spain?"

Jack smiled at him. "There's a war going on," he said gently. "Have you heard of it?"

Tidwell wasn't listening. He was busy with his horses. When they were under control again, he nodded to the major and started off.

"One moment, Tides!" Jack called. "Know any good inns on the road north?"

Tidwell slowed his horses. "Dashed good place near Bramby Swale, near Morecombe: Dry sheets *and* good ale. Morecombe's about where you'd reach by nightfall. Called the Fox and Hare. Anyone can tell you where it is."

Jack Beresford was at the door of Tattersall's when it opened the next morning. Fifteen minutes later he had a horse, a big rangy black monster that reminded him of the first horse shot out from under him at Ciudad Rodrigo. Fifteen more minutes added a saddle, bridle, and reins to his acquisitions.

London was still foggy with morning mist from the Thames and smoke from breakfast cooking fires when Major Beresford started toward home on the Great North Road.

Leaving Lady Daggett and Sir Matthew caused Onyx Hamilton so little pain that she spent the first hour of her journey toward Chalcott wondering if there was a heart left in her body.

She knew that Lady Daggett would miss her. Now there was no one except Amethyst—who was notoriously undependable—to fetch her shawl, her netting, no one to listen to her complain about the price of beeswax candles or the difficulty of keeping good servants. No one would be there to mediate when the cook suffered some insult— real or imagined—at the hands of the butler.

Onyx also knew that Lady Daggett was relieved to see her go. Gone now, finally and at last, was the tangible reminder of an act of unforgivable kindness by her first husband, the late Reverend Hamilton. Now Lady Daggett would no longer have to be ever vigilant against the smiles and stares. Surely the polite world would soon forget Onyx Hamilton and leave the field clean for her own daughter, Amethyst.

Onyx rested her cheek against the tiny pane of glass in the carriage, a relic from Sir Matthew's past that he grudgingly loaned for the journey. "I don't know why that . . . that girl cannot ride the stage to Chalcott," he had fumed at Lady Daggett, almost, but not quite, out of Onyx's hearing.

"I own it would be more fitting, considering her station," Lady Daggett had replied. "But what would our friends and neighbors say if they heard of such a thing?"

And so Sir Matthew had whined and complained for the better part of two days about the personal inconveniences and dreadful expense that he was incurring, and all for "your stepdaughter." Onyx wondered all over again, as she had since she came, wide-eyed, into his household when she was twelve years old, if Sir Matthew even knew her name.

When she could not bear another one of his tirades,

Onyx became an earlier riser and avoided him at breakfast. As she was seldom included in the family circle for dinner if anyone of any consequence was present, she succeeded in staying out of range of Sir Matthew's hurtful tongue until the morning she left for Chalcott.

Her trunk had been packed for two days. She had packed twice. The first time, her clothes had been in one trunk, neatly folded with tissue paper. She had filled Gerald's trunk too, this one with his dress uniform and his books and the bird nests he had collected.

She got no farther than the upper landing with Gerald's trunk. Sir Matthew stopped her. "See here, girl, put that trunk back. Do you want to break the carriage springs and ruin my horses? You'll take your things, and nothing more. We'll take good care of poor Gerald's things."

She knew they would not. As soon as the carriage rolled out of the driveway, Sir Matthew would order Gerald's effects burned, and he would be lost to her.

Kettering helped her get the trunks back to her room. Swiftly, she unpacked her dresses and put them back in the clothes press. When her trunk was empty, she put Gerald's books in, the letters he had written from Spain, and his dress uniform. There was enough room for half her dresses, shoes, and the fabric that would become her wedding gown.

Alice Banner, Lady Daggett's one grudging contribution to Onyx Hamilton's upbringing, had helped Onyx repack the trunk but drew the line at Gerald's bird nests. "Onyx, some things we can't save. And don't look at me like that!" She smiled and patted Onyx's cheek. "Here, help me shove these under your bed. Won't that make Mrs. Clouse furious when she finally cleans your room?"

The two conspirators laughed like schoolgirls as they pushed the ragged nests into a dark corner under the bed.

"There, now. It looks like an invasion of hedgehogs," said Alice, peering under the bed on her hands and knees.

Onyx smiled. "Mrs. Clouse will throw up her hands and scream and run to the Gorgon. She'll threaten to resign and Lady Daggett will be forced to raise her pay." She sat on the trunk while Alice buckled the straps. "Lady Daggett may have spasms."

"Oh, I hope so," said Alice.

As Onyx took her leave of Sir Matthew's household, her mother offered her cheek. Onyx kissed her, leaning forward carefully so as not to disrupt the perfection of Lady Daggett's muslin morning gown. She curtsied to Sir Matthew.

"Mind you be a good girl. Lady Bagshott, I don't mind telling you, doesn't have much use for inferior behavior."

That was too much. "My behavior has never been a trial to you, Sir Matthew," she said and allowed Kettering to help her into the carriage.

"Good for you, miss," the butler whispered as he helped her arrange her skirts. "The servants and I—we want to wish you the very best."

She touched his hand. "Thank you, Kettering." She wanted to say more, but she couldn't.

"Did you get all of Gerald's—"

"Everything except his sword," she whispered back.

"Hurry up, Kettering, you old dodderer," Sir Matthew roared. "We haven't got all day to stand about! My breakfast is getting cold!"

The butler placed a light carriage robe over her lap. "We'll find a safe place for Gerald's sword in the servants' hall, miss."

"Thank you, Kettering, thank you," was all she could trust herself to say.

A wave to Lady Daggett, who was already turning to go into the house, and they were off, lumbering down the long driveway. Onyx looked back only once, when they were some distance from the manor.

"I leave with no regrets, Alice," she said simply to her companion.

"Oh? Well, I have a regret, Onyx," replied her servant. "I regret that you have to marry that paralyzing bagpipe!"

Onyx looked at her for a long moment. "Let's not think about it right now. August is a long time away."

"Not far enough," muttered the woman, settling herself in the corner and folding her arms emphatically. After a few miles her head nodded forward and she slept, snoring lightly, as the countryside moved slowly by.

As much as she loved Alice Banner, Onyx was glad for the solitude, glad for the fact that, even if for only a few days, there was no one to tell her what to do. *I'm on my own*, she thought, and the notion filled her with no fear. *Even if it's only until I exchange the tyranny of Sir Matthew's house for Lady Bagshott's rule, I will enjoy the moment.*

She smiled to herself, thinking of the wish game she and Gerald began to play after Papa's death. Her smile turned militant. No matter how Lady Daggett had railed at her and scolded, Reverend Hamilton would always be Papa. The game had started out simply enough. "I wish Papa would come for us," Gerald had said after the funeral.

"I wish that he would come for us and take us to Bath," she had chimed in. They had all been to Bath once for Papa to drink the waters, and to her young mind, it had seemed the most magnificent of cities.

"Well, I wish he would take us to Bath and buy me a horse."

And so it went, until they were laughing at the extravagance of dreams that would never be fulfilled but were pleasurable because they shared them with each other.

"I wish that Reverend Littletree would fall headfirst into a bog wallow," she whispered out loud.

That was hardly kind, even as much as she detested him.

"No. No. I take that back. I wish instead that something exciting would happen." What, she did not know. "Something exciting enough to get me through this summer," she added, glancing over to make sure Alice was still asleep. Onyx knew she was too old for such games, but it was fun, even if for only a moment, to forget that she was twenty-two years old and headed toward a future not of her choosing.

Her wish came true almost as soon as the words had left her lips. As the coach negotiated a curve in a wooded area not far from Morecombe, the back axle gave a sudden creak and Sir Matthew's elderly carriage crashed to a halt.

They were tipped at an alarming angle. Alice Banner, fully awake now, shot out of her corner and into Onyx's arms. "Onyx! What can be the matter?" she shrieked as she struggled to right herself. Onyx and Alice were crammed together against the squabs, from which the dust rose in alarming puffs. Alice began to sneeze.

"God bless you," said Onyx as she struggled to help Alice straighten herself.

The servant's hat was askew and perched over one eye, giving her an almost piratical look. She again tried to right herself and fell to the carriage floor with a plop.

Against her will, Onyx Hamilton felt laughter welling up inside her. She knew it was the height of impropriety to laugh at a servant, especially one as dear to her as Alice Banner, but she couldn't help herself. There was her beloved Alice, sitting on the carriage floor, sneezing. Each explosion dropped the hat lower and lower over her eye.

A valiant attempt at control succeeded finally. Onyx helped Alice to her feet. Alice glared at her and perched her hat back where it belonged.

"I thought I taught you something besides rag manners, young lady!" she barked in commanding tones.

Onyx wiped her eyes. "Oh, you did, Alice, but I have to confess, this little accident is entirely my doing!" She abandoned herself to another gust of laughter that abated only when John, the coachman, opened the door and looked in.

The coach was far enough on its side so that the door appeared to be in the roof. John leaned inside, reaching for Alice. "Are you ladies all right?" he asked anxiously.

"Quite well, thank you, John," said Onyx, with only a small giggle betraying the well-bred tones of her voice. "Nothing the matter with us except that our pride is slightly wounded."

She helped Alice stand and leaned back as the servant grasped the coachman's hand and scrambled out of the carriage with a flash of petticoats and striped stockings. Onyx untied her hat and tossed it out the window after Alice. She straightened her skirts, dusted off her pelisse, and then held up her hands for John, who pulled her out and set her carefully on the roadway.

All of their luggage had tumbled off the coach's luggage rack. Onyx's hatbox had burst open, scattering her few hats across the road, where they perched like feathered birds too large to fly. The sight made her laugh, but she put her hand to her lips. She could tell from the look that Alice was giving her that the servant was in no mood for additional levity.

John Coachman was unwise enough to address some prosaic comment to Alice, who turned on him. "This is outside of enough, sir," she raged. "Suppose Onyx had been killed! Must you drive like a Corinthian?"

John blinked his eyes, and Onyx was forced to turn away to keep from laughter. In his shabby livery a size too large, a hat that sat squarely on his ears, and his obvious state of agitation, John was as far from a sporting dandy as That Beast Napoleon was from Father Christmas.

"Oh, dear," Onyx said faintly to herself. "I must set a better example." When she felt fully composed, but still not trusting herself to look at the aggrieved coachman, Onyx gathered her hats from the road and brought them back to the coach.

John had retreated from Alice Banner's wrath to his beloved horses, where he stood talking to them and casting darkling glances at the servant. "Wasn't my fault!" he muttered as Onyx approached him, hats in hand.

"I'm sure it was not," she said soothingly, petting one of the horses, which still trembled in agitation. "Should you not unhitch the animals? Wouldn't it be better for them?" she inquired kindly.

She handed the hats to Alice and returned to help the coachman.

"'Tis no task for a lady," he protested as she helped him remove the traces that held the horses to the whiffletree. Gathering up the long reins, she led the horses to a tree by the edge of the road and looped the ribbons over a sturdy branch, making sure that the animals had length enough to graze. When she was sure they were comfortable, she returned to the carriage, where John was gazing at the back axle.

"Snapped clean in two, miss," he said. "That's what comes from using ancient equipment last fit for the road when our good old king was sane!"

"Is that any way to address Onyx Hamilton?" asked Alice, still in her high ropes.

"Never mind, my dear," said Onyx. "I understand quite plainly what John is saying. One can hardly argue with his logic." She turned back to the coachman. "The question is, sir, what should we do about this?"

He took off his hat and held it in front of him like a beggar. "Well, miss, I can ride one of the horses for help."

He looked doubtful. "I think that is an admirable idea, John," she said to encourage him.

John shifted his overlarge hat from one hand to the other. "But, miss, that will leave you and Alice alone here on the roadway." His face clouded again, and he crammed his hat back on his head. "I asked Sir Matthew about post-boys, but he only laughed at me! Even after I reminded him about murderers and thieves!"

Onyx touched his arm. "John, it's only early after-noon, and we will be fine. Surely you do not have to go far?"

He shook his head. "No. At least, I do not think so, miss. We are only a few minutes from Morecombe. It's a middling place, to be sure, but there must be someone about handy with tools."

"Well, then," she urged, "if you hurry, we'll be on our way soon enough."

He left with real reluctance, sitting atop the gentler of the two coach horses, looking back at them until the newly leafed trees swallowed him from view.

Alice had removed the trunk from the fastenings where it hung. She dusted off the top and sat down on it, patting the remaining space. "Come sit, my dear; we may be here for a while."

Onyx did as she said, hitching herself onto the trunk. She raised her dress and surveyed the ruin of her stockings. "I'm glad they weren't silk," she said, fingering the rip that ran from her knee to her ankle.

Alice snorted. "You've never had a pair of silk stock-ings in your life!" she exclaimed.

"No," Onyx admitted, "not unless Amethyst decided she didn't care for the color of hers." She smiled to herself. "Remember when everything she wore had to be peri-winkle blue? And how she pouted and stormed until Sir Matthew gave her a curricle of matching color?"

"I remember," said Alice grimly, looking about her for

villains and cutthroats. "And here we sit on a cast-off carriage, at the mercy of whatever brigands choose to wander by. It's not a fair world, miss."

"No, it's not," said Onyx. "But the sun is warm today, and I don't mind."

She didn't. Every hour idled on the road was one hour farther from Sir Matthew and one hour stolen from Lady Bagshott. Onyx had learned early in childhood to count her pleasures in small thimbles instead of bushel baskets.

She knew so little of Lady Bagshott, a woman of middling age and height who appeared at Sir Matthew's only for special events. Or at times of great sadness. Onyx closed her eyes and thought of Gerald.

The shadows of afternoon were lengthening across the road when Onyx heard the sound of horses approaching. She looked up from the needlework in her hands. John must have found help and was returning at last. She put her embroidery hoop back in her reticule and glanced up again as Alice sucked in her breath.

Four men rode toward them, all of them with pistols ready. The scissors fell out of Onyx's hand. She got down off the trunk and watched them as they rode closer and dismounted.

She heard a small sound beside her as Alice slid off the trunk in a swoon and lay in a heap at her feet. One of the men laughed, but it was not a pleasant sound. Onyx wanted to kneel down and straighten Alice's dress, but her legs already felt like jelly. She stood where she was, leaning against the trunk, and watched the men.

Two of them were clad in ragged uniforms patched with bits and pieces of other uniforms. One of the other men, the leader obviously, was swathed in a black cloak that was almost green with age. His boots were patched, and his hat was as small as John Coachman's was large.

Interest almost overcame the sick feeling in Onyx's stomach. Highway robbery obviously wasn't a paying concern in this part of England. *And they want to rob me?* she thought. *Oh, dear.*

She stood absolutely still, frozen into marble, as the men came closer. They came toward her without any fear or stealth. They had probably been watching her for some time and knew that there was no one around to help.

When he was only a few paces from her, so close that she smelled his unwashed body, the leader stopped and pulled back his tattered cape with a flourish. Onyx watched him, fascinated. He pointed his pistol at her and pulled back on the hammer.

"Stand and deliver, miss," he growled.

"Oh, my," said Onyx Hamilton. "This is indeed an awkward situation."

Chapter 3

⁓

THE HIGHWAYMAN BLINKED AND lowered his pistol. "What did you say?"

Onyx would have backed away, but she was up tight against the trunk, and there was poor Alice, even now moaning and shaking her head. Onyx knelt by her servant, and the man shuffled backward a few steps.

"You certainly frightened my companion, sir," she said as she brushed the hair from Alice's eyes. Alice opened one eye and then the other, moaned, and closed them both again.

The highwayman remembered himself and raised the pistol. "I want all your valuables, miss, and no putting me off."

Onyx rose to her feet. "I would never do a thing like that, sir," she replied. Her heart felt as if it were fluttering in her throat. "It's just that I have nothing of any worth."

He pushed the pistol against her shoulder and moved her forcibly away from the trunk. Onyx grabbed Alice under the arm and pulled her away, propping her up against the carriage wheel. A glimmer of light in the road caught her eye. With a smooth gesture, Onyx picked up the embroidery scissors she had dropped and pocketed them. It wasn't much defense against four brigands, but she felt better.

Standing in front of Alice, Onyx watched as the men surrounded her trunk and broke it open, spilling the contents on the road. Her nightgowns and petticoats tumbled out in a froth of lace. The muslin dresses she had sewn and mended over and over with such care were picked up and tossed aside.

Her gold necklace with one pearl, a christening gift from Papa, went in one soldier's voluminous pocket. She wanted to protest, but the other soldier was watching her closely, and she did not like the look in his eyes. *I will hold very still*, she told herself.

Her only other pieces of jewelry were a garnet necklace and matching bracelet, and both disappeared as fast as the pearl. As the highwayman stood close by, the remaining brigand tossed out the rest of her dresses. When he came to the brown-wrapped package of silk that was to be her wedding dress, he gave a shout and tossed out the whole bolt like a party streamer. The delicate fabric shivered in the breeze and caught and tore on the bushes by the roadside.

Onyx brushed aside angry tears. She knew there would not be another such piece of cloth from Sir Matthew. She knew, from years of living on the fringes of his household, that she would never be given such a present again, and that she would be berated and hounded and nagged about the loss of the silk until she was completely dragged down by the weight of his displeasure. The thought of being forced to throw herself on the charity of Sir Matthew or her future husband to replace that silk made her tears flow faster.

The soldier-brigand who stood holding the horses looked at her. "I'm sorry, miss, real sorry about that silk," he murmured in a low voice.

Onyx glanced at him in surprise. She could never explain to anyone that it wasn't the silk, but the humiliation that made her cry. She looked away. This was one of the men trying to rob her. How dare he?

The leader had reached the contents of the trunk that belonged to Gerald. With an oath, he threw out the books and the letters that Gerald had written her from Spain and which she had carefully saved. The letters scattered across the highway and into the woods, far beyond her reach ever again.

"No, please!" she said, starting forward. The other soldier, the one who had been watching her so intently, grabbed her by the arm. She tried to shake him off, but he gripped her so tight that she cried out.

And then the leader was holding Gerald's good dress uniform, the one that his regiment had shipped home to her. He fingered the fine fabric and touched the row of buttons.

"A Light Bob, eh?" the man asked.

She nodded, the tears streaming down her face now. "Please," she begged, "it's all I have left. Don't take it!"

The leader only gave her a look of great disinterest and ripped off the gold epaulets. Onyx shrieked and struggled to free herself.

The buttons were next, little gold pellets that scattered to the road as the highwayman slid his knife down the double row.

Quicker than her captor could see, Onyx pulled out her embroidery scissors and stuck the scissors in his arm. With a scream of his own, he let go of her and dropped to his knees as Onyx ran toward the leader, who was busily engaged in tearing off the fancy goldwork on the sleeves of the mutilated uniform. Crying and yelling, she pummeled him with her fists.

The horses reared up and distracted her for a moment as she realized the other soldier had loosed the reins and was running toward her. He grabbed her and shook her until her hair came loose from its pins. Still she fought him, trying to bite and scratch, as the leader imperturbably continued his destruction of Gerald's uniform.

The soldier pulled her away from the leader and pinned her arms to her sides. "Don't, miss, he's a bad one," the man said.

"But you don't understand," she gasped, trying to shake loose. "That's all I have!"

When Gerald's uniform was in tatters in his hands, the leader tossed it away and sauntered toward Onyx. He grabbed her around the waist. As she struggled, he grabbed her chin and forced her to look him full in the face.

"Is that all you have for us, miss?" he asked, his voice softer and more frightening at the same time.

She nodded, pinned into submission.

The highwayman rested his free hand on her hip. "I'm sure my mates and I could find something else." He looked over his shoulder at his other men. "But I'm first."

There was no mistaking his meaning. With a smile he let go of her.

Onyx sucked in her breath and took a step backward until she was up close against the highwayman who held her. She thought he was trembling as much as she was, but she couldn't be sure.

She looked around in dismay as the man she had stabbed came closer too, like a wolf circling a wounded deer. He raised his hand to slap her, but as she waited, flinching, the blow never came. He made a queer sound in his throat, even as he still stood with his arm raised. Onyx looked up and watched in horror as a dot of red bloomed on his forehead and his eyes went strangely blank. He fell face forward at her feet.

She shook herself free and looked beyond the man into the woods, where she could barely make out the shape of another man on horseback. She spotted him only by the puff of smoke that lingered in the air, which was still filled with the swirling letters Gerald had written to her.

She couldn't tell what he was doing, but his hands were moving swiftly; he was reloading his pistol. When he guided the horse onto the road, the man was ready to fire again.

"Stand back," he called to her, and she darted toward the coach and Alice.

He was dressed as the other highwaymen, in a tatter of several uniforms. There was nothing about this person that would have distinguished him from those who were already robbing her and threatening her virtue, except that he seemed to be on her side. She did as he said, crouching down and making herself a smaller target.

The leader pulled up his pants with one hand and picked up his own pistol. Without a word, he fired at Onyx's savior.

The man stayed in the saddle, but Onyx knew he had been hit by the ball. His sleeve ruffled above his elbow and she watched little spatters of blood rise in a sudden rush. The man grabbed at the horse's mane and looked at Onyx. Carefully he transferred his gun to the other hand and tossed it to her.

"Shoot him," he commanded, even as he fell from his horse.

They all watched the pistol rise and fall in a lazy arc.

Alice tugged at her dress, trying to stop her, but Onyx ran into the road and caught the pistol.

"Pull back the hammer," said the man from the ground where he lay.

She did as he said, turning on the leader, who was running across the road to her. The man stopped and watched her, a smile spreading on his face. He held his own pistol by the barrel now, ready to swing it at her.

"You wouldn't," he said. His voice was silky soft and the most irritating sound to Onyx.

"I would," she replied, amazed at the coolness of her own voice. "Don't take another step." Onyx raised the gun with both hands and pointed it at his midsection.

He smiled at her. It was the same condescending smile that she had tolerated for so many years from Sir Matthew Daggett. He took another step. She fired.

Her aim wobbled, but she did not miss entirely. The leader fell to his knees and grasped his side with both hands, calling out to his cohorts to aid him. Neither man moved.

Onyx turned to the man on the ground. "I don't know how to load it," she said.

"Bring it here," he said.

She knelt by him and handed him the gun. With an effort, he turned onto his back and reloaded the weapon as the blood ran down his arm and spread in a dark pool alongside his body. The other men in the clearing had not moved, but as he handed her back the weapon, one of the robbers ran to the leader, who was swearing and moaning. He helped the highwayman to his feet.

Onyx stood away from her injured savior and in the road alone. She pointed the weapon at the highwayman's head. "I won't miss this time," she said, her voice as steady as the bloody weapon in her hand. "Not from this close." She lowered the pistol until it was aimed directly below his belt. She heard the wounded man behind her chuckle. "Do it," he said.

The highwayman lurched toward her and she pulled back the hammer. He shook his head and muttered something to one of his fellow brigands. The two of them turned and stumbled toward the woods, where their horses had bolted when the firing began.

Onyx continued to follow the leader with the pistol, walking within a few paces of them as they melted into the forest. She heard the leader groan as his henchmen threw him onto the horse. She waited until they were gone and then turned her attention to the one remaining brigand who had not fled the clearing.

He put his hands up high over his head. "No, miss, no," he said.

"I wish you would leave," she said. Her voice was not as steady now, and the pistol began to shake in her grasp.

"Come toward me, lady," said the wounded man on the ground who had come to her rescue.

She did as he said, backing up, not taking her eyes off the bandit, who would not leave. She knelt by the man, crouching close to him, so close that she could feel his warmth. His blood was soaking into her dress, but she felt strangely safe beside him.

"J-just stay close," he said. "We'll see what his game is."

The soldier-bandit made no move toward them. He lowered his hands and in a moment he was crying.

"I meant no harm!" he sobbed. "Truly I did not! There was nothing else for me to do!" He cried until Onyx thought her heart would break.

"Poor man," she said softly.

"Poor man, my happy backside," snapped the man beside her. "B-beg your p-pardon, lady. Too many years with the Forty-fifth."

The crying soldier looked up. He wiped his eyes and rose to his feet. Onyx pointed the pistol at him again, but he seemed oblivious of the threat.

"Did you say the Forty-fifth?" asked the brigand, coming closer.

The wounded man rose up halfway on his good elbow and looked at the soldier. "Yes, the Forty-fifth, the b-best regiment in the whole . . . the whole army," he amended, with a glance at Onyx. "So you had b-better get out of here," he concluded, dropping back to the ground again.

"Major Beresford!" gasped the brigand.

"Well, bless me," said the major weakly. "Lady, let me put my head on your lap,"

She cradled his head in her lap, and he took the gun from her. She put her arms on his shoulders in a protective gesture, which was not lost on him. He tilted his head back and smiled up at her. "We . . . we'll be all right," he said.

The brigand stood up slowly, his eyes on Beresford's pistol. He brought his heels together smartly and saluted. "Private Kit Petrie," he said, "late of His Majesty's Forty-fifth Foot." He held the salute for a moment and then came closer, dropping to his knees in front of the other man. "I'm sorry, sir. I've been looking for a job for six months, and I was hungry." He watched for some reaction. "Don't you remember me, sir?"

Beresford lowered the hammer on the pistol and laid it across his lap. He closed his eyes for a moment. "I remember you, Petrie," he murmured. His voice sounded drowsy now, his words slurred. "You . . . you'll have to help us, Private."

Petrie saluted again. "That I will, sir!"

"He's fainted, Private," said Onyx quietly. "Can you quit saluting please and help me stop the bleeding?"

The ex-infantryman sprang to her side. "Help me get him out of this coat," he said. The two of them tugged at the garment. "I'm glad he fainted," whispered Onyx. "Else how could he bear this?"

When the coat was off, she folded it and placed it under the major's head, which still rested in her lap. "We need some cloth." She looked up at the silk, torn and fluttering from the bushes. "We have plenty of that."

Without a word, the private ran to the bolt of silk. He ripped off a large chunk. Onyx cringed at the sound, and sniffed back her tears again. *Poor, dear man*, she thought, immediately ashamed of herself. *This Major Beresford probably saved my life—my honor, certainly—and I'm caviling about material. Goodness, how petty I have become. I sound like Amethyst.*

The private was aided by Alice Banner, who had come to her senses and seen what needed to be done. They worked quickly and gathered a large handful of the beautiful material. Onyx leaned across the major and slowly ripped the torn sleeve, trying not to jostle him. She exposed the wound, which continued to bleed copiously. The smell of blood made her light-headed, but she turned her head, took a deep breath, and stayed where she was.

Private Petrie was at her side then. He folded a hunk of the silk into a thick, neat square and handed it to her. "Put it right on the bullet hole and clamp down. I'll wrap it tight after you do that."

She bit her lip and did as he said, leaning forward with the heel of her hand on the wound, pressing down until the bleeding slowed and then stopped.

"Members of the Forty-fifth are the best clotters in the army," said the private. He had a dreamy expression on his face, remembering other battles, obviously.

He was jerked back to the present by Alice Banner, who slapped him on the shoulder. "Watch your gutter language around Miss Hamilton," she snapped.

Petrie only blinked at her. Alice put her hands on her hips and looked at Onyx in exasperation. "He hasn't the slightest notion of his impropriety!" she exclaimed as her bonnet slid, pirate-like, over her eye again.

"It scarcely matters, Alice dear," Onyx replied. She pressed down on the wound again and then took away her hands as the private deftly wound a strip of silk around the major's arm. "You've done this before, haven't you, Private?" she asked.

"Oh, many times, ma'am," he said proudly, pleased that someone admired his handiwork. "Fixed up the major's thigh once before. That bullet nearly took off his . . ." He paused, reddened, and then glanced at Alice, who was already looking grim about the lips. "I've . . . I've doctored him before. He's a rapid healer."

43

I should be so offended by this vulgar man, thought Onyx as she held the major in her arms, *but I'm not. What can be the matter with me?* "Maybe it really isn't important," she said out loud.

"Pardon, ma'am?" asked Private Petrie.

"Oh, nothing. Nothing. Private, we need to get the major to shelter and find a doctor. He is bleeding so badly."

"There's a farmhouse not far from here," he offered. "The farmer's not what I'd call a generous soul, but—"

"Surely he will not turn us away," Onyx interrupted.

"I hope not, ma'am," said Petrie. He didn't say anything more, but Onyx wondered what was troubling him.

The major's horse had not strayed. Petrie helped her mount the horse. She straddled the big horse, blushing with embarrassment as Major Beresford regained consciousness and winked at her. "Beautiful legs, ma'am," he said. His voice sounded far away, but there was a chuckle in it.

She considered all manner of replies but chose the simplest one. "Thank you, sir," she replied as Petrie helped him into the saddle in front of her.

"Can you hold him, ma'am?" he asked anxiously as the major sagged against her.

"I think so, Private," she replied, wrapping her arms around the man and grasping the reins.

Major Beresford was still conscious. He rested his head on her chest. "I have died and ascended to heaven," he said in a low voice before he fainted again.

She couldn't help laughing at the major's outrageousness. "What kind of man is this?" she asked out loud to no one in particular.

"The very best, ma'am," replied Petrie. "Take good care of him, mind."

She nodded and tightened her grip around the major.

She held him and watched as Alice and Private Petrie gathered as many of Gerald's letters as they could and stuffed everything back in her trunk. The clasp had been broken off, but Alice sat on it as Petrie strapped it down.

"What should we do now, Onyx?" Alice asked as the private helped her down from the trunk.

How odd, thought Onyx. *They are asking me for advice. No one ever asked me for advice in my life. I have always done what I was told to do.* She looked down at the man in her arms as he stirred and tried to sit up. "Can't imagine why I'm such a baby about this," he muttered before he lapsed into unconsciousness again.

"We must find a doctor," she said, guiding the major's horse closer to the carriage. "Just leave everything. We can't wait for John Coachman to return."

"But your clothes, Onyx, your possessions!" exclaimed Alice. "I should remain here."

"No, and that's final," Onyx replied, her lips set in a firm line. "It's too dangerous. Nothing I have is worth your life."

"Bravo," said the major softly. She hadn't realized that he was conscious again. "You're a trooper."

She patted his chest, "Private, you said you know where there is a farmhouse. Lead us there and be quick about it."

"Yes, ma'am," said Petrie. He saluted smartly, and Onyx turned her face into the major's hair to hide her smile.

The farmhouse was not far, and never was a sight more welcome to Onyx than the thatch-roofed house with smoke curling from the chimney. She could see a man in the barnyard. He stood still, hands on hips, watching them as they approached, Private Petrie in the lead.

When they were within hailing distance, Petrie dropped back. "I can't go on, miss," he said to Onyx.

"Oh, how is this?" she asked. "Private, I need you."

Petrie shook his head. "Ma'am, you don't understand.

He might . . . he might recognize me. We've been hanging around these parts."

She didn't have to ask who "we" was. "You can't abandon the major," she said, throwing out her trump card.

"Well, no," he admitted, "I can't." He sighed. "Maybe they won't know me. Soldiers all tend to look alike, don't they, ma'am?"

"Rather like Chinese," said Major Beresford. He sat up and leaned away from Onyx. "Why don't you leave the talking to me and the lady?"

Major Beresford turned his head slightly, and she could tell that every movement pained him. "My name is Jack. What is your name?" he asked when he got his breath back.

"Onyx," she answered, "Onyx Hamilton."

"Onyx? What an odd name. Did your mother have a predilection for semiprecious gems?"

She shook her head. "My . . . father was rather a romantic."

"And you're not?"

"I never thought about it." Onyx felt her face redden, and she rushed on. "I have a sister named Amethyst."

She waited for comment. There was none, and she realized that Major Beresford was grimacing with pain.

"I will tell the farmer that the major is my brother," she said to Petrie. "I do not think he would approve of any other explanation." *How strange this situation must seem to others*, she thought. *How strange it seems to me.*

Petrie eyed her doubtfully. "You two don't look anything alike. He won't believe you."

"Well, what should I do?" she snapped. There was no reply from the private. *It's up to me, then*, she thought as they came closer and stopped in front of the farmer.

The man did not appear pleased to see them, and in spite of their need, Onyx could understand this. They were a ragged mob, a bloody gathering of shabby people. She remembered then that her hat was back at the carriage, and her stockings torn. Her gloves were so bloody that she had thrown them away back by the carriage.

"Sir," she asked, as the man approached the fence with some reluctance, "can you help us, please? We have met with an accident."

The man climbed over the fence, but he did not come close. "Indeed you have. What on earth has happened to your husband?"

Onyx was ready to tell him the truth, or at least less of a lie, but there was something in the farmer's swift and minatory appraisal that told her there would be no welcome if they appeared any more out of the ordinary than they already did.

She handed the reins to the farmer, who looped them over the fence. "I'm Onyx . . . Beresford, and this is my husband, Jack," she explained, amazed at her glibness. She threw aside every bit of breeding she had been taught and rushed headlong into certain destruction. "Major Jack and his batman, Private Petrie here, are just back from the Spanish wars. We're on our way home to . . ." She paused. *Dear heaven above, where did they live?*

"To Sherbourn, in Yorkshire," said the major. "I . . . it's been four years. My d-dear wife met me in London. We were set upon by thieves." His voice trailed off again, and his head sagged forward.

"I don't know," said the farmer, rubbing his jaw and looking at Petrie, who tried to stay well back. "This one, here, he looks familiar. I don't know. I don't want to be party to any havey-cavey doings. The wife and I, we're Methodists," he said, as if that were sufficient explanation for his reluctance to be party to any nonsense.

"Private Petrie has relatives in the vicinity," Onyx lied. "You may have seen him about in years past. But see here, sir, we need a doctor. Is there a bed somewhere for my husband?" She put her hand in Jack's pocket and drew out his wallet. "We have money to pay. Please help us."

It was an easy matter to allow the tears to spring to her eyes. She had watched Amethyst practice her art in front of the mirror on many occasions and knew just how to make her lip quiver and when to sob out loud. But as the tears pooled in her eyes, she realized that lessons from Amethyst weren't necessary. Either way, the farmer didn't have a chance.

The farmer, after another moment's long consideration, pulled the major over his shoulder like a sack of meal and started for the house. Private Petrie helped her down.

"Pretty good, ma'am!" he said. "A body would think you'd been lying all your life!"

Alice sniffed and thumped him. "Mind your tongue, Private!" she hissed.

They followed the farmer into the cottage and up the stairs to a small bedroom under the eaves. The farmer put the major down as gently as he could, but the wound reopened and began to bleed heavily again. Onyx sat down on the bed and pressed down hard on the bloody bandage.

"Oh, sir, go for the doctor at once! If anything should happen to my beloved husband, whatever would I tell little Ned!" She cast herself across Jack Beresford's body and sobbed.

The farmer turned and ran down the stairs. "A bravura performance, Onyx," said the major, his lips close to her ear. "I didn't know we had a son. Does he favor you or me?"

She sat up quickly and would have laughed if she wasn't so distraught. "I . . . I thought that would hurry him up." She paused and watched him. "I wish you would not look at me so! I cannot imagine what possessed me! What else was I to do?"

He shook his head. "Onyx, you are truly magnificent.

You have my permission to conjure up any number of sons and daughters, as long as the daughters look like you." He smiled at her. "The sons too, f-for that matter."

He closed his eyes again and did not reopen them, not even when the farmer's wife came upstairs with a basin of warm water and several towels. The woman was large and red-faced and smelled strongly of yeast. Little pills of dough clung to her apron, and Onyx realized she had been taken away from the family bread-baking. She set the basin on the little table by the bed. "Here, madam," she said, handing Onyx a soft cloth. "I'll help you get him out of those clothes, and we'll clean him up."

Onyx gulped and did as she was bid. The farmer's wife—her name was Mrs. Millstead—had few questions. She was more gentle than her appearance would have led Onyx to suspect, and she carefully took a pair of shears and slit the major's shirt and pants off him. Onyx tugged off his boots as Mrs. Millstead began washing Jack Beresford, talking all the while.

"Mrs. Beresford," she said as she scrubbed his legs, "do you suppose he has a scar from every battle?"

"It's very likely," said Onyx softly. She touched the infamous scar to which Petrie had already alluded. "The wonder to me is that he survived." She thought of Gerald and tears sprang to her eyes. She turned away.

Mrs. Millstead stopped. "I may be forgetting myself, Mrs. Beresford. Would you prefer to do this by yourself?"

Onyx whirled around. "Oh, no, no," she said hastily. "I mean, Jack's such a big man. I'll need help turning him. Please don't go."

When the major was clean, Onyx covered him with a sheet and gently cut away the silk bandage. The bleeding had stopped, and she could see torn muscles and bits of bone. She bit her lip. "Will the doctor be here soon, do you think, Mrs. Millstead?"

The woman put her arm around Onyx's shoulders.

"Oh, don't you fret. He'll be here directly. Why, before you know it, the major will be home in Yorkshire playing with little Ned."

"Oh, yes, little Ned," said Onyx, recalling her fictitious son.

"How old is the dear boy?"

"He's . . . he's three," said Onyx as she dribbled water around the gaping wound and wondered how much deeper this path would lead her.

"Oh?" said Mrs. Millstead. "Didn't my husband say the major was only just returning after four years?"

Onyx blushed and stared down at Jack. "You see, Mrs. Millstead, he was on leave only just before that. He's never seen little Ned, who is really three and a half."

The major shifted his weight and gave out a groan that sounded suspiciously like a laugh. Onyx bent over him, and he winked at her. She glared at him and then looked up at the farm wife, who was wringing out the bloody cloth.

"Dear madam, could you not fetch me a small glass of port? In the event that my dear husband regains consciousness?"

Mrs. Millstead opened the window and threw the water into the courtyard below. "I will. Here, I've wrung out this clean cloth. For his face, my dear. I'll be right back."

She left and Onyx pulled up a small stool and sat down near the bed. "Sir, you are incorrigible!" she whispered.

Beresford opened his eyes wide. "I? Incorrigible? My-my dear wife, I must also be a dedicated lover. So little Ned was conceived on my last wild fling before returning to Spain?"

"I did not say that!" she said, mortified completely, her state of mind wavering somewhere between laughter and tears. "Oh! I may strangle little Ned before you even get a chance to see him!"

The major began to laugh, holding onto his arm. "It hurts to laugh. You will kill me yet, fair Onyx."

"I'd like to," she retorted, softening the blow by wiping his sweat-stained face gently with the damp cloth.

"But be kind to our child," he said from the depths of the washcloth.

She couldn't help laughing. "Serves you right if it hurts," she gasped and then covered her mouth so Mrs. Millstead wouldn't hear.

The major was only warming to his subject. "And not in recent memory has anyone . . . anyone . . . fingered any of my less-obvious scars. Ladies of quality have changed since my last furlough."

That was too much. She picked up the stool and carried it to the far side of the room, plunking herself down. Mrs. Millstead came into the room then and handed her a glass of port. "For your dear husband," she whispered and tiptoed out of the room again.

"How thoughtful of you, wife," said the major wickedly. When she didn't come any closer to the bed, he smiled at her. "I'm sorry, Miss Hamilton. I've put you in a terribly awkward and embarrassing position." He paused a moment. "I *am* thirsty."

She stood, paused, and then came back, pulling the stool next to the bed again. She put her hand under his head and raised him up so he could drink, wiping his lips when he finished.

"I am sorry too, Major Beresford," she said quietly as his eyes slowly closed. "How can I forget so quickly that you saved my virtue and probably my life?"

She could tell he heard her because he smiled. He was still sleeping when the doctor came. Onyx eased herself out into the hall, where she stood shivering in the warm light until Mrs. Millstead claimed her and took her downstairs.

Chapter 4

ＯNYX COULD NOT BRING HERSELF to sit quietly in the little front room of the farmer's house. Alice sat there calmly enough, sipping tea and silently keeping her reflections to herself, but the room seemed too small, too confined. Onyx felt like an exhibit at a zoological garden. She knew that if she remained a second longer in the parlor she would begin to pace back and forth like a panther.

Onyx caught a glimpse of herself in the tiny mirror just inside the room. Her hands went immediately to her hair, and then she noticed the blood that flecked her arms from nails to elbows.

"My stars," she said out loud, surveying the ruin of her once-neat-and-proper traveling dress. "I look as though I have been in battle."

The farmer's wife was still hovering nearby. "Mrs. Beresford," she announced in the tone of one not accustomed to any disagreement, "you'll want to follow me into the kitchen. I have some nice hot water in there."

Onyx meekly did as she was told, thankful for something to do while the doctor was upstairs. She scrubbed her arms and face until her skin glowed pink. There wasn't much she could do about her dress, but she did remove her ruined stockings and wash her legs.

She was sitting there wondering how soon she could locate clean clothes when she remembered John, the coachman. Her hand went to her mouth. "My stars," she said again, and leapt to her feet, forgetting her shoes. She ran into the farmyard, calling for Private Petrie.

She found him in the barn, where the farmer had taken Beresford's horse. He sat huddled on an overturned milk pail, complete in his misery. When he looked up at her, she saw that he was on the verge of tears. Wordlessly she sat next to him on the straw-covered floor.

"He's . . . he's . . . dead?"

The words were wrenched out of him. Onyx took his hand. "Oh, no! The doctor is with him now." She squeezed his hand. "Private, I don't know anything about wounds . . ." She shook her head and amended, "I don't know anything about anything, but I do not think he will die from this."

He looked at her then, and the wretchedness in his eyes made her want to turn away. To her credit, she did not but continued to hold his hand.

"Don't you understand, Miss Hamilton?" The words were torn out of him. "I could have killed him! And you! I don't know how I came to be in such low company!"

"Except that you were hungry, Private Petrie, and no one in England would hire you," she said in excuse. "Everyone gets hungry. Everyone has to eat. The important thing is, you helped us instead." She raised herself to her knees and touched his shoulder. "I don't know the major very well. Surely not as well as you must. But I do know him well enough to be confident that it will be your kindness to us that he will remember."

Petrie sighed and let go of her hand. "I hope you are right, miss. I don't want it any other way."

It would have been easy then for both of them to succumb to melancholy, sitting there in the dark barn, but Onyx hadn't time for melancholy. She stood up suddenly and pulled Petrie to his feet.

"You must help me now," she said. "Please, Private, you must go back to that clearing and wait for my coachman to return. I cannot imagine what he will think if he returns there and finds that dead man." She paused. "And we are gone, and the place is so . . . bloody."

Her plight recalled Petrie to his duty. "I will leave at once on Major Beresford's horse," he said, eager to be doing something. He pulled the saddle off the hook and hurried to the stall. "What on earth am I to tell your coachman?"

What indeed? "I . . . I don't know . . ." She faltered. He waited for her to continue. *Why is it nobody makes decisions but me?* she thought, half in exasperation and half in vexation at her own shortcomings. "Just tell him what happened and get him to follow you here. I'll think of something by then."

"Perhaps if I were to move that corpse into the shrubbery?" he asked.

"Oh, yes, Private. I think that would be best."

Onyx stayed in the barn until Petrie left. She almost wished she had gone with him. Anything would better than standing around and waiting. *How odd this is*, she thought. *For years and years I have waited on people and been a paragon of patience. I have cajoled the servants and calmed the family tempests and tolerated insufferable Amethyst with complete equanimity. Look at me now. I cannot even collect my thoughts. And I have become a hardened liar.*

She hurried back to the farmhouse, pausing in the kitchen only long enough to clean off her feet, pull on her shoes again, look in on Alice in the parlor, and then bolt the stairs two at a time to the little bedroom under the eaves.

The door was open. She looked in. The doctor was kneeling by the bed, hunched in great concentration. As quiet as could be, she sidled into the room, hugging the wall. She was incapable of remaining outside or downstairs, beside herself with worry for this man she scarcely knew.

The doctor glanced around. "Mrs. Beresford," he said in a low voice. "Come closer. I think your husband is trying to say something to you."

She did as he said. With his good hand, Beresford reached for her. She came around to the other side of the bed and took his hand, holding tight to him and sitting carefully beside him.

"Yes, Jack?" she said softly. The room was so quiet she could hear the clock ticking.

Beresford had already soaked the pillow with his sweat. When he did not say anything, only watched her intently, hungrily almost, she looked at the doctor.

"The ball is embedded in the bone. I've been removing bone fragments."

She winced at his words and clung tighter to Jack's hand. He seemed not to mind. She wondered why he did not say anything, until she noticed how tightly his teeth were clenched together, as if he were just barely holding on to his own composure.

"I've removed most of the fragments. I think," he added. The doctor's glasses had slipped far down his nose. "But I have old eyes. Mrs. Beresford . . . would it be too much? Or could you come over here and have a look yourself? I daren't leave any fragments. They'll just cause trouble as they work themselves out."

In a dream, she unlaced her fingers from Jack's, put his hand on his chest, and came around to the doctor, sitting down when he stood up and peered into the wound.

Her stomach heaved in revolt, but she ignored it and stared resolutely into the wound until the horror became almost abstract. "I see fragments," she said suddenly. Her voice was high-pitched and tinny to her ears. "What can I use? What do you have?"

"Here." The doctor slapped a pair of long-handled tweezers into her hand. "Get them out. I just can't see them."

She put one hand on Jack's bare shoulder and took a firm grip on the tweezers with her other hand. She hesitated, her lips drawn into a thin line, until Jack reached up with his other hand and touched her face. "Go ahead, wife," he said. "I can manage. You are here."

The doctor sighed. "He's been telling me what a bonny lass you are, Mrs. Beresford, what a game goer."

She was too terrified to feel any shame at their deception. Working slowly and carefully, she removed the remaining fragments, thinking as she did so of the endless games of jackstraws she had played at Amethyst's insistence when her stepsister was much younger. *I must not move anything that is not a fragment or I will lose this game*, she thought.

The sweat trickled down her neck. The doctor dabbed at it. She smiled her thanks to him but did not turn her head. One by one, she dropped the tiny bone chips into the ceramic bowl the doctor held close to her elbow. Her back ached from hunching over. Doggedly, Onyx continued until she was done. She looked up at the doctor and put the tweezers in his hand.

Her own hands began to tremble then, so she held them tightly together until the moment passed. She moved aside for the doctor.

"You're a wonder, madam," he said, wiping the tweezers on his blood-speckled waistcoat. "Now, I will remove the ball, and then we'll see. Perhaps you would prefer to wait outside?"

She would have much preferred it, but she could not leave Jack by himself. His eyes pleaded with her to stay, even if he could not say anything. Already his lips were pressed tight together and the muscles in his jaw worked.

Onyx tiptoed around to the other side of the bed and sat there again, holding Jack's hand against her leg. When the doctor probed for the ball, Jack's fingers dug into her thigh. She winced as he ground his teeth. He gasped and relaxed his grip on her leg as his eyes rolled back in his head.

"Thank heavens," said the doctor. "I thought he would never do that. Your husband is a tough man, Mrs. Beresford."

She nodded, not really hearing him. In another moment he raised the probe in triumph and plinked the little lead ball into the basin. Onyx felt the sweat break out on her back, and she shuddered.

The doctor spent some minutes just staring at the wound, turning his head this way and that, inspecting it from several angles like a sculptor scrutinizing a piece of art. Finally he shifted his scrutiny to her.

"If the major were alone, I would suture this right now and leave him to the mercies of this household." He paused and cleared his throat. "Since you are here, I will wait a day or two."

She waited for him to continue. He dabbed around the wound. "There may be other fragments. I want you to keep this clean and look for them several times a day." He smiled at her over the rims of his spectacles. "I'll leave you some fever powders, for I know you will need them."

If she had thought of escape to Chalcott and Lady Bagshott's mercies, she had already scotched that scheme by declaring Jack her husband. She had to remain, no matter what. As she gazed down at Jack and wiped the hair back from his forehead, she wasn't sure she could have left anyway.

"You must only tell me how to go on, doctor," she murmured. "Surely we will manage."

"I know you will," he replied. The doctor ran his hand down Jack's sheeted leg. "He has been wounded many times before—and worse than this, from the look of him." He nodded and smiled at her. "I do not suppose he has ever been in better hands before, madam, and I do not speak of mine."

He told her what to do then, how to care for Major Beresford. She listened intently, knowing that she was absorbing only one word in ten, praying that she would overlook nothing that was vital. The weight of her responsibility descended, and she knew that in some way she did not even question, she would never be free of it again.

The doctor left. Alice Banner came into the room, her eyes wide. "What are we to do when John Coachman arrives, Onyx?"

Onyx looked up from the end of the bed where she sat. "We'll remain here until the major is better." She met the mutiny in Alice's eyes and calmly stared it down. "I have promised."

There was nothing to say. Alice took a chair by the window and remained silent while Onyx cleaned around the wound, covered it with a layer of gauze, and pulled the sheet up higher on Jack's chest. She wanted to change his soaking pillow for a dry one, but she did not wish to disturb him in any way.

She came downstairs that evening only long enough to make a few remarks that she couldn't remember the moment after she uttered them and to push the excellent meal around on the plate. She finally excused herself and went back upstairs. Jack was feverish. Onyx stirred the powders into warm water and with Alice's help roused him enough to get him to drink the mixture.

When the moon was casting its shadows in the room, Onyx heard Sir Matthew's coach rattle into the farmyard. She closed her eyes in relief. "Dear God, I thank thee," she breathed.

Mrs. Millstead came into the room. "I'll stay here with your husband while you go downstairs," she said. "Your coachman is most particular on insisting that you talk with him, even though I told him how ill your husband was."

Onyx was glad the darkness of the room hid her guilty embarrassment. She could imagine what John was making of Mrs. Millstead's talk of her husband.

John stood in the kitchen, tapping his whip against the table. "Miss Hamilton!" he shouted. "What doings are these?"

She put her finger to her lips and hurried out the back door, knowing he would follow. Private Petrie stood in the yard, eyeing them both.

"I told him the truth," he blurted as John glared at him. She turned to the coachman, her hands raised in appeal.

"I did not know what else to do. The farmer was so suspicious, and I was so afraid he would not help us."

John grunted. He took off his hat and twisted it in his hands, turning it round and round, his agitation apparent to all who chose to see. His face screwed up into an expression that reminded Onyx of nothing so much as a dried apple, and he began to sniff.

"I told Sir Matthew that nothing good would come of pinching pennies by leaving off the postboys!"

"It doesn't matter," Onyx broke in. "The deed is done, and you can see that I cannot leave Major Beresford. Not after he saved our lives." She eyed the coachman shrewdly. "Particularly since you were not there to protect us."

The force of this argument was not lost on the coachman. "It may be so," he admitted. "But what are we to do?"

"We're closer to Chalcott than we are to Bramby Swale, aren't we?" she asked by way of answer.

"Yes, miss, much closer."

"Then in the morning you will take a message to Lady Bagshott," Onyx continued. "You will tell her there has been an accident, but that we are well. You will remain there. I will write to you again when we are ready to travel."

"She won't like it. No more do I," he replied, remorse replaced by stubbornness again.

"She'll have no choice in the matter," Onyx replied decisively. "You will deliver her that message on the morrow. I have spent entirely too much time out here in the yard, and I am going in now."

She allowed John no time to continue his protestations but turned on her heel and hurried back into the house.

Mrs. Millstead had prepared a low cot for Onyx next to Jack's bed. "I know you don't want to disturb him," she whispered in explanation, glancing over at the still form that seemed not to have moved since Onyx administered the fever powder.

"How good you are to us, Mrs. Millstead," said Onyx.

The woman handed her a nightgown. "It is big enough for two of you, I imagine, miss, but you may use it until your trunk is unpacked tomorrow."

She whispered her thanks and sank down on the cot, exhausted right through to her shoes. Jack was sleeping. She knew she should sleep too, but as she lay there in the darkness, she could only review over and over again the strange events of the day that had begun in such prosaic fashion. Again and again she watched the robber fall dead at her feet. Over and over she removed bone chips; over and over she watched Gerald's letters flutter by, enveloped in a bolt of white wedding silk. All the events jumbled together and chased each other around and around as she stared at the ceiling and tried to make sense of it all.

Jack woke toward morning and mumbled to himself. She rose from her cot and felt his forehead. "You're burning up," she murmured out loud. He made no reply as she mixed another dose of fever powder and made him drink it.

He slept then, and she slept too, until the sun was high.

Jack Beresford was conscious the next day, but he did not say anything. It was as though the horrors of the day before had left him mute. She fretted about this at first, as she carefully cleaned his wound, removing several more fragments. But as she watched him drift in and out of sleep, she noted how tightly clenched his jaw was, and she realized that he was concentrating all his efforts on withstanding the pain and literally had no time to waste on speech. His eyes followed her around the room, but his gaze was inner-directed. She could tell he was adjusting himself to the rhythm of his own body, massaging his own pain from within. She understood and did not blight his time with words of her own. He seemed to realize that she knew, and he relaxed little by little.

By nightfall, Alice had finished washing and ironing some of the dresses from her trunk. Onyx took time out to change clothes and swallow a mouthful of Mrs. Millstead's good cooking. She hurried back upstairs again.

The second night passed much as the first one, but she noticed a difference in the morning. When she opened her eyes and looked up at Jack, she knew that he was better. His breathing was regular, his color good, and best of all, his face was relaxed. Onyx let her breath out slowly in relief and gratitude.

When she came back into the room after breakfast, his eyes were still closed. She quietly took her seat by the bed and reached for the mending that Alice had not finished yesterday. Onyx applied herself to a torn flounce on her favorite muslin gown, drawing her chair up closer toward the window, looking out from time to time at the field where the farmer was sowing oats.

"Where have I seen you before?"

She jumped and stuck the needle in her thumb, turning half around in her chair to look at Major Beresford. He struggled to sit up, and she dropped her mending and ran to him, tucking the pillow up higher and helping him.

His tone was normal almost, except that his voice sounded unused, rusty. "I have been puzzling it over in my mind this last half hour and more, watching you, and wondering where I know you from."

She smiled. "Major Beresford—"

"Major? Wasn't I your dear husband only two days ago? Or was it a month ago? And what of little Ned?"

"Two days," she replied firmly, ameliorating her severity by adding, "Little Ned has taken himself off somewhere. That is, I believe, much in the style of three-year-olds."

"But I *have* seen you before," he continued relentlessly.

"That is quite the oldest faradiddle that any soldier ever told a girl," she protested, smiling in spite of herself. "I imagine it even predates Hannibal."

"You're probably right," he agreed. He raised his wounded arm gingerly, eyeing it with some distaste.

"It's much better," she assured him. "I think all the fragments are out. The doctor left word that he would be by today to stitch it."

"I am filled with eager anticipation," he replied.

She smiled, again. "Prevaricator," she said.

"When you smile, you look especially familiar," Beresford insisted. "The devil take me, I wish I knew where . . ." His voice was growing drowsy, and he allowed her to help him lie down again. He was asleep before she had time to wipe his face.

While he dozed, she went downstairs and retrieved Gerald's uniform from her trunk. It looked beyond repair, but she gathered together the pieces and took them up to the little bedroom. She pulled her chair quietly up to the window and arranged the jacket on her lap, fingering the torn shoulders where the epaulets had been ripped off.

Onyx raised the uniform to her face and smelled it.

When it had first come from Spain with the rest of Gerald's pitifully few effects, it had smelled of his perspiration, and the cologne he sometimes wore. The odor was gone now. She sighed and put the uniform in her lap, leaning back in her chair and staring across the fields again, seeing nothing this time.

Before he spoke this time, Major Beresford had the grace to cough and announce that he was awake. Onyx looked over at him.

"Who . . . who was the Light Bob?" His voice was almost a whisper, as if he was doubtful of the wisdom of his question.

"He was my brother," she replied in a voice as low as his own. She spread the tattered uniform carefully on her lap, stroking the sleeve, brushing off the dirt.

Major Beresford said nothing, but he watched her in that intense way of his that she was growing accustomed to. He had such expressive eyes. She looked into them and could almost watch his brain working.

He pulled himself upright again, tucking the sheet around his waist, never taking his eyes from her face. She began to feel uneasy, and then he spoke.

"T-tell me his name," he asked, "although I think I know it."

"Gerald," she replied, chilled to her heart at his words. "Gerald Hamilton."

He nodded, as if it were no surprise. "I knew Gerald. Everyone did."

After two years of convincing herself that she could withstand Gerald's loss in silent calm, his simple words were like a knife, twisting in her heart.

There was a moment of quiet, and then the major continued, his voice softer. "That is where I have seen you before—your blue eyes, the shape of your face, that way you have of sitting so quietly and really detaching yourself. Although I believe Lieutenant Hamilton's hair was quite dark. Black."

Onyx nodded. Tears came to her eyes, and she brushed them away.

"I noticed it in your profile. You bear a strong resemblance to Gerald." He watched her face and then patted the bed. "Come here."

She did as he said, as if pulled from her chair by strings, and sat by him. She spread her hands out in front of her. "He was my twin."

"I am so sorry," he replied, taking hold of her hands.

"It's nothing," she said quickly, too quickly. She knew that her eyes were bright with tears. She knew that in a moment she would cry, even though Sir Matthew had forbidden it. Onyx wanted to leap up and run from the room, but Jack held her hands and she could not move.

The moment passed and she felt her calm returning.

"Did you . . . did you know him well?"

He shook his head. "No, not really. He was much younger than I, and a lieutenant. But everyone knew Gerald. He was so much fun."

She nodded, feeling herself relax again, and also feeling no inclination to work her hands out of Jack's. She felt strong and safe. Her words tumbled out, almost before she realized she was speaking. "He used to tease me because I was too serious." She laughed. "He called me Brother Onyx the monk, Onyx Sober Sides. I . . ." She stopped, looking at Jack in embarrassment. "You don't want to hear me go on like this."

"But I do. And why do I have the feeling that you need to talk?"

"No," she insisted. "I don't need to." Suddenly she felt as though the room was caving in, and she could not breathe. She rose to her feet quickly, and Jack released her hands. "I'm not permitted to. It's forbidden. Sir Matthew says I may not." She clapped her hand to her mouth and stared at him, horrified at her ill manners in such a revelation. Suddenly she was filled with anger. "You're horrid to try to force me to say what I should not! You and Gerald both!"

Her outburst shocked her. "What am I saying?" she whispered.

Major Beresford tried to struggle to a sitting position.

"Onyx, Onyx, come here," he said, holding out his hand.

Onyx ran from the room, slamming the door behind her. She leaned against it and covered her face with her hands. *I should have left yesterday. Just left*, she thought. *Abandoned him. Let Mrs. Millstead think what she would. I can't stay here.*

She heard Jack stirring around in the room, and the floorboards creaking. He had no business being out of bed.

She put her cheek against the door panel. "You had better not be out of that bed," she said, swallowing her tears.

"I am," he said, "and I'm coming out that door." His voice sounded faint, and she knew he would do himself injury if she did not go back. "Please, Jack, lie down," she pleaded.

He was silent for a moment. "On one condition," he said. "You come back in here right now."

She said nothing.

"If you do not, I will wrap this sheet around me and follow you."

She knew that he would. She struggled to gain control of her feelings, and when she had them in order again, she spoke. "Very well. Lie down, Major. I will come back in."

She waited until she heard the bed creak again and opened the door.

His movements had caused his arm to bleed again. With a cry of vexation, she hurried to his side and held a gauze pad against the wound until it stopped bleeding. "This won't do," she said severely.

"No, it won't," he agreed. "We're going to talk."

Her hands began to shake. "No!"

With unspeakable relief, Onyx heard heavy footsteps on the stairs, followed by the doctor's voice. She almost ran to the door to let him in.

"Mrs. Beresford, you look a bit hagged," the doctor said, handing his hat and cane to Mrs. Millstead, who had followed him up the stairs. "And how is our patient?"

"Stubborn," she replied.

The doctor smiled beatifically, as if she had uttered the magic phrase. "Ah, good. That means he will get well. The stubborn ones never fail me." He adjusted his glasses and began to probe around in his black bag. "Well, sir, shall we get on with it?"

Jack sighed. "I suppose." He looked at Onyx, who stood by the door. "My dear, this time I think you would be better off somewhere else."

Wordlessly she turned and fled down the stairs. Jack called to her several times, and she cringed at the alarm in his voice, but she ran into the farmyard and did not stop until she was deep in the barn, wedged up tight against the back wall and the feed bin. She covered her ears with her hands and made herself small in the corner, gritting her teeth against the sound of Major Beresford's screams as the doctor stitched the open wound.

She did not move from the corner, even when all was quiet again, until the afternoon shadows gave way to twilight. Alice had been looking for her. Onyx heard her companion calling to her, the voice drifting in and around the barn and then fading away.

She knew that if she returned to Major Beresford's room, and if he began to talk to her about Gerald, she would disgrace herself further. Since that dreadful day when Sir Matthew had forbidden her to cry, she had not dared mourn Gerald. To spare the sensitivities of Lady Daggett, to avoid troubling Sir Matthew, to maintain her shadowy place in their world, she had been forced to surrender all memories of Gerald. It was as though he did not exist except in the shabby remnants of his effects sent from Spain.

And now suddenly, after two years of slamming the door shut on her brother, the pretense was over. She knew that when she walked into Major Beresford's room, as she knew she must, her great grief would be exposed. It was ill-bred and unmannerly, but she knew it would be so. The game she had been forced to play was over, and she was not certain of the new rules.

Chapter 5

ONYX KNEW THAT MAJOR BERES-
ford would be awake when she returned to the
room. Some instinct she had never been conscious
of before told her that he would be waiting.

She had lived a well-regulated life; nothing had ever
happened to Onyx Hamilton before. Every action, down
to the smallest nuance, was carefully planned, if not by
her, then by Reverend Hamilton, and then the Daggetts,
in their reluctance. Nothing was ever left to chance. The
smallest details were thoughtfully planned and dutifully
executed. Everything in her life, even Gerald's death, had
been tidy and bloodless. Until now.

It was as though the delicate stream of her life had
suddenly tumbled into a river in flood, with each twist
and turn of the bank adding new currents to the stream
that bubbled and frothed. The clear water was muddier
now, and no longer was it possible to see downstream so
easily. Anything could happen. The uncertainty of that
both vexed and thrilled her.

I can't go in there, she thought as she quietly climbed
the stairs in the darkened house. At the top step she sat

down and rested her chin in her palms. *I am a wondrous coward*, she thought.

"Onyx?"

She raised her head. *Gracious, but the man's hearing is acute. And I was so quiet.* She looked toward the closed door, sighed, and stood up.

Moonlight filled the little room and threw a wide band of brightness across the blanket that covered Major Beresford. His hands were resting on top of the blanket in that moonlit space and were the only part of him that she could see.

"Onyx."

It wasn't so much a question this time, or even just her name. It was an entire sentence—subject, verb, and direct object.

She sat down on the end of the bed, careful not to jiggle the mattress, mindful of the need to spare him any further pain. She felt an absurd desire to reach for his hands; instead, she twined her arms around the bedpost.

The silence unnerved her. "I am so sorry I ran away like that," she said.

"Don't be. I . . . I seem to recall requesting that you leave."

His voice sounded tired, but that edge of pain was gone from it.

"You did ask me to leave," she agreed, "but I don't think you meant it."

He chuckled, as if she had caught him by surprise. "You are right. How . . . how is it that we understand each other so well? Our acquaintance is so . . . precipitously brief."

She walked right into the opening he created. "Not really, sir. You knew Gerald. He and I were very much alike."

A long silence followed. The hands on the bed covering moved out of the moonlight then, and a moment later returned, this time palms-up, in a gesture of supplication.

"C-could you fetch me that pitcher of water? I've been eyeing it this last hour and more, but it's so far away."

Her guilt at abandoning him in his time of great need gnawed at her, but she did not apologize for it. Without a word she poured him a glass of water, raised his head, and cushioned him against her so he could drink it.

"Thank you."

She arranged his pillows, and he settled himself again. At some point during the long afternoon he had acquired a nightshirt, so she was spared the sight of his bandaged arm.

"I feel like a pincushion," he said, as if following her thoughts, something he did with disconcerting regularity. "I'm all done up right and tight with black thread."

She said nothing.

"Who begins?" said Major Beresford when the silence threatened to stretch out. "It should be ladies first, if I have not completely forgotten my good English manners."

Onyx sat down again, regaining her comforting grip on the bedpost.

"You look rather like a figurehead sitting there," the major commented.

She scarcely heard him. "I know nothing of Gerald's death. Nothing."

"Did you not receive a letter from his colonel? From Colonel March?" He sounded surprised.

"Yes. The post brought it to Lady Daggett. She read it, screamed, and fainted." Onyx turned toward the major and sat cross-legged with her skirts tucked around her. The major's eyes were on her face.

"I ran to her room." She paused and her voice caught. "That was when Sir Matthew grabbed me and told me . . . about Gerald's death." Onyx felt her heart grow numb again, as it had on that day. "I started to cry. He shook me hard and ordered me to stop it." Her voice broke. "He said he would . . . would take a stick to me if I caused Lady Daggett any more grief."

"Blast him," said the major.

"Gerald was never spoken of again." Onyx leaned against the bedpost. "I don't understand . . . how that could help . . ." She faltered. "Was it to spare the Daggetts pain by not ever mentioning him again? As if he hadn't even existed? Oh, surely not! But there was . . . no one to talk to me about it."

She was speaking too loud. She sat still a moment until she had regained her composure. Major Beresford had never taken his eyes from her face. Ordinarily such scrutiny would have sent her into transports of embarrassment, but she knew only a feeling of protection, something she had not felt since the Reverend Hamilton's death, and it gave her courage to continue.

"I . . . I wanted to find out what happened. I needed to find out. Once, when they were gone, I went into Mama's . . . Lady Daggett's room and found the letter from Colonel March."

"And?" he prompted when she was silent.

She leaned closer so she could see his face better. "It said something about an honorable quick death on the field of battle." Onyx noted how Major Beresford's eyes wavered for a moment. "I thought it was all a hum. It sounded so . . . rehearsed."

"It was a hum," he said. There was pain in his voice then, coupled with resignation. "I've written those letters myself. It was what we thought you families in England wanted to hear."

"Can you tell me how he died?"

There. I have said it, she thought.

The major settled himself a little lower in the bed. "Yes, I can. I . . . I remember it quite well."

"Then tell me."

He sighed, and again she felt a chill ruffle up and down her spine. "I d-don't even remember the name of the town we had taken. Something small and dirty. It was winter. Gerald got too close to the charcoal brazier in his tent and set himself on fire."

"Oh mercy," she breathed, her hands to her face.

"Come to me, Onyx," urged the major, reaching for her.

She shook her head. With an effort that caused him to suck in his breath, he sat up and took her by the arm, pulling her closer to him.

"I wasn't there when it happened. None of us were. We heard him, though. We heard him."

She was crying. "Was he dead?"

"No, and more's the pity," Beresford said with another sigh. "He was so badly burned that I honestly don't think there was any feeling left in his body. Anyway, the light artillery was pulling out first, and they had to leave him with us."

He looked away from her then and absently rubbed his chest. "Marshal Soult was coming on a quick march. We knew we had to retreat, and right smartly too, but we could not leave Gerald. Shame on us, I remember us wishing he would die."

"And . . . did you? Leave him, I mean," she asked, wiping her eyes on her dress.

"Oh, no. We officers sent most of the men ahead and stayed with him. He told us to send his good uniform and sword to his family." Beresford ran his hand up and down her arm. "It gave me a start this morning to see that uniform on your lap."

She could think of nothing to say.

Beresford leaned his head back on the pillow, exhausted from the effort of speaking. "And do you know, Onyx, now that I think of it, he mentioned you. It was almost the last thing he said."

"You're not telling me another tale, are you?" she asked, the numbness overtaking her again.

"No! I would not!" His voice was harsh at first, but then that innate understanding of his seemed to take over and he spoke more softly. "I could not lie to you. He was hard to understand. His face was . . . so swollen. But, oh, those blue eyes! So bright. Like yours. He said, 'I wish,' and then he said, 'Onyx.' " Beresford looked at Onyx, his face close to hers. "I was about as far away from him as I am from you right now. I know he said 'Onyx,' but at the time, it made no sense. Onyx, none of us knew him well enough to know your name."

"An odd name," she said softly. "Remember, my father was a romantic."

"And you are not."

"No," she agreed. "I am supposed to be sensible and mindful always of others."

"How tedious for you," he murmured, his face still close to hers. She slid away from him.

"That is almost all," he continued. "We took his body with us when we retreated over the mountains to Portugal. It was winter and cold. We thought to turn the body over to Colonel March." He paused then, as if wondering what he should say next, hesitating until honesty won out. "We assumed that the family would claim the body, and it would be shipped to England. But no one ever did."

Onyx sat up. Again the cold rippled down her back, followed by a feeling of great shame. "I begged Sir Matthew to retrieve Gerald, but he would not. He said the expense was too great and I was not to discuss it."

"Well, we wondered. I saw to it that your brother was buried in the little church cemetery in Resende. It's a village not far from Oporto."

For two years she had wondered where Gerald was, and now the answer was before her. "I wish I could see his grave," she said, her voice heavy with tears waiting to be shed.

"Perhaps someday you shall, Onyx, when conditions

are different there. And now, will you cry? You'll feel better."

She did as he said, tucking her skirts under her and sobbing until her dress front was soaked. Through her muffled tears she vaguely heard Major Beresford murmuring something to her. The last thing she remembered before she fell into exhausted sleep was his hand on her hair.

She woke early, before the sun had cleared the newly sowed fields. The room was cloaked in shadow. She was still curled in a comfortable ball, her head resting on Major Beresford's legs. Onyx sat up slowly. Major Beresford did not stir. She did not wish to wake him, so she climbed off the end of the bed.

Onyx wondered what Lady Daggett would think, or Alice, if they had known how she spent the night. As she brushed at the wrinkles of her dress, she made the womanly decision that some things were no one's business but her own. The thought pleased her, as nothing else had in many days. She was smiling as she looked at Major Beresford, made sure he continued to slumber, and left the room on tiptoe.

After changing into a fresh dress, she paused on the landing to look in the mirror, turning her face this way and that, regarding her inelegant nose, her firm chin, and her dimples with more understanding and less criticism. It was her face; it would not change, and for the first time in many a critical year, Onyx decided that she did not want it to. It was Gerald's face too.

Her eyes were blue, as blue as Gerald's. She touched the mirror, thinking of him, but not thinking of him in sorrow anymore, but in a recollection so fond that she closed her eyes against the sheer delight of it.

Onyx looked back at Major Beresford's room. She wanted to tell him how she felt, knowing that he would understand. Good sense took over. She continued down the stairs, leaving him in peace.

Mrs. Millstead presided over the kitchen and over Alice Banner. They looked up from their breakfast as she entered, Alice with relief in her eyes. The relief was soon replaced by a militant gleam that warned Onyx of a rare trimming to come from her unexplained absence of yesterday.

Mrs. Millstead pulled out a chair, poured a large mug of tea, and offered her toast. Onyx sipped the tea, wondering why it was that everything seemed so fresh and new to her this morning.

"How is our dear Major Beresford this morning?" the farmer's wife asked as Onyx nibbled on the toast.

"Much better," Onyx replied, stung again by the deception—well intentioned or not—that she and the dear major were working on Mrs. Millstead. "He seems almost himself," she finished, not looking at Alice.

How on earth was she to know what Jack Beresford would be like when he was himself? She had known him four days, four days that even the most relentless adventurer would have to call exceptionable. What was Jack Beresford like when he was in good health? She had no idea.

She ate in silence and then excused herself and went outside, walking alongside the kitchen garden and into the shrubbery that gave onto the haying meadow. The air smelled of cows and grass and wildflowers. She took a deep breath.

"You worried all of us, Onyx."

It was Alice. Her companion had followed her, as Onyx had known she would. Better to spill the budget away from the house and not disturb any of its inmates.

"I'm sorry. I just couldn't face anybody." Onyx had planned to tell Alice all that had happened that night, but when confronted with the prospect in the light of day, knew that she would not. Some things were for treasuring personally, especially since soon there would be no more such diversions. Jack Beresford would heal and go on his way. She was headed to Chalcott and marriage. She sighed and could not look her dear Alice in the face.

"You're becoming quite missish, Madam Prevaricator," scolded Alice, plumping herself down on the rustic bench that Mrs. Millstead used as a shelf for her gardening tools.

"I suppose I am, Alice," Onyx replied quite calmly. "I am sure it will pass."

She said nothing more. She did not join her companion but went into the house again and up the stairs to Major Beresford.

He was awake and looking around when she opened the door. He smiled at her, and she smiled back, noting with some personal confusion his openness of expression and the way his eyes lighted up as she came toward him. He reached out his hand to her, and she took it, much against her better judgment.

"You're . . . you're much cooler," she said, shy again.

"I'm also about ready to gnaw the bedclothes," he said. "Do you think you could find me something more substantial than the everlasting gruel and porter I am offered around here?"

He tugged on her hand until she sat down on the bed, as she knew he must have intended. She was still too shy to look at him. "Thank you, Major," she said. "Thank you for . . . Gerald." She slid her hand out of his and hurried back to the safety of the kitchen.

Major Beresford ate everything she brought to him. He ate quickly, with no conversation. Halfway through the dishes on his tray, he looked up at her and wiped his lips with the back of his hand. "Should I be carrying on with a little breakfast chatter?" he asked. "I've forgotten what to do during an English meal." He laughed. "I own I'm accustomed to eating fast before the next barrage begins—or ends." He winked at her. "I've been known to duel for a piece of cheese. Don't try me, Onyx, or make any sudden moves! I'm a dangerous man over plate and fork."

Onyx laughed and fell into the spirit of his banter. "Silly! You should sit at a table and read the newspaper, grunt a little, and then animadvert on the weather, and make disparaging comments about your tenants."

"I need to know these things, Mrs. Beresford," he said, teasing her. "Suppose Mrs. Millstead were to come in here? We must preserve our fiction of connubial enchantment, at least until I have mended."

Her conscience strove with her mightily again. "I . . . I think I would feel more at home with myself if I confessed to Mrs. Millstead," she said. "I feel so deceitful with my Banbury tale."

He did not argue. "It is an awkward pass, Mrs. Beresford."

"You must stop calling me that!" she protested, feeling the unruly blush rise up her neck and into her cheeks.

He regarded her. "You color up so . . . delightfully, Mrs. B.," he said. "I am told that comes from an uneasy conscience." He laughed at her confusion. "But in total fairness to your sex, I must say that you have been an amiable and well intentioned spouse during the past—what is it?—three or four days. I think I lost a day."

He buttered the remaining square of toast and popped it in his mouth. "But you are right, Onyx B. We must make a clean breast of it to our hostess. Throw ourselves on the mercy of the Methodists."

She laughed. "You wretch!" She rose and he took her hand again.

"Onyx," he began, and he was serious this time. "Call her up here and tell her. I don't want you to face the wrath alone."

Not since Gerald had been her childhood companion had there been an advocate in difficult situations. She mentally forgave him all his teasing, nodded, and patted his hand.

Mrs. Millstead came when she was called, huffing up the stairs and talking to herself as she wiped her hands on her apron. The anxious way her eyebrows came together gave Onyx another bad moment.

"It is not serious, Mrs. Millstead," Onyx said as she stood at the top of the landing. "I need, or rather, we need to talk to you."

The woman came into the bedroom right on Onyx's heels, looking over Onyx's shoulder to make sure for herself that the dear major was not lying dead on her second-best sheets.

When she saw that he was looking rested and running his little finger around the rim of the jam pot, her sigh of relief was audible. Mrs. Millstead clapped her hands together to see this display of culinary enthusiasm from the man brought bleeding and half-conscious into her house only three days ago.

"Major Beresford!" she began, and then words failed her. She dabbed at her eyes with her apron. "I love to see a sick man eat!" she sobbed into her apron.

Onyx touched her shoulder. "The major is ever so much better," she said, "and we have you to thank for it."

The obvious promise of Jack Beresford's return to health and vigor seemed to unnerve the woman. She sobbed into her apron all the more. "He finished off the toast and the jam," she marveled as she wept. "God bless us!"

Jack set down the jam pot and gave Onyx such a droll glance over Mrs. Millstead's bowed head that she could scarcely contain herself. Resolutely Onyx turned her back on him and took Mrs. Millstead in her arms.

When Mrs. Millstead was reduced finally to an occasional sob or sniff, Onyx released her. The woman's eyes filled with tears again. "Only think, Mrs. Beresford, soon you will be reunited with little Ned."

The silence that followed was broken at last by the major.

"M-Mrs. Millstead," he began, picking his way carefully over stony ground, "there isn't going to be a reunion with little Ned."

Mrs. Millstead gasped, threw up her hands, and sank onto the bed, narrowly missing the major's legs. She sobbed into her damp apron. "Little Ned is . . . dead?" she shrieked.

Onyx hurried to her side, mortification growing by the minute as the woman sobbed and the major lay on his back staring at the ceiling, soundlessly laughing and holding his arm to assuage the pain of it. He looked at her only long enough to launch into another painful fit of silent mirth. Onyx tried to stare him down, but the effort proved fruitless. She turned her attention again to the distraught farmer's wife, who grabbed her about the waist and pulled Onyx to her.

She rocked back and forth, hugging Onyx to her. "My dear Mrs. Beresford, there will be other children for you and the major. I'm sure it will be so."

Onyx knew better this time than to even shift her eyes in the direction of the unrepentant Jack Beresford. She let herself be smothered in Mrs. Millstead's fleshy embrace and then gradually disentangled herself. When Mrs. Millstead was reasonably composed, Onyx cleared her throat, thought fleetingly of her fiancé as she did so, and forged resolutely ahead.

"Mrs. Millstead, you misunderstand me," she began. "We have . . . misrepresented ourselves. You see," she struggled on, "the major and I are not . . . we're not married."

Mrs. Millstead turned as pale as her second-best sheets. Her eyes widened. "Then little Ned . . ." She couldn't bring herself to say it. ". . . out of wedlock?" She ended the sentence on a whisper, as if afraid the laborers working in the barley field one mile distant would overhear.

Onyx sat up straight. With great force of will, she ignored the muffled choking sounds behind her from the general vicinity of Major Beresford. *If he opens his stitches, it will serve him right*, she thought to herself as she took Mrs. Millstead's hands in her own.

"Oh, ma'am, it's nothing like that, I assure you! I never met the major before three days ago."

Mrs. Millstead continued to stare at her, her mouth wide open.

"I . . . I didn't intend to tell you a tale, but your husband assumed . . . he asked what happened to my husband . . ." Onyx knew she was fumbling about, but she forged on. "I thought that if he continued to believe that Major Beresford and I were married, he would not turn us away. You see, Mrs. Millstead, the major was bleeding so much, and we did look like . . . like down-and-out irregulars. Oh, please say you understand, Mrs. Millstead. I'm dreadfully sorry!"

The silence was awful. Onyx knew that her face was flaming red. Mrs. Millstead pulled her hands away and lodged them firmly in her lap.

"You mean . . . there is no little Ned?" she asked finally.

Onyx shook her head. "I really don't know why I said that. I don't think I've ever lied in my life. I was desperate for you take us in. Oh, Mrs. Millstead, suppose the major had died?"

The thought seemed to soften the woman's heart again. She sighed and looked at Onyx. "Then who are you?"

Onyx couldn't look at her. "My name is Onyx Hamilton, from Morecombe. Alice Banner and I were on our way to Chalcott when we were set upon by highwaymen."

"Major Beresford and Private Petrie came to your rescue?"

"Yes," lied Onyx. She could see no harm in allowing

Private Petrie a less-checkered past, particularly in light of his sincere repentance. "I do not know what we would have done if they had not come along."

The woman looked from Onyx to Major Beresford, who had composed himself and was lying supine with an interesting, pitiful air of suffering on his face.

"Is this so, Major?" she asked.

"Yes," he replied. "We . . . we're sorry for any inconvenience we may have caused you. I'm riding north to Yorkshire as soon as I'm able."

"And you?" Mrs. Millstead shifted her gaze back to Onyx.

"I'm going to Chalcott. I am to marry the vicar of Chalcott."

"What?" said the major, abandoning his studied agony long enough to sit upright and stare at his former wife.

"Yes," she replied quietly. "I'm to be the vicar's wife. Dear me."

"'Dear me' indeed!" exclaimed Mrs. Millstead, rising to her feet. "I fear you're going to lead that poor man a merry dance!"

Onyx could not disagree, so she made no reply. The silence continued. Onyx heard the bees humming around the hollyhocks growing toward the window. *How could I have been so deceitful?* she flagellated herself. And why does Major Beresford continue to stare at me? She wished herself away from the little bedroom, but even Gerald's game of "I wish" had no comfort.

Onyx swallowed hard. "Mrs. Millstead," she began, quite overcome with her deception and chagrined as never before, "I will write to John, the coachman, and we will be away from here tomorrow afternoon at the latest. Only please . . . please allow Jack . . . the major to remain here until he has healed."

The silence was awful. Mrs. Millstead looked at them

both and shook her head. "I cannot say this is anything to be proud of, but if I own the truth, I'm glad enough to have you here." She pointed a finger at Onyx. "The follies of youth!" she exclaimed, and then left the room.

Onyx couldn't bring herself to look at Major Beresford. With a studied air, she examined the wallpaper. She could think of nothing to say. She was not a witty person, however lively her mind; she had never pretended to be. Nothing in the calm of her life had prepared her for someone like Major Beresford. More than anything, she wanted to be alone by herself for a while, to reflect on the chaos of the last few days. At the same time, she was already regretting that tomorrow she would be leaving.

"It *is* fascinating wallpaper, isn't it, Onyx?" the major ventured at last.

She turned around then, smiling. "Major Beresford," she said, "I am chagrined to reflect that now there is one region of England in which I dare not show my face ever again."

"But only one," he rejoined, adding outrageously, "I have many." He grinned at her shocked look, showing no remorse. "I haven't had so much fun since . . ." He paused. "Never mind. I'll not b-bore you with Spanish stories."

"I have benefited from your Spanish stories," Onyx said quietly.

"Not these you wouldn't," he said. "Wait. Before you go. Could you l-loosen my bandage? It's beginning to feel sharpish."

She came over to him, pulling a chair up to the bed, bending over her work seriously, thankful not to have to look him in the eyes.

"Before—when you were still my wife—you sat on my bed," said the major. He was smiling, but his eyes were gentle.

Onyx refused to rise to his teasing this time. "I did. I think I should not do that anymore."

When Onyx finally came downstairs, she had a letter in her hand for Private Petrie. "Take this to my coachman at Chalcott," she instructed. She laid a hand on his arm as he turned to go. "And if you please, Private, come back with John and help the major."

He looked at her in astonishment. "Did you think I would not, Mrs. Beres . . . Miss Hamilton?" He put his hand over his heart. "I am his forever."

She covered her mouth to hide her smile. "I think only until he is well enough to sit his horse will be sufficient, Private."

Major Beresford was dozing when she took his dinner to him. By the time she set the tray on the table and lit the lamp, he was awake and watching her. She could tell by the brightness of his eyes that the fever had returned with evening. She sighed and mixed some powders for him. He drank the potion and offered no objection until she began to gather up the dishes when he had finished.

"I own I feel a trifle ill-used, Onyx," he said at last. There was no mistaking the pout in his voice.

"And why is this, Major?"

"Are you so sure that I am sufficiently recovered to be thrown on the mercy of an amiable but overworked farmwoman?"

She was not so sure, but she did not tell him. "You have had far worse wounds, Major."

"I wondered when we would return to my thigh," he said wickedly and winked at her. "It's not the same," he continued. "I've grown . . . used to you," he declared, the force of his argument dulled because the fever powders were making him drowsy. He kept his eyes open with an effort. "Tell me something, Miss Hamilton," he said, long after his eyes had closed and she was sure he slept. "This vicar—is he good to you?"

His question startled her. "Really, Major, whatever do you mean?"

"I hope he's good to you," said the major, his voice far away. He slept.

Alice made room for Onyx in the parlor that night. Onyx pretended she was asleep so she would not have to talk to Alice. She finally drifted off, wondering to herself what color the Reverend Mr. Andrew Littletree's eyes were. She chastised herself. How strange that she could not remember such a mundane detail, when she had no trouble with her recollection that Jack Beresford's eyes were quite, quite brown.

Chapter 6

NYX WONDERED AT FIRST WHAT had woken her in the middle of the night. One moment she was asleep, and the next moment she was wide awake, listening. The room was quiet except for Alice's regular breathing. Onyx yawned and rolled over, and then she heard it again.

Someone was talking upstairs. It sounded like Major Beresford, but she could not be sure. She sat up on her cot to hear him better and then found herself by the door, listening as his voice rose.

"My stars," she whispered out loud. "What can be the matter? Who is he talking to?"

No one answered her questions, but the voice became louder, more insistent. There was an air of command in it, sharp and to the point. Onyx threw a sheet around her nightgown and quietly climbed the stairs, hand over hand on the railing, avoiding the squeaky tread that she was already familiar with. Major Beresford was shouting now. Onyx bolted up the stairs two at a time and burst into his room.

He was sitting up in bed and staring at her. But no,

not at her. He didn't know she was there. He was looking beyond her, beyond the wall even, to a place she had never seen before. She resisted the very real urge to look over her shoulder. Through some alchemy of the night, she feared what she would see.

Still staring beyond her, the major started to get out of bed. "Come on, my lads, come on!" he called to troops she could not see. "We'll take it and be back in time for supper!"

The terror in his eyes made her gasp. She was filled with fear of her own, but she closed the door and ran to his side, pushing him back down on the bed. He resisted, muttering something about the French, but she kept her hands on his shoulders, talking to him, murmuring words that made no sense to her, soothing sounds.

After what seemed like ages to her, she felt the tension leave his shoulders. He relaxed and leaned forward as if the springs that wound him had suddenly snapped. He rested his head on her chest, and soon he was breathing steadily again. Gradually, still whispering to him as she would to a child, she lowered him back to his bed and covered him.

There were tears on his cheeks. She wiped them off with the sheet and touched his forehead. He was cool now and damp with perspiration. She wiped his face carefully and tiptoed to the window to close it against the chill of the night.

"Onyx, forgive me."

She whirled around. He was sitting up in bed again, and he frightened her. For only the smallest moment, she felt that she was in the room with someone strange, someone she did not know.

He shuddered then, and she forgot her own fear. Onyx hurried to his side again and took hold of his shoulders, hoping that her presence would wake him from whatever nightmare still possessed him.

The major put his arms around her and held her tight, as if afraid that she would vanish. She made no objection but clung to him and tentatively placed her hand on his hair as he rested against her. As she held him, Onyx thought to herself: *A week ago, I would have screamed and swooned if someone had grabbed me like this.* She knew that nothing could force her to leave his side now. She would cling to him like this as long as he needed her.

After a few moments, his breathing changed. In another moment she could feel the flutter of his eyelids against her. She loosened her grip on him, and the major sat up, fully awake.

He didn't say anything for a long time, but he watched her. His direct gaze troubled her, and she almost said something but then realized that he was trying to decide if he could trust her. She remained silent, not moving away from him, returning his gaze.

"I . . . I . . . just w-want to go home," he said at last. His hair was so rumpled. She reached out impulsively to smooth it down, and he took her hand and held it against his cheek, letting out a long shuddering sigh.

"You'll have to wait until you are able to travel," she reminded him.

He shook his head, kissed her fingers, and let go of her hand. "No. I want to go n-now."

His look of longing unnerved her. "Oh, Jack," she whispered, close to tears. "Perhaps we can work something out."

He didn't say anything else, only continued to regard her. He opened his mouth to say something and then thought better of it. Onyx sat in silence. When he said nothing else, she rose to go.

Jack Beresford took her hand and pulled her back down. She sat beside him on the bed and rearranged the coverings. She reached around to pull up the other pillow and then was still.

"Tell me, Jack," she said simply.

It was as though he had been waiting for her to ask him. He allowed himself to lean back on the pillows, although there was no peace or relaxation in the lines of his face. His eyes bored into hers. *Whatever he tells me, I must not flinch*, she thought to herself as she watched him.

"I don't know how long the siege of Badajoz had gone on," he began, his tone conversational as he strove for a calmness she instinctively knew he did not feel. "We were all pretty sick of one another. Tired of the way we smelled, I guess. I hate sieges."

He took her hand in his again, running his thumb over her knuckles, feeling the indents between them. "The orders came finally. We were to move on the walls again. Again! We had tried and tried . . ." His voice trailed off and he let go of her hand.

"I knew it wouldn't work. I mean, why should it?" Beresford moved restlessly. "But it was an order. It became my privilege to stand in front of all those mothers' sons and tell them to climb those walls." He closed his eyes and was silent again.

"But . . . but surely you had given orders like that before, Major?" she asked.

He opened his eyes and then passed his hand in front of them. "Oh, yes. I don't know what it was. Maybe the latest recruits just looked younger than last year's. Maybe I was finally s-sick of war."

Beresford sighed and stared out the window. Morning was coming. Birds were beginning to wake up in the ash tree outside the window.

"They looked at me with such . . . trust, Onyx B," he said and turned his head toward her again, his eyes filled with anguish this time. "They were ready to follow me anywhere. I lined them up, led them out, and watched them die."

"Oh, Jack, no," she said, taking both of his hands in hers.

"That wasn't all," he went on. "When that first wave was lying dead under the ladders, I got to send out another, and another. Finally we were just putting down those ladders on lads of mine who were lying there still alive."

He looked at her. "Have you ever planted a ladder on someone who is dying?"

Onyx knew her face had drained of all color. She shook her head and clung to his hands, her eyes wide.

He didn't even notice. "And every time you move up a rung on the ladder, it slips a little bit down?" Beresford shivered and slid lower in the bed. With an automatic gesture, Onyx pulled the covers higher on his shoulders, careful not to bump his bandaged arm.

His voice altered then and became practically toneless as he stared out the window again, looking well beyond the fields into another country that she could not see. "We were the first ones over the wall. And I'm a hero of Badajoz. Merciful heaven help me."

He found her hand again. "Your hands are cold," he commented, a little more life in his voice. "Could it be that you are not used to such stories?"

She could only shake her head as her eyes filled with tears.

He watched her. "Poor Onyx B, with eyes as blue as Wedgwood," he said softly. "Whatever did you do to deserve all of this?"

It was not a question to answer, and she did not try.

"As long as our association continues, my dear," he began, choosing his words carefully, "give me no more fever powders, even if I'm burning up. I only sleep too long . . ." He swallowed and tightened his grip on her fingers. "And then I dream."

Onyx waited for him to continue, but he did not. She put her other hand over his. "Tell me. You must, you know." She had no money to repay Major Jack Beresford for all he had done for her; all she could give him was an ear for his own misery.

"I d-dream that I am climbing up the ladder. I climb and climb, and slip lower and lower." He could not meet her gaze as his eyes filled with tears. "Onyx, soon I'm hip-deep in bodies. They . . . they suck me under. And then someone is putting a ladder on me. I struggle and it's so hard to breathe." He let out a long shuddering breath. "Usually someone shakes me awake by then. As you did."

He let go of her hands and made a gesture, as if to push her away. She refused to move, and when he began to cry, she gathered him close and held him tight. She smoothed down his hair as he sobbed, turning his face into her nightgown to muffle the terrible sound. She had felt inadequate before, of small use to the major. But as he cried and she held him, she felt herself grow strong and whole again for the first time since Gerald's death. Someone needed her.

As the major sobbed in her arms, Onyx heard someone open the door. It was Alice. Onyx looked over the major's head and put a finger to her lips. Alice nodded and closed the door quietly.

When the major finished crying, Onyx wiped his face and made him blow his nose. She covered him again, tucking in the sheets as she remembered Reverend Hamilton tucking her in when she was a small child. She sat beside him in silence until he finally fell asleep, this time deep, restful sleep.

She thought she would leave the room then, but the sun was coming up, and the room took on such a comfortable rosy glow that she pulled up the chair to the window and watched the land begin to live again. She opened the window a crack again and sniffed the air. It was filled with the perfume of apple blossoms. The fragrance mingled with the lilacs until the pleasure of it made her want to pick up her nightgown by the flounce and dance around the room. There was a sweetness to the coming season that she had never even suspected before, and she smiled through her burden of Jack Beresford's sadness.

Onyx looked back at him. He was totally relaxed now, his uninjured arm flung wide across the other pillow. There were still tears on his face, but she did not wish to disturb him by wiping them off. She sat in her chair and watched the morning cross the fields. Soon she found herself breathing in rhythm with Major Beresford, and then she slept too.

Onyx woke hours later to the sound of a carriage in the farmyard. She had tucked herself into a comfortable corner of the chair with her head resting on the arm of it. For a moment she couldn't remember where she was or why she was sleeping in the middle of the day. Then she looked over at Major Beresford, who still slumbered.

If he had moved in the intervening hours, it had been only a minor adjustment. She sat up and watched him, wondering that anyone could sleep so solidly, especially with that old creaking carriage practically under the window and the Reverend Mr. Andrew Littletree speaking so loudly and rudely to John Coachman.

Her eyes widened. "Dear me," she said out loud and leapt from the chair. She hurried to the window and peered out, careful not to be seen, hoping that it really wasn't her fiancé standing below, berating the coachman.

It was no one else. In horrified fascination Onyx opened the window a crack wider and leaned over, wishing the vicar away even as she wondered how she would explain her nightgown—she looked at the clock—at two in the afternoon.

She had never seen Andrew Littletree from such a view before. When, in some agitation, he removed his hat and ran his fingers through his hair, she noted again that it was thinning on top. *He'll be bald as an egg before he is thirty*, she thought. *He will blind his congregation.* The idea made her giggle. She jerked her head inside the window before he looked up and saw her.

She sobered immediately. The bigger challenge lay ahead. She would have to descend the stairs in her bare feet, dressed in her nightgown, and wrapped in a sheet, under the gaze of a man of the cloth who appeared to be in remarkable ill humor. "Dear me," she said again faintly.

The absurdity of her situation kept her from growing entirely numb with fear. *I have spent my life in an unexceptionable manner*, she thought as she draped herself in the sheet she had worn upstairs hours before. *I have become positively hoydenish.*

She was halfway down the stairs when Mrs. Millstead let in the Reverend Mr. Andrew Littletree. His eyes fell on her immediately, and he staggered backward and would have fallen if John had not captured him in a clumsy embrace.

"Put me down, you clodpole," he shrieked, his face going from white to red and white again, leaving ugly splotches. He regained his footing and stared up at her.

Words nearly failed him, but not quite. "Miss Hamilton," he uttered in failing tones, "you have forgotten yourself!"

To Onyx's logical mind it seemed a supremely silly thing to say. "No, indeed, Andrew, I have not."

The vicar launched his attack. "I suppose then, Miss Hamilton," he declared, "that there is some reasonable explanation for the fact that you are standing on the stairs barefoot in your nightgown?" He paused and struck an indignant pose as he snapped open his pocket watch. "At two o'clock in the afternoon?"

"Indeed there is," she replied serenely, resisting the urge to bolt and run. She opened her mouth to say more— what, she had no idea—when she was silenced by a low moan from upstairs that seemed to stretch on and on.

Everyone was quiet then, listening, the vicar frozen in his indignant pose, Mrs. Millstead with her eyes wide, and Onyx with her mouth open.

"Onyx!" It was the last word of a dying man. Onyx turned and without a word raced back up the stairs, followed by the vicar, who clapped his watch on his head and tried to stuff his hat in his pocket.

Onyx burst into the bedroom and threw herself on her knees beside the bed. The major was stretched out straight as a poker, his hands folded across his broad chest. Before she could say or do anything, he opened one eye and winked at her.

She choked back the laughter that threatened to spill out of her and took his hand as the vicar ran into the room. "Jack! Jack!" she said, as if trying to summon her patient back from some nether region.

The major turned his head from side to side. "I'm so hot," he muttered as the vicar retreated to a far corner of the room, still holding his crumpled hat.

Onyx put her hand on Jack's cool forehead and turned to her fiancé. "Reverend Littletree," she said, her eyes cast down only because she knew she would laugh if she looked at him, "this is Major Beresford, the man who saved my life." She ran her other hand across her forehead. "You see how he is. I cannot leave him like this."

The vicar stared at her and then at Jack. "You have been tending the sick, Miss Hamilton," he said, "through the long and dismal night. How noble of you, how like the future wife of a clergyman. How wise, how very wise of me to select you as my bride, even overlooking your lamentable background," Littletree congratulated himself.

Jack gave a choke that sounded to Onyx suspiciously like a growl of real indignation. She tightened her grip on his hand. "Don't task yourself, Major," she whispered in sweet, urgent tones and then glowered at him.

With the greatest force of will, she controlled the urge

to box the major's ears and turned back to her fiancé. "My dear, you see how things are. I cannot leave the major in this state. Consider what he has done for me."

The vicar moved closer to the deathbed, stepping warily, as if expecting the floor to open up and swallow him whole. Jack shifted in bed and exposed his bandaged arm, which was still streaked with flecks of dried blood. Reverend Littletree swallowed, paled, and nimbly sidestepped until he was out of sight of the wound.

"Onyx," he began when he had sufficiently recovered. "Setting all this aside, we must leave right away. Do you realize that I have lost nearly three days to my homiletics lectures? When that disreputable-looking private showed up at Lady Bagshott's with your very cryptic message, she summoned me immediately. I came, of course," he added righteously.

"I should hope so," murmured Jack under his breath for Onyx's benefit. She shot him another withering glance.

"Only by the greatest exhibition of my powers was I able to prevent Lady Bagshott from lapsing into spasms," Littletree added.

"Heaven help me," whispered the irrepressible major. Onyx dug her fingernails into his wrist, and he gave her a wounded look that rendered her incapable of comment.

As usual, the vicar made comment superfluous. "I must return to Cambridge immediately," he continued, backing up as Jack stirred and moaned again. "You'll gather your things together and come at once, my dear."

Onyx released the major's hand and arranged the bedcovers around him, careful to leave the bloody bandage exposed. "Only if the major comes with us," she said. "Mrs. Millstead is much too busy with the management of this farm to have any time to devote to Major Beresford."

"Out of the question," snapped the vicar, his short supply of righteousness exhausted.

Onyx took a deep breath, avoiding looking at the

major, and opened her eyes wide in a remarkable imitation of her stepsister, Amethyst. She leaned toward the vicar. "I do not say it will be so, my dear, but suppose word should get out that you were remiss in your Christian duty to this poor man?" She came close to the Reverend Littletree and twined her hands in his coat front. "Suppose somehow tattlemongers carried the news that you abandoned . . ." She paused to give the word time to sink in. ". . . abandoned one of God's most miserable . . ." She paused again as Jack Beresford choked and groaned. ". . . most miserable creatures surely at the brink of a deep decline." She rolled her eyes heavenward and clasped her hands together. "Your parish would surely waver from the effect of this example!" She paused again. "If word of this were to get out," she added, ameliorating the effect by leaning her head against his chest.

The vicar blushed and put her to one side. He advanced toward the bed again and peered down at Jack. "Would he survive the ride to Chalcott?" Littletree muttered, not entirely comfortable with the role of savior yet.

"I think he would, my dear," said Onyx. She clapped her hands together and the vicar jumped. "And only think, Andrew! Next Sunday, you can take your text from Luke Ten: the Good Samaritan!"

He considered this and found favor in the idea. "I could, Miss Hamilton, I could."

The mention of sermonizing wrought a marvel. The vicar put one foot forward and clutched his lapel. He closed his eyes against the ecstasy of it all. "A wretched man, fallen among thieves . . . ," he mused as Jack glared at him. Littletree opened his eyes and pointed suddenly at Jack. "'Which now, thinkest thou, was neighbor unto him that fell among the thieves?'" He turned to Onyx. "Oh, my dear, you are right, of course. We will take him with us. Think what a sermon this will make." He rubbed his hands together. "And if he should die, why, I can preach on the many mansions awaiting sinners in God's house. There is no end of topics!"

"What a wonderful idea, Andrew," Onyx said, staring at him in total admiration until the major began to cough and groan. "My dear, you are a wonder," she said. "Now, if you will be so good as to go downstairs and summon the farmer and Private Petrie, I am sure that you can make Jack Beresford comfortable in the carriage."

He did as she said, fairly floating out of the room, already wrapped up tight in the sermon he would preach to his eager parishioners Sunday next. "'Which one among you,'" he repeated as he left the room, stabbing the air with appropriate gestures. He repeated the phrase all the way down the stairs, changing the emphasis from syllable to syllable.

Jack clapped his hand over his wound and held it tight as he shook with silent laughter. "It hurts!" he whispered as he struggled to remain silent. When he almost had control of himself, his shoulders started to shake again, and he abandoned himself to silent mirth.

Onyx frowned at him. "You are the most disreputable man I ever met!"

That set him off again. Beresford rolled over and lay with his face in the pillow. The bed shook as he laughed. When he finally surfaced for air, there were tears in his eyes. He rested his cheek on the pillow. "Onyx B, I am the *only* disreputable man you have ever met! Barring that ugly customer on the highway, of course. Come sit down."

She did as he said, her back straight, her lips tight together. Correctly judging her mood, he made no motion to touch her. "Thank you," he said simply. "I heard the carriage in the yard, and I knew he was coming for you. I would feel much better if you were close by. At least for a while, Onyx B."

"You must stop calling me that," she said and touched

him on the shoulder. "And turn over, please, before you open that wound."

He obeyed. "You are right, of course. I must survive so the vicar can have his good example." He took her by the wrist. "My dear Miss Hamilton, did anyone ever tell you that you are a complete hand?"

"No. Until now I was no such thing," she retorted, and stood up. "Sir, I would advise you to compose yourself along more pitiful lines. If you can manage to cry out a few times as they are carrying you downstairs, it would help. Perhaps you could even faint."

She looked around the room. "I imagine Mrs. Millstead will sacrifice her husband's nightshirt for you, but what are we to do with your pants and shirt? Mrs. Millstead reduced them to ribbons."

"Do whatever you please," he said, "only save the boots and the coat. That uniform coat belongs to a former tentmate of mine, and I am sworn to forward it to his little brother when I am through."

"Blood and all?" she asked, picking up the uniform jacket with thumb and forefinger.

"Obviously you are not acquainted with the ways of little boys, Miss Hamilton," he said, grinning. "Only think how much more valuable it will be now. We will not tell young Master Wilton that the blood is English and not Spanish." Beresford pointed a finger at her in the style of the vicar. "Would you have denied our own dear little Ned the youthful pleasure of such a bloody treasure? For shame, madam wife!"

She laughed and then sobered immediately. "But we have disposed of little Ned, Major," she reminded him. "And you must remember yourself."

"So I must," he agreed. "But for how long?" he added outrageously.

She drilled him with a minatory glance and stalked downstairs to pack.

Chapter 7

THE REVEREND ANDREW LITTLE-
tree chose not to accompany them to Chalcott.
That was his original intention, but when Jack
moaned and then fainted as he and Farmer Millstead carried the wounded officer to the carriage, the vicar had a
sudden change of heart.

"I will return to Chalcott next Saturday in time to
prepare my sermon," he said, eyeing the major as he hurriedly removed his belongings from the carriage and then
turned his attention to the farmer. "Surely I can convince
this worthy rustic to drive me in his gig to the nearest
coach stop. I own it does my consequence little good to
ride the common stage, but everyone must make a sacrifice now and then, my dear."

"I suppose one must," Onyx agreed, offering him
her cheek to kiss, which he did, after looking around to
make sure no one was watching. She let him help her into
the carriage and Alice after her. Private Petrie mounted
the major's horse and waited close by as John Coachman,
grumbling as he always did at the start of any journey,
heaved himself into the box and unlimbered the whip.

The first miles were covered in silence. Propped up with pillows, Jack Beresford reclined on the seat opposite Onyx. His eyes were closed, but she had no idea if he slept.

Alice Banner spent those early miles scolding her charge until she was satisfied that she had done her duty. When she finished, Alice leaned back in her corner and was soon snoring.

Onyx glanced at the major then and saw that his eyes were open. "You heard every word of that!" she accused in a low voice.

"Certainly," he replied. "Beau Wellington always advised us to cover heavy ground as lightly as possible, so I thought it prudent to keep my eyes closed until she was finished. I too had a tyrant for a nursemaid once."

She said nothing, only sighed and looked out the window.

"Poor Onyx. Does everyone bully you?" he asked.

"Almost," she answered. "You do not." She spoke without thinking and then looked at him in confusion.

She wanted to tell him that she had been bullied since the death of Reverend Hamilton. Bullied by Sir Matthew into conformity; bullied by Lady Daggett's velvet threats into obedience; bullied by Alice, who loved her but treated her as a child; bullied now by Andrew Littletree, who took every opportunity to remind her of her good fortune in accepting his proposal. She was not slow of thought; she knew that a long look down the years ahead would show her years of gibes and reminders to come of her lower station and meager expectations.

Onyx looked into the major's eyes, and it was almost as if he read her thoughts. But there was sympathy in his eyes, and it stung her.

"Don't feel sorry for me," she said, raising her chin higher.

"I don't," he said, "but I do wish you trusted me enough to tell me all of what's bothering you."

"I . . . I don't know you well enough," Onyx stammered, and then she thought about the few days they had spent together. She realized with a pang that she knew this man better than anyone she had ever known before, even better than Gerald.

It would have been easy to say nothing, or to smile and turn the subject, as she had always been taught to do. She was too honest for that.

"No. I know you better than anyone," she said, and he did not disagree. It sounded so bold, but it was honest. "And yet, at the same time, I know so little about you."

The carriage jolted, and she held her breath as the pain crossed Jack's face. "That's true," he said when he could speak again. "What do you want to know?"

"Where are you going? Where do you live?"

"North of here. Yorkshire, in fact. Can't you tell by my accent?"

She shook her head. He sounded evasive, but perhaps it was her imagination.

"My brother . . . I own s-some land in Yorkshire. Not far from York."

"Are you married?"

He grinned then. "Well, I was only yesterday, but the lady cried off."

It worked. He coaxed a smile out of her. "Silly! That doesn't count!" she exclaimed. "Can you never be serious?"

"You know that I can be, Onyx," he said, sitting up and stretching his long legs out straight in front of him. "Now, tell me why you are so meek and biddable, and yet so entirely brave, and such a complete paradox?"

She ignored the latter part of his question. "I have to be 'meek and biddable,' Major. You see, I'm not really here."

He cocked his head to one side, as if inviting her to continue.

Onyx glanced at Alice and lowered her voice. She

took a deep breath. "Sir, Gerald and I were found on the steps of the Reverend Peter Hamilton's church in a little village near Bath. We're illegitimate."

There. She had said it. Onyx looked at Jack Beresford, wondering how he would take that piece of news.

If she had expected surprise or the repugnance that she had come to expect when someone discerned the family skeleton, she saw none of that in Jack Beresford's eyes.

"I have even heard of such things in Yorkshire, Onyx B," he said. There was amusement in his voice, but she knew it was not at her expense. "Surely there must be more to your story than that, or I shall be sorely disappointed."

"Oh, much more," she said. "Papa, or rather I should say the Reverend Hamilton, took us home and sentimentally kept the names for us that were pinned on our blanket. But he considered us his own children."

"An estimable man," stated the major.

"He was all that we could ever have hoped for," Onyx said simply. "I loved him dearly."

There was a moment's pause. "And did he adopt you two?"

She shook her head. "He wanted to, but Mama—Lady Daggett—would have none of it, especially after Amethyst was born to them."

"Then Amethyst is your . . . well, I suppose she is no relation."

"True. Papa considered Gerald and me his children as much as Amethyst. He chose the name Amethyst to match mine. Mama cared for us only because he did."

"So that was how the wind blew."

"Yes." Onyx ventured a look at him. "This doesn't seem to be bothering you. Why is that?"

"Why should it bother me?" he asked in turn. "How is any of this your fault?"

She knew that surprise showed on her face. "I really

can't say. I don't know that I ever thought of it that way before."

"Tell me where Sir Matthew Daggett entered the picture."

"When we were ten, Papa took ill and died. Mama returned to her home." Onyx sighed. "I think she was glad enough to go. She is the daughter of a baronet, and many had been whispering for years that in marrying Papa she had married beneath her station. Yes, she went home."

"And you two went with her and Amethyst?"

"What could she do?" asked Onyx. "She could not abandon us, although I . . . well, I do not know." Onyx rubbed her arms, as if to ward off a chill. "When Sir Matthew married her, she warned Gerald and me that we were to stay away from the rest of the Daggetts, and not to call attention to ourselves. This is . . . difficult when you are twelve."

It was not a time she remembered with any pleasure, so she was silent then, until Jack recalled her to the moment.

"Onyx, when you are deep in serious thought, your eyes turn from Wedgwood blue to stormy gray."

She glanced up from the contemplation of her hands, surprised, forgetful for the moment where she was. "Are you always so poetic, Major?"

He carefully lowered himself to the pillows again. "No, and that's the surprise of it. You seem to bring out the Byron in me."

Her eyes widened. "That would be a terrible thing, Major! My . . . the Reverend Littletree says Byron is a shockingly bad man."

"In this instance, I must agree with the vicar's superior knowledge. But tell me, lovely Onyx, what do you mean when you say, 'I am not really here'?"

"Mama remarried someone more in her own style, but Gerald and I were always a reminder of her earlier marriage, and what she considered the Reverend Hamilton's folly. We soon learned to avoid family gatherings when anyone of importance was present, anyone titled or in any way distinguished. Anyone who might cut her dead if the issue of our background were raised. Mama insisted."

Onyx was not looking at Major Beresford when she made this artless confession. If she had been, she would have been troubled by the expression in his eyes. As it was, the harshness in his voice startled her.

"And so you vanished when company came, eh?"

"That's . . . about it," she replied, uncertain of his tone. "Mama didn't want anyone to remember us. I think it even troubles her now that Gerald and I were—are—called Hamilton."

Onyx clenched her fist. "But what are we to call ourselves? Everyone must have a last name. Even . . . even Gerald and Onyx." She fell silent, looking out the window at countryside that might well have been a blank wall, for all that she saw of it.

"I am still puzzled about one thing, Onyx," Major Beresford said finally, interrupting her highly unproductive thoughts.

"Sir?"

"How is this your fault, that you should be punished? Did these circumstances make Gerald less of a soldier? I know they did not. Does it make you less of a woman? I cannot see that it does."

She stirred, uncomfortable, confused again under the intensity of his gaze. "I've cried myself to sleep on many occasions, Major, wondering that very thing."

He sat up again and held out his good arm to her. "Come over here and sit by me, Onyx B. You look so lonely over there."

She did as he said and was soon curled up under his good arm. "I suppose this isn't very dignified, my dear

Miss Hamilton," he said. "If Alice should wake up, we can say that I needed someone to lean against."

"Gerald went to war then," said Onyx, scarcely hearing him. Somehow it was easier to talk when she didn't have to look at Major Beresford. She felt protected now. "Papa had left him enough money to buy a pair of colors. It was a small legacy that Mama could not touch. She was so glad to see him go." Her voice broke and she drew a long breath as Jack's arm tightened around her. "That was four years ago, when we were eighteen. And then one of Papa's cousins invited me to London for the Season."

"Did you go?" Beresford prodded when she fell silent again.

"I was almost all ready, and then Mama changed her mind. She was afraid such notice of an illegitimate child would reflect ill on her. And so I unpacked everything."

"I'm sorry. Would you have liked a London Season?"

She turned to look at him for the first time, her face alive with the glow from her eyes. "Oh, yes! Above all things. I've always wanted to see Vauxhall Gardens, and the opera, and the Elgin Marbles, even if they are stored in a shed." She touched his arm. "Have you seen them?"

"Yes, I have. I escorted my totty-headed aunt, who only wanted to make sure that she was seen there. I think I would enjoy even more the opportunity to show them to you. We could even witness a balloon ascension. Would you like that?"

"Oh! Indeed I would." She sighed with pleasure. "I own I would not care to dance until dawn, but I would like to look in at Almack's and drive down Rotten Row during the fashionable hour."

"And buy a poke bonnet with feathers?"

"Yes! And not even have to mind the expense. Just walk into a milliner's and say, 'I'll take that one, and that one, and . . .' Oh, but I am rambling on in a fearsome way," she concluded.

"And I enjoy it, Onyx," the major replied simply. "Do you realize that I have not thought about Spain in quite a while?"

She smiled but said nothing. The major looked at her, watching the way she blushed under any scrutiny. "And do you know something else?"

She shook her head.

"I have hardly stammered since you woke me out of that nightmare," he said softly.

Onyx worked her way out of his grasp so she could regard him better. "I did not know that you stammered in the first place, Major. It could not have been very noticeable."

He had no answer for her except to take her hand and raise it to his lips. "God bless you, little lady," he said, kissing her fingers lightly.

He laughed softly when she retreated in confusion to the other side of the carriage and resumed her place next to Alice Banner. With a wink to her, he lowered himself to his pillows again and closed his eyes, leaving her to her own disordered thoughts.

When her agitation lessened, she observed the sleeping man across from her, wondering about him. That he was a gentleman, despite his rough language, was obvious. He had been at war; he was used to male company, the talk of men who had no time for frivolities. He must be somewhere in his late twenties or early thirties, but she could not be sure. She remembered Gerald's one visit home before his death and her discomfiture at observing how much older he seemed. It was the same with the major.

By no exercise of the imagination could she call Jack Beresford a handsome man. His features, though regular enough, did not come together in any way remarkable. The lines at the corners of his eyes and mouth were attributable to long hours in harsh sunlight. His skin was leathery and well-tanned, his hair auburn. He was quite tall, but much too lean.

As she analyzed the major's appearance, Onyx told herself that in no way did he come up to anyone's criterion of male beauty. The Reverend Littletree, for all his little tics and quirks and thinning hair, was probably a better looking man. But the vicar lacked Beresford's cachet, that indefinable something that a woman of Onyx's inexperience with men could not put into words. Whatever it was, she knew that when Major Beresford finally said good-bye, turned his back to her, and continued his journey to Yorkshire, he would be hard—perhaps impossible—to forget.

Alice woke up when the afternoon was blending into early evening. She watched her charge, who was looking out the window.

"Have you decided what you plan to tell Lady Bagshott about this little delay?" Alice asked finally in her dry fashion.

"The truth, of course," replied Onyx, "except where Private Petrie is concerned. No good will ever be served by involving him with the brigands." She sighed. "I hope Lady Bagshott is of an understanding mind. Jack needs a place to rest, and I still feel responsible."

Alice patted Onyx. "I know that you do."

Onyx smiled on her sleeping charge. "Do you know, Alice, it is too bad we are not sufficiently beforehand in the world to command Lady Bagshott's services." The smile left her face. "As it is, we will hope for the best."

They did not stop for the night but continued on by the light of the full moon to Chalcott, arriving there, as near as Onyx could judge, at about the time when at home she would have been beaten at the whist table by Lady Daggett for the second and final time of the evening.

Her uneasiness increased as they turned off the main highway beyond Chalcott village and traveled down a well-graveled road with hedges of sweet-smelling orange blossoms. Major Beresford was awake and sitting up, but he was not speaking. His gaze was inner-directed again, and she knew he was in pain. She did not trouble him with words, but in the little voice inside her mind, she urged John Coachman to hurry.

They turned off the gravel road and Chalcott Manor was before them.

"Alice, look!" Onyx exclaimed.

The house rose before them like a giant wedding cake, all arches and ogives, comings and goings of massive walls and mullioned windows. It was such a house that she, in her prosaic way, would never have imagined. She could only fold her hands together in her lap and stare at it. She began to feel the familiar discomfort that overtook her whenever the Daggetts prepared for an evening's entertainment and she knew she was to be excluded.

Private Petrie had ridden ahead of them and already dismounted in front of the main entrance. With an insouciance that quite took her breath away, he swung off the major's horse and strode up the front steps to ring the bell. *I would have found a servants' entrance*, Onyx marveled as she watched him.

By the time Sir Matthew Daggett's venerable traveling coach creaked to a halt, Petrie's peremptory summons had been answered. A servant, looking quite as antique as the house, came onto the driveway, followed by another retainer equally ancient. Before either of them could open the carriage door, John leapt off his box and shouldered them aside. He flung open the door, muttering something about "showing these old furriners how we as come from Bedfordshire do things."

With a glance back at the major, who watched her, but still said nothing, Onyx accepted John's hand and stepped lightly to the ground. She smoothed her wrinkled skirts about her and looked up in time to watch the majesty that was Lady Amanda Bagshott silhouette herself in the front door and pause.

Onyx would have known her anywhere. Lady Bagshott and her brother, Sir Matthew, shared the same long nose and pointed chin. As she stood in awe, watching Lady Bagshott descend the steps, Onyx was reminded of the time Gerald threw her into whoops by declaring quite solemnly, "If ever Sir Matthew loses all his teeth, his nose and chin will surely meet. Perhaps they will grow together."

As the image rose before her eyes, Onyx resisted the urge to lean against the carriage and laugh until her sides hurt. Such foolishness would never do. Even as she wondered at the majesty before her, there was something about Lady Bagshott, some resemblance that she couldn't quite place.

But this was hardly the time for philosophy. Gathering her courage about her like a threadbare robe, she came toward the formidable dame, dropped a graceful curtsy, and extended her hand. "Lady Bagshott, I am Onyx Hamilton," she said in her soft voice.

The dowager did not accept the proffered hand. She came closer and at her leisure looked Onyx over from head to foot. Never was Onyx more conscious of her shabby clothes, the meek little hat with no plumes to recommend it, the gray pelisse with the tear at the elbow she had so artfully mended, but which now seemed to stand out like a windmill on a Spanish plain. She knew that her face had no blemishes, and she wondered why she worried anyway, as Lady Bagshott's eyes lingered on it and then passed down to her generous amplitude, where they paused.

Lady Bagshott's voice boomed out as she stared at Onyx. "Young lady, such bosoms are not the fashion!"

A week ago, Onyx would have dropped over in a dead faint if anyone had said such a thing to her. In her anger, Onyx whipped off her gloves and held them in one hand. Lady Bagshott stepped back one pace, as if half-expecting the overendowed Miss Hamilton to slap the gloves across her face.

Lady Bagshott's sudden movement recalled Onyx to her present dilemma. She slapped her gloves in her other hand, bit her lower lip until it hurt, and raised her chin higher.

"Lady Bagshott, we can find ample time in the future to discuss my physical failings. I regret the intrusion at this late hour. I regret that I must disturb the tenor of your household in any way, but I have brought with me the man who rescued Alice and me on the road some days past, and he is in need of a place to sleep."

Again the dowager fixed her with a formidable stare that, if Onyx had only known, Lady Bagshott used to employ to great advantage on her little brother Matthew.

"And I am to be the recipient of your tawdry adventures, girl? Is this how you would repay my condescension in allowing you here in the first place?"

"Oh, cut line, Lady Bagshott," growled a voice from within the carriage.

Onyx could almost feel the blood from her face draining into her shoes. "Oh, no, Jack!" she squeaked, horrified. "Oh, please, madam, he did not mean it."

"Yes, I did," Major Beresford assured her. "Alice, quit gaping like a fish in a net and lend me a hand."

Onyx watched in stunned silence, bereft of the power of speech, as the major hauled himself from the carriage and sat down quite suddenly on the coach step. He looked up at Lady Bagshott and smiled.

"Amanda Bagshott, how are you this evening? Blooming, as usual?"

The dowager stepped back another pace. She rummaged around in her reticule and took out a man's spectacles, which she propped on her nose. The officer and the dowager stared at one another as Onyx looked from one to the other, unable to take her eyes from them.

Amanda Bagshott's gaze wavered first. A little smile came to her lips but did not linger there long. A deep-throated sputter forced its way from between her lips. In someone else, Onyx would have thought such a sound to be the reminiscence of a recently eaten meal, a sound to be followed immediately by an apology. But the sound came again, and Onyx realized it was laughter.

And then the voice trumpeted forth again. "Jack Beresford! You are every bit the scapegrace and rakehell your father was before you!"

"You should know, Lady Bagshott," he murmured. "We'll have time for more pleasantries in the morning, I am sure. Will you kindly do as this little lady here suggests and find me a bed before I collapse at your feet?"

"I recall your father doing that once!" Amanda boomed and uttered that peculiar laugh again. She clapped her hands, and two slightly younger menservants appeared. "Find this man a bed. Tell Mrs. Dowling to bring a warming pan. Lud, the night brings strange creatures to my house. Come, girl, don't just stand there with your mouth open!"

Wordlessly Onyx watched the servants help Jack to his feet and followed the dowager into the mansion. Onyx trailed after them up the stairs and stood in the hallway as the men undressed the major and put him to bed. When they were done, she went in.

Amanda Bagshott stood by the bed, looking down at the major. "Can I get you anything, Jack?" she asked, her voice no softer but muffled a bit by the hangings that drooped around the bed and over the windows like crepe in a funeral establishment.

"Just Onyx," he said, starting to roll up his sleeve. Without a word to either of them, Onyx removed her pelisse and sat down on the bed. She pulled the sleeve up the rest of the way to Jack's shoulder and gently pulled back the bandage. In another moment there was a servant at her elbow with a tray of medicinal supplies. She took the scissors and snipped away the bandage. As Amanda Bagshott loomed over her, Onyx dabbed at the oozing cut.

Lady Bagshott's breath was hot on her neck as Onyx touched the skin and then sighed in exasperation. She picked up a pair of tweezers from the little tray, pressed down on the skin, and slowly extracted a bone fragment.

"I knew there was something rubbing on that bandage," was all Jack said before he closed his eyes.

Onyx wrapped his arm again after spreading on a thin layer of ointment Mrs. Millstead's doctor had concocted for her. She felt Jack's forehead. It was warm.

"I have fever powders, Miss Hamilton," said Lady Bagshott. In deference to the sleeping man, she spoke in a whisper, but the tones rolled across the room like reverberations from the belfry of the York Minster.

"No," Onyx said, "he will not need them." She straightened up and regarded her hostess. "And if I may have the room next to this one, I will look in on him during the night."

"Such a thing, of course, is highly irregular," began Lady Bagshott.

"Yes, it is, isn't it?" broke in Onyx before Lady Bagshott had further opportunity to unburden herself. "I have been his nurse these past few days, and I know his needs." She was almost unaware of it, but a certain militancy had crept into her voice. The sound of it caused Jack to open his eyes.

"I suggest you listen to the sergeant here, Lady Bagshott," said Jack. "I always used to listen to mine."

Lady Bagshott offered her odd laugh. "Very well, girl, for tonight," she capitulated. "But in the morning, it is off to the vicarage with you."

"That is all I ask," Onyx replied. The quelling tones of Lady Bagshott's voice made the gooseflesh rise and march up and down her back, but she was not about to surrender Jack to someone who had no notion of his situation. She was tired; she wanted nothing more than to find a bed of her own. She started to follow Amanda Bagshott from the room.

Jack called her back. With his good hand he gestured to her to lean closer. Her ear was practically on his lips.

"I don't care, you know," he said.

She drew back slightly. "Care about what, Major?"

"I don't care that you are not the first stare of fashion, Miss Hamilton," he said, his voice a conspiratorial whisper. "Next to your Wedgwood eyes, I must admit . . . to dropping a glance now and then at your unfashionable—" He winked at her. "But just now and then."

"Jack!" she gasped. "What will you say next? No . . . don't answer. Just go to sleep." She left the room hurriedly, hardly knowing whether to laugh or cry.

Lady Bagshott awaited her in the hall. She gestured toward the next room. "You will find this adequate." She sniffed. "Probably nicer than anything Sir Matthew ever thought of. He has no notion of true splendor."

Onyx put her hand on the doorknob. All she wanted was sleep, but she turned to address the dowager. "I was so afraid," she confessed. "You see, I did not know how you would like the idea of a wounded man in your house."

Amanda Bagshott gave several barks of laughter; "Oh, girl, I do believe the joke is on you! Your good vicar said you were used to the sheltered life. Have you even the smallest idea who that is sleeping in my second-best bedroom?"

Onyx shook her head as that chilly feeling of exclusion began to descend on her again.

Another bark of laughter. "That is John Beresford. He's the richest man in Yorkshire." More laughter. "His brother is Adrian, Marquess of Sherbourn. Between the two of them, I do believe they own most of the northern marches all the way to the Tees. Good night, Miss Hamilton. Pleasant dreams."

Chapter 8

⌒

THE BED WAS COMFORTABLE, THE little coal fire in the grate more than she was used to, the walls thick enough to keep the world from intruding, but Onyx Hamilton was still lying wide awake in bed staring at the ceiling when the sun rose.

As far as she could tell during her hours of tossing and turning, Jack Beresford had slept peacefully through the night. As she lay there with her hands folded precisely across her middle, she wondered if she would have gone to him if he had been in need of her.

Just thinking about the night before made her eyes close in humiliation. *How he must be laughing*, she told herself for the hundredth time as she shifted her gaze from the ceiling and watched the wallpaper turn from muddy dots to brambles and roses as the light of morning filled the cozy room.

It was a new role for her. During the ten years of Lady Daggett's marriage to Sir Matthew, Onyx had been relegated to the back of the room, the darker corners, where no one of any consequence ever chose to look very closely. She lay in bed and wished herself back in the corner again, far away from Jack Beresford.

Even her brief acquaintance with him, strained as it was by circumstance, had shown her how much he loved a good joke. *How he must be laughing now*, she thought. *He can tell his army cohorts and his brother how he led on a silly woman of utterly no consequence.*

The thought so unnerved her that it propelled her out of bed in such a rapid motion that she was standing by the window before she was aware almost of having left the warmth of the blankets. She leaned her head against window frame and looked out, refusing to cry. It was not difficult; she was too angry at herself to cry.

A servant scratched on the door. Onyx gave herself a mental shake and opened the door. It was the maid, with a can of hot water and several towels. She curtsied. "Miss Hamilton, when you're ready, Major Beresford told me to tell you to step into his room before you go down to breakfast."

Onyx smiled and nodded and then closed the door behind the maid as she left. *That's the last thing I will do*, she told herself as she washed and dressed. For the first time ever, she wished that the Reverend Littletree were closer than Cambridge. He was prosy; he was boring; he was endlessly right; he was also a buffer against the man next door. As trying as the vicar could be at times, he never gave her any reason to think she was more than what she was.

She buttoned up her dress and savagely attacked her hair, brushing it until it crackled and stood out from her head. She looked in the mirror, leaning closer, the hairbrush in her hand like a weapon. "Wedgwood eyes," she muttered. They were blue and nothing more. Still . . . She touched her face and sighed.

Her good gray morning dress was quite wrinkled from the ordeal of the journey, but she draped Lady Daggett's cast-off Norwich silk shawl around her shoulders to hide the more obvious lines and creases and carefully let herself out the door.

"Onyx?"

She sighed, bit her tongue, and resolutely continued down the hall.

"Onyx, please," he said, louder, his voice with an edge of command to it. "I must talk to you."

Her rage got the better of her. She stalked back to the door. "You're not going to bully me, Major Beresford," she said on her side of the door. "You're in excellent hands now."

If there was a reply, she did not hear it. Gathering her shawl about her, she ran down the hall, assuming a sedate pace only when she had descended two floors and located the breakfast parlor.

Lady Bagshott waited within, standing by the sideboard and twitching the skirt of her morning dress with the air of one who seldom is called upon to wait for anyone.

"I trust, Miss Hamilton," she began, as if she had been rehearsing, her speech, "you are not in the habit of late mornings. It is hardly becoming in the wife of a clergyman."

"No, madam, indeed I am not," Onyx replied, wishing that the unruly color would leave her cheeks. She thought about making excuse, but something in Lady Bagshott's bearing stopped her. "I am sorry," was all she said as she inclined her head toward the dowager and allowed the footman to seat her at the table.

"Baa!" Lady Bagshott dismissed the man with a wave of her hand as Onyx poured herself a cup of tea and nibbled at the buttered toast.

When it appeared that she could not further intimidate Onyx, Lady Bagshott sat down. She accepted without a word the cup of tea Onyx handed to her.

There was a certain militancy in Lady Bagshott that someone of Onyx's straightforward nature could not understand. Beyond wondering about it for a brief moment, Onyx did not try. Instead, she finished her bread and butter in silence and waited.

"Aren't you even curious about the major?" the dowager asked at last, her voice full of accusation.

Onyx looked at her and smiled. "I am sure, Lady Bagshott, that he is in excellent hands now," she said calmly, willing her heart to stop its fluttering about. "He is back among his own kind now and surely can lack for nothing in the way of proper attention."

"The doctor has already been to see him," said Lady Bagshott, waiting for some reaction. "Ahem, don't you wish to know how he is?"

"If you choose to tell me, Lady Bagshott," was the calm reply.

"Well, I do not!" snapped the other woman. When Onyx made no reply, but calmly continued eating, she shifted in her chair. "He is fine, Miss Hamilton. Dr. Meers says that he is young and healthy, and will heal rapidly."

"Oh, such excellent news," said Onyx. She raised her Wedgwood eyes to the dowager. "And now, madam, I do not wish to take up your valuable time, but perhaps you could acquaint me with the vicarage? The Reverend Littletree tells me I am to be responsible for seeing to its refurbishing."

So adroitly had she dismissed the subject of Jack Beresford that for Lady Bagshott to retrieve the thread of that conversation would have been poor manners indeed.

After a moment of stunned silence, Lady Bagshott cleared her throat with a sound reminiscent of distant cannonading. "Indeed, Miss Hamilton. Your . . . companion has already gone ahead this morning."

"I shall follow her then," said Onyx. "I have not unpacked my trunk. Can you have it removed to the vicarage? I assume, of course, that the vicar has not yet taken up residence there?"

"Oh, goodness, no," Lady Bagshott replied. "He said

he was partial to lung inflammation and would wait until the residence was in better repair."

If ever anyone had waved a clearer warning signal, Onyx had never known of it. For all she knew, the building was falling down. She smiled, knowing with a feeling of delicious naughtiness totally foreign to her nature that such a smile would irritate Lady Bagshott. It was summer now; her lungs were strong. She wouldn't remain one more minute under the same roof that sheltered Jack Beresford. Not if she could help it.

"I am certain that I can make the best of this situation, Lady Bagshott. You have only to point me in the right direction."

The vicarage lay two miles distant across the wide expanse that was Chalcott's back lawn. The day was fine. Onyx took a deep breath of the garden fragrances, raised her skirts to keep her hem dry, and set off.

She looked around her. It would be a pleasant walk anytime of the year, except perhaps in the deep of winter. *I will be married by then*, she thought. She shivered, wondering if it was from her thoughts of cold or her thoughts of life with the Reverend Andrew Littletree. She gave herself a little shake and hurried faster.

The front door was open when Onyx arrived at the vicarage, a half-timbered two-story house of uncertain age and questionable lineage. Ivy in early, tentative bloom twined all over the little windows, rather like cataracts in old eyes, she thought. The pathway was overgrown with weeds poking up through the cobbled stones.

The total effect was Gothic enough to please the most case-hardened reader of Mrs. Winslow or Fanny Weatherington, but as Onyx stood on the path and watched the play of sunlight over the weathered building, she knew that she could contrive enough to make a pleasant home.

Once indoors, she was less sure. Her eyes went immediately to dark patches on the ceiling and the unsightly fingers of rainwater that had flowed down the walls, leaving the wallpaper in discolored streaks. Over all these defects was the gloom created by the profusion of ivy that allowed in only a begrudging amount of light. *Rather as if Lady Bagshott were in charge of lighting*, Onyx thought and smiled slightly.

The furniture, what there was of it in the saloon off the entrance, was shrouded in holland covers, contributing to the air of general dishevelment. Onyx stood in the doorway to the parlor and marveled at how abandoned the room looked. She thought of Egyptian ruins pictured in one of Gerald's old textbooks. The remembered sarcophagus and jumble of funerary jars looked no more antique than the display spread before her. *How old things appear when they are not cared for*, she thought as she wrote her name in the dust of a small uncovered table.

But this was to be her home. She gave herself another shake and crossed the hallway to the other, smaller parlor. She peeked in the partly open door and gasped.

Before her was a pianoforte, a handsome, dignified instrument that not even a thick layer of dust could disguise. From the looks of the padded bench, mice had staged periodic raids for nesting material, but the piano appeared intact. Onyx came closer and pulled off the rest of the holland cover that was draped over it.

The dust rose in clouds. She coughed and stepped back to the room entrance until it settled slowly again. Stepping closer, she raised the lid and played a major chord.

As she had feared, the pianoforte was badly out of tune.

Onyx could see no sign of water damage from the

leaking ceiling, but the beautiful instrument had suffered several years of neglect. She patted the piano bench to make sure that all mice had long since vacated it, and sat down, resting her fingers lightly on the keys.

Onyx looked around her. The room was small, but there was a good enough fireplace, and with the encroaching ivy stripped away, she knew that the little saloon could become the heart of the house.

"I can see that you are already imagining a winter evening."

Onyx looked around and clapped her hands. "Alice, isn't it famous? Who would have thought to find such a treasure in this old place?"

Alice had removed her hat and was swathed in a long apron. "Onyx, I knew that you would overlook every defect once you saw that piano."

Onyx turned to her, holding out her hand. "You know how I am," she replied simply. "It is a little enough pleasure."

"Indeed it is!" Alice retorted. "My dear, when you see the rest of this place . . ." Words failed her. She sat down on the bench with Onyx.

"Surely it cannot be that bad," said Onyx.

It was that—and more. Onyx trailed behind Alice as the older woman led her from the bedchambers upstairs, completely at the mercy of the leaking roof, to the kitchen, a gloomy dungeon with its cavernous fireplace that must have done duty during the reign of good Queen Bess.

Onyx stood upright in the fireplace, holding her dress tight around her. "Alice," she exclaimed in awed tones, "we could probably cook a meal for Wellington's entire army at one time in this fireplace."

"There isn't enough firewood left in England," was Alice's tart rejoinder. "Onyx, come out of that fireplace. Only think how dirty you will get your shoes!"

Onyx did as she was bidden, removing her bonnet

and setting it carefully on the table. The mention of Wellington's army reminded her of Gerald. She wished with her whole heart that he were here. She sat in silence, looking into the fireplace.

"Well," she said at last, "this place will not clean itself. Perhaps you can find me another apron, dear Alice. If we clean up one bedroom first, at least we'll have a place to put our belongings." She stood up, careful not to disturb the ashes from many fires that lay about the tiled floor. "Oh, do you think Lady Bagshott will send someone to help us?"

"Not in our lifetime," was Alice's reply.

By the time the underfootman arrived, puffing and bug-eyed, with their luggage, Onyx and Alice had swept the floor of the main bedchamber. Onyx had to admit that her shabby trunk, somewhat dented from its disaster on the highway, looked right at home against the tattered and water-stained wallpaper. She found her oldest dress and put it on, mindful that the wrinkles didn't really matter. There was no one to impress. The thought reminded her of Jack Beresford, and she winced in spite of herself.

Onyx was descending the stairs, treading carefully, listening to the creak and groan of each step and wondering at what instant the stairs would part company with the peeling walls, when someone tapped on the doorframe.

"Yes?" she called.

A youngish woman poked her head in the front door, which still stood open. "Miss Hamilton?"

Onyx hurried down the stairs. "Yes?"

The servant curtsied. "I've been sent to help you clean."

Onyx sighed with relief. "There will be plenty for you to do, as soon as we can find where things are."

"Oh, miss, that's easy. My mother was cook here, and I was born on the property. My name is Daisy."

"Daisy, you are welcome indeed."

With only a moment to reflect, Daisy located the cleaning equipment in the closet under the servants' stairs and started on the kitchen. Alice Banner watched her, nodded, and then took pencil and paper from an open drawer and handed it to her charge. "Here, Onyx, you had better be the one to take inventory. Write down what is in good repair and what needs to be fixed."

"I'm not sure there is enough paper, Alice," she replied.

She started for the stairs and then turned back to Daisy. "I will certainly have to thank Lady Bagshott for sending you to us."

Daisy laughed and then put her hand over her mouth, looking around her. "Oh, miss, it wasn't her lady-ship! It was that man, that man upstairs, the one with the wounded arm."

"Oh, no," said Onyx under her breath.

"Oh, yes, ma'am! I was cleaning out the ashes in his grate when he told me to come to the vicarage. Said he would make it right with Lady Bagshott. And then he gave me such a wink." She giggled.

I know that wink, Onyx thought. The man thinks he can get anything he wants by winking. Her innate honesty won out over her momentary pique. *Well, he can, drat his hide.*

"Then I must . . . you must . . . tell him how grate-ful I . . . we are," Onyx finished in a rush. She could not understand why she should be standing there blushing in front of the maid.

The inventory, a document boding to be even more complex than William the Conqueror's Doomsday Book, was only partly finished when the sun disappeared from the sky. Onyx straightened up from counting lacerated sheets and mothy towels and went down the stairs.

The little parlor with the pianoforte was swept clean and well dusted. The ashes were gone from the fireplace, and Alice was just removing the last of the sun-faded draperies from the window.

"Daisy says these can be washed and mended," Alice commented from her perch on the ladder.

"I am sure she is right."

The piano was a magnet that drew Onyx across the room, even when she thought she was too tired to take another step. She approached it and ran her fingers gently across the keys, barely touching them. She did not want to press down hard enough to make a sound. The piano was so badly out of tune that she could not bear it. But at least the wood of the instrument glowed now, following the application of a dust rag and several coats of polish.

"The kitchen is in order," Alice continued briskly as she climbed down the ladder and handed the curtain to Onyx. "Daisy seems to think that we will be able to stock it tomorrow and then we can take our meals here."

"If we can find a cook equal to that monstrous fireplace," said Onyx. "Whatever will we pay her?"

Alice had no answer. She merely shook her head and pulled the ladder away from the window.

When they had changed clothes and shaken all the dust from their hair and shoes, Onyx and Alice started back across the lawn. The air smelled of late-spring flowers and newly cropped grass. Onyx breathed deeply. "How nice not to smell mildew and bat soil," she declared.

Alice snorted. "I can't imagine what the Reverend Littletree had in mind to have you do this."

"I am sure he had no notion of how great was the state of disrepair," was Onyx's quiet reply. "Hush, Alice. We can listen to the birds singing."

Her head throbbed, and she longed for a soaking bath and the comfort of clean sheets. The birds reminded her that it was summer, and she stood still long enough to enjoy the little pleasure, wondering, as she did so, why she was poised so precariously on the edge of tears. It was more than the emotion felt in the beauty of an early summer night; it was something else she had never felt before, but she was too tired to question it.

Lady Bagshott's butler informed them that her ladyship was enjoying dinner at a neighboring residence and that dinner trays had been prepared for them in their respective rooms. Onyx thanked him, said good night to Alice, and climbed the stairs.

She paused at the top, turned, and sat down on the top step, her chin cupped in her hands. With tired eyes she noted how clean and straight was the wallpaper, how well polished the sconces with their neat little beeswax candles. She closed her eyes.

"Onyx, do you make a habit of sitting on stairs?"

She wasn't even startled. "Why, yes, I do, Major," she replied, not looking around. "In Sir Matthew's house I spent many evenings watching guests coming and going. They didn't see me because I was at the top of the stairs."

She stood and continued up the stairs, wondering where he was. She grew more accustomed to the darkness and saw the major sitting in a chair outside his room. He looked so exhausted that her own discomfort vanished.

"What are you doing there, sir?" she asked.

"Waiting for you," was his brief reply.

She could tell by his clipped words that his arm was paining him. "Well, I wish you would go to bed."

"I wanted to see you first," he replied and then paused a moment. "I want to apologize."

"There's no need, Major," she answered, and there wasn't. A day spent cleaning her future home had cleared her mind of any cobwebs. If even for a moment she had harbored any pretensions about her position in this household or any other, they were gone now, swept away. She was Onyx Hamilton again, shadowy nondaughter of Lady Marjorie Daggett. The heroine of the highway, the ministering angel, was gone now. *I'm sure that in a month or two, I won't even remember this adventure at all*, she thought as she looked at Jack Beresford and then reached out for him.

"Come on, sir. You're tired and have no business sitting here," she scolded gently. "Just lean on me. I'll help you."

She got the major to his feet, and he draped his arm across her shoulders. Her arm went around his waist, and she could feel his ribs.

"You're too thin, you know, for your size," she said.

"It's a thin war, Onyx. They'll feed me when I get home."

He said the word *home* with so much longing that she felt tears starting in her eyes again. She helped him to his bed, made sure the covers were up around his shoulders, and took a look at the fire glowing in the grate.

She was mindful of his eyes on her the whole time she moved about the room, closing the window against the breeze that had come up, making sure the curtains were drawn and that there was water in the crystal carafe by the bedside.

Onyx hesitated and then put her hand on the major's forehead. "You have the fever again," she said. "Oh, I wish you did not."

"That is the wish of us both, then. No fever powders, though. I'll manage."

"I never doubted that you would, sir," she said formally.

"I wrote, or rather, Lady Bagshott wrote to Sherbourn today. She dispatched Private Petrie with the letter. I expect I will have clothes that fit me soon. I do grow weary of Mr. Millstead's nightgown."

His eyes were closing. "I am sorry, Onyx," he said. "I didn't mean to lead you on, truly I did not, but when you told me how it was for you in your house when anyone of any particular distinction came to visit, I was . . . afraid you would not . . ." His voice grew quieter. ". . . like me anymore."

She didn't know what to say. She blew out the candle by the bed. "Go to sleep, Major," she said.

"I wish you would call me Jack again," he said.

"I think not, sir," she replied, feeling again those absurd tears and grateful for the darkness.

"Can we be friends at least?" he asked. His voice was slow and thick, and she knew he was close to sleep.

"Yes. Surely we can be friends."

She could not trust herself to say more. She quietly closed the door behind her.

In the middle of the night, Onyx heard Jack Beresford talking out loud, commanding his soldiers. She woke up, tears on her face, but she did not go to him. In another moment he had wakened himself, and the talking ceased. She lay back down, drew herself into a little ball, and let sleep overtake her again.

Chapter 9

ONYX FELT MORE CHARITABLE toward Major Beresford in the morning. Dressing quickly, she pulled her long hair back in a simple chignon at the nape of her neck. She stepped into the dress she had laid carefully across the end of the bed and buttoned it. All her other clothes were at the vicarage. Indeed, she had planned to return there the night before, but when she finished eating in her room, she lay down on the bed just to rest a moment. Other than her brief awakening in the middle of the night when the major started to talk in the room next door, she had slept soundly.

Onyx grabbed up her shawl and left the room. Without giving Jack Beresford the chance to call to her, she knocked on his door.

"Come in, Onyx," he said.

She opened the door. The major was sitting up in bed with the remains of a breakfast tray still across his lap. She removed it without a word and then opened the curtains. Sunlight streamed in. The warmth made her sigh with pleasure.

"A beautiful day, Major," she said.

"Now it is," he replied. "You came in."

She ignored his flattery, chiding herself for the way her heart thumped at his words. *How singular*, she thought. *Hearts don't thump. I must be experiencing a moment's indigestion.* She made a mental note to mix herself some soda and water that evening.

"Is it so awful at the vicarage?" he asked.

She laughed. "It is dreadful! But imagine, Jack, there is a pianoforte! It is something I never expected. It is fearsomely out of tune, but I am assembling a list of things that need to be done about the place, and a piano tuner is high on the list."

"Bravo, Onyx," he murmured.

She curtsied to him playfully and enjoyed the sound of his laughter.

"Oh, and I should thank you . . . for Daisy," she said, her hand on the doorknob.

"Will that work out?"

"Oh, yes. How did you ever convince that . . . Lady Bagshott that we needed help?"

Beresford hitched himself up higher and leaned back against his pillows. "Nothing simpler. After all, I have been watching you manage the redoubtable vicar, so I merely employed your tactics."

"Wretch!"

"Call me what you will. I am a fast learner," he responded virtuously, but not without a twinkle in his brown eyes. "I waited until Lady Bagshott *and* the doctor were in my room and then remarked to her how kind, how truly Christian, she was to approve of Daisy's going to the vicarage." He smiled broadly. "What could she do? Deny it? Embarrass herself in front of the good doctor—who, by the way, tells me that you are an excellent nurse. Oh, no. She bowed and smiled. The only thing I did not do was fling myself upon her chest, which I recall worked quite well with the vicar."

She blushed and he laughed again, throwing his head back and letting the laughter ring in the room. "Onyx, you're good for me," he said.

"You, sir, are incorrigible."

"So, Miss Hamilton, are you. We are a pair of rogues. Now, get along and finish that inventory. Daisy stopped in earlier this morning to inform me that she might have found you a cook."

Daisy had certainly found a cook.

"Miss Hamilton, this is my mother," she said when Onyx reached the house and let herself in by the kitchen entrance. "My mother, Mrs. Sable. She's a bit troubled by the joint ache, and Lady Bagshott pensioned her off."

"But I am bored, miss," stated Mrs. Sable. "When Daisy tells me what's what here in the vicarage, nothing will do but I come down here myself. After all, this was used to be my kitchen." She looked around defiantly. "I'd like to see another work *that* fireplace! Plain food, Miss Hamilton, plain food is what I cook." She looked over her shoulder in the general direction of Chalcott. "Plain food what was good enough until Lady Bagshott went off to London and got some airs and polish and a French cook. French!" She spit out the word as though it tasted bad on her tongue. "Plain food, that's all."

Onyx took both of Mrs. Sable's hands in her own.

"That is precisely what we will be wanting here. The Reverend Littletree has a dyspeptic nature. I am not sure that a French cook would be at all to his liking. I'd be pleased if you would join us." She paused and her face reddened. "I . . . don't know what I'll be able to pay you . . . at least, not until I am married later this summer and I am provided with a household allowance."

Mrs. Sable freed her hand and waved it. "Don't be

fretting! I have no needs that won't keep. Look at it this way, miss. You've saved me from boredom."

Jack must have been working further miracles. All morning, a stream of footmen and underhouse-maids carted staples and dishes to the kitchen. Mrs. Sable, holding court at the head of the kitchen table, examined each dish. "Cast-offs and Gypsy-mended pans," she sniffed. "But what can you expect when a Frenchman governs the kitchen?" She glared about her as if expecting to see French chefs in every cubbyhole. "The enemy!"

The vicarage inventory was complete after dinner—a simple roast chicken removed with sole—was a dim and satisfying memory to Onyx and Alice. When they had finally forced themselves away from Mrs. Sable's "plain food, just plain food," they had continued the inventory. Onyx covered several pages with her neat script. She handed the list to Alice finally, who perused it, frowning all the while, and then handed it back.

"I wish you good fortune in convincing Lady Bagshott to agree to anything beyond the roof repair and new wallpaper, and I wouldn't hold my breath on the wallpaper," she said.

They slept together in the big bed in the main upstairs chamber. The mattress sagged in the middle.

"Daisy tells me that the last vicar was a bucket of guts," Alice said as they struggled to keep from rolling together in the middle.

"Alice!"

"Why else would this old bed sag so alarmingly?" Alice retorted. "Put a new mattress on your list tomorrow."

Onyx was awakened toward morning to the sound of thunder and then cold rain on her face. She burrowed under the covers; but the sound of dripping water came at her from all sides. She poked Alice awake, and they draped themselves in blankets and went trailing downstairs to the parlor, where they listened to rainwater running down the walls and waited for morning.

The storm stopped by midmorning. Before the rainbow had faded from the sky, Onyx presented herself in Chalcott. Jenner, the butler, bowed her into the house, raising his eyebrows at the wet hem of her dress.

"Lady Bagshott?" he asked in quelling tones.

Onyx nodded; Jenner looked so clean, pressed, and starched. She was painfully aware that her dress was wet, and her stockings splashed with mud, but she pulled her shawl tighter around her and clutched the inventory.

"Bookroom, miss," he said, striding toward the back of the house as she hurried to keep up with him.

Lady Bagshott sat behind a heavily carved desk, her accounts spread before her. She looked up when Onyx entered, and then sighed and held out her hand. "The inventory, I suppose?"

Onyx nodded and handed it over. Even as it left her hands, she knew that it was too long. She wanted to snatch it back, run away, and take another look at it, but Lady Bagshott had snapped open the document. She said nothing as she perused the document, only pausing every now and then to fix Onyx with her eagle's stare, rumble deep in her throat, and continue her journey down the document.

The door opened. Lady Bagshott looked up and nodded to Major Beresford, who came in and sat down.

He was dressed at last in clothes that fit him, the elegant but definitely casual buckskins, high-top boots, and unruffled shirt of a country gentleman. His hair had been cut and he was clean-shaven again, smelling faintly of bay rum.

"These garments came from Sherbourn by morning post," he said. "I couldn't get my coat on over the bandage," he whispered to Onyx. "I'm a trifle old-fashioned, it is true, but my tailor refused to come to Spain with me for four years; so here you are."

"Hush, Jack," bellowed Lady Bagshott. "How can I think when you are carrying on in that rackety way?"

"Beg pardon," he replied and winked at Onyx.

She scarcely noticed. Her eyes were drawn again to Lady Bagshott, who continued her stately way down the inventory. The rumblings in her throat grew louder. Onyx felt the blood drain from her face as Lady Bagshott picked up her pencil and began to mark heavily through several items, muttering something under her breath.

She reached the bottom of the last page. The ensuing silence lasted long enough for Jack Beresford to cross and uncross his long legs twice.

"This is outrageous!" Lady Bagshott said at last, her voice rising to a timbre that made the window shiver. "Repairs on the vicarage will propel me into the poorhouse!"

"Madam," ventured Onyx, "the house is falling down. Alice and I spent last night in the parlor because the bedroom was deluged. The roof leaks, the floors are rotten because of it, the fireplaces all draw wickedly, the wallpaper hangs in tat—"

"That is enough of your impertinence!" exclaimed Lady Bagshott.

"Did you get wet, Onyx?" Major Beresford asked. She nodded, too afraid to speak.

Lady Bagshott banged her fist on the desk. "Name me the three most important repairs, young lady."

"The roof, the upstairs flooring, and . . ." Onyx paused, and then sat up straight and looked the irate woman right in the eye. ". . . and the piano wants tuning."

Lady Bagshott gasped and slammed the list down on the desk. "You are a frivolous baggage!" she said. "How distressed I am that my vicar has so obviously been led astray by a pretty face! I will not spend one farthing on sheets and towels and these countless other little idiocies. You can use whatever money your stepmother has settled on you for fripperies."

"I have not one pound note of my own," Onyx said quietly.

"Then, Miss Fine Airs, I suggest you unlimber your needles and start patching the sheets and towels. And as for that piano, you can chop it into kindling to feed the kitchen fireplace." Lady Bagshott rose to her feet. "The Reverend Littletree will be thoroughly ashamed when I tell him of your behavior! For a vicar's wife, you do have airs! Remember who you are!"

"I am reminded all the time," was Onyx's reply. Her words seemed to hang in the air like fiery darts after Lady Bagshott's windy tirade. Onyx rose to go. The room seemed small and close.

"Sit down," ordered Lady Bagshott. "We are not through!"

"Oh, we are!" said Onyx. She turned and fled the room, bumping into Jenner, who was discreetly watering potted plants within earshot of the door.

"Excuse me!" she gasped and hurried out the side door, running across the back lawn.

"Wait, Onyx!" It was Jack Beresford, but she did not look back. She ran faster, gathering up her skirts as she darted across the wet lawn, scattering the sheep grazing there, and setting the geese to hissing and arching their long necks.

"I . . . can't keep up with you, Onyx!"

She stopped, looking back at Jack, who was standing with his hand clasped over his bandaged arm. Without a word, she turned and walked back to him, already ashamed of her action.

He managed a grin, but she saw, with anger at her own thoughtlessness, how tight the muscles were around his mouth, and that the strained look was back in his eyes.

"Onyx B," he began when he caught his breath, "take my arm like a good girl and find me a bench."

Still silent, she did as he said, walking him to one

of the rustic stone benches crafted to look like wood that Lady Bagshott had placed throughout the grounds.

He lowered himself to the bench and sighed. "Now, if I were a gentleman, my dear, I would sweep off my coat and place it here so you could sit without soiling your dress. But I do not have on a coat, and if I did, I am certain the act of sweeping it off would cause me to topple over in a dead faint. Sit at your own risk."

She sat, head bowed, and waited for him to ring a grand and glorious peal over her.

"Come, come, Onyx," he said after a moment's pause. "You're supposed to sit on my other side by my good arm. That way I could take you by the hand and you would not dash away again. Did anyone ever tell you that you are remarkably fleet for a woman?"

His gentle banter did cause her to smile briefly. "I'll sit right where I am, sir, because you can tell me from either side what a fool I was."

He shrugged and then winced from the pain. "I hate this," he muttered under his breath. "Pardon, Miss Hamilton. I am, as you have probably well noted, a less-than-exemplary patient. And no, I have no intention of calling you a fool. But do you know what I will tell you?"

She shook her head, too shy to look at him.

"I think you are magnificently brave, remarkably courageous, and full of delightful surprises."

Her eyes looked into his in perfect amazement.

"Heaven help me," he exclaimed. "How did you manage to come by those Wedgwood eyes?"

She laughed and dabbed at the tears that glistened in her eyes.

"That's much better. I'd lend you a handkerchief, but the inmates of Sherbourn did not send me one. Seriously, Miss Hamilton, I'd have been privileged to have you serve under me in Picton's Brigade. You're brave, even though you're powerless, and you maintain dignity and countenance even though people about you have done their best to reduce you to . . . to their level." He paused and gazed across the lawn, as if thinking of something else.

"I didn't have much 'dignity and countenance' in the bookroom just now," she reminded him.

"I contend that you were superb. A roof over your head, floors you won't fall through, and . . . Beethoven. What a salvo you fired at Lady Bagshott!"

She laughed again. "Jack, did you see how her eyes started out of her head when I mentioned the piano?"

He laughed with her, holding onto his arm again. "I've simply never met anyone like you. Every other woman I ever had any dealings with—my mother included—was devoted to frippery things and ideas, comforts and pleasures. I remember how Mother would pout and rage when Father denied her any little thing. How different you are! If you have Beethoven, you would be as happy as a grig, even if your house fell down flat around you. I like that. You're a great campaigner."

"I seem to have lost this encounter with the enemy," she said, and the flush rose to her face again as she remembered the humiliation of the bookroom.

"I can think of a few I have lost," Jack agreed, "and the cost was greater." He turned slightly to face her on the bench. "The important thing is to win the war." He winked at her. "Perhaps if you throw yourself on the Reverend Littletree's chest when he returns this Sunday or next for a sermon?"

"You will never let me forget that, will you?" she asked.

"Well, it worked," he said. "Your scheme wouldn't work with me. I'd see right through it, Onyx B, and you know it. Of course, I suspect that I know you better than the Reverend Littletree does. Besides, I'm a campaigner too."

He was sitting so close to her, and she had always liked the smell of bay rum. Jack's voice was such a pleasant combination of clipped North Country burr mingled with public-school polish, and the assurance of someone used to giving commands. The funny feeling in her chest returned again. *I simply must take some baking soda and water tonight*, she said to herself.

The thought was enough to recall her to her present situation. She had no business sitting so close to a man not her husband or fiancé. She moved away slightly, noting as she did so how his brown eyes crinkled up with laughter.

She stood up then, considering it the better part of valor, and with the hope that her indigestion would subside. "I think you have jollied me out of my miseries, Major," she added and held her hand out to him.

He took her hand and kissed it. "Wellington always told us to serve valiantly in whatever capacity needed. It is my pleasure, Onyx B."

"And you promised me you would stop calling me that!" she exclaimed, stamping her foot.

"Did I? Very well, plain Onyx. Tell me how you will plan your campaign."

"That will bear thinking on, Major. But I will return to the vicarage, mop the water from my bedchamber, wash the windows, and patch the broken ones with pasteboard. And then later this evening, I will sit myself at the piano, leave the lid closed, and hum to myself as I go through all the fingerings of Beethoven's Sonata in G. 'Chop it up for firewood' indeed! Who does she think she is? And I will *not* go back to Chalcott until I can be well-behaved, calm, sensible, and so thoroughly irritating that it will drive her to Bedlam. Adieu, sir."

Major Beresford laughed so loud that the sheep looked up from their grazing. She joined in, noting that her indigestion subsided when she laughed.

He stood up slowly, carefully, and with his good hand

on the back of her neck, pulled her toward him before she had a chance to dart away. He kissed her on the forehead with a resounding smack. "It feels so good to laugh again, Onyx! You can't imagine."

The baking soda and water can't wait until tonight, she thought as he released her, saluted, and started back to Chalcott.

"Are you sure, Major, that you are able to . . . to return to Chalcott?"

"Decidedly. I feel better already, as long as I run no footraces with irate women. And besides, Onyx B— Onyx—if I tire, I can plop myself down on these ornamental Iron Maidens that Lady Bagshott has placed artistically about for strollers' discomfort."

She was still laughing to herself as she went into the vicarage and stared at the pianoforte. She touched its shining surface, sat down, and rested her cheek on the magnificent instrument. The wood was soft, almost like a human touch on her face.

Onyx stayed in the little parlor, the door closed, her head resting on the piano, until she felt almost calm again. Part of her longed to be in the Daggetts' house again, back in the house, however unfriendly, that she was familiar with. It was easy to dissolve into the woodwork or vanish quietly, unobtrusively, when Lady Daggett arched her eyebrows or motioned with her hand. Onyx realized for the second time in as many days that she had never before been called upon to experience much emotion. Whereas her life had been calm and bloodless, it was now unsettling, tumultuous. Another part of her yearned for . . . What? She did not know.

Because there was no sign of rain that evening, Onyx and Alice remained at the vicarage, mending the tattered sheets when possible and tearing them into cleaning rags when there was no choice.

"Do you know," said Alice suddenly, after a long

moment of silence, "I think the former vicar had very sharp toenails that he never trimmed."

Onyx laughed and held up a ragged towel. "Yes, and a sharp chin. Oh, Alice, we should not think ill of him, I suppose. He had a piano."

"Yes, he had," agreed Alice, "and only imagine the trouble it has already caused."

"That is my doing," Onyx replied. "Perhaps it will teach me to hold my tongue."

The next day, Mrs. Sable and Daisy washed, brushed, and aired the curtains, and Alice and Onyx scrubbed walls, washing off several years of grime and carefully cleaning wallpaper that was not in total ruin. Onyx thought briefly of Jack Beresford and wondered if he would visit the vicarage. When he did not come, she began to worry, although Daisy assured her that the other servants said he was strolling about the house.

The evening was quiet, as before. The women of the vicarage mended until their eyes began to blur from the flickering light of cheap candles. Onyx would have preferred silence to mull on her sins, but Alice was in a voluble mood.

"Onyx, have you taken a thought to what we will make your wedding dress out of, now that all your beautiful silk was ruined on the highway?"

Onyx looked up from the tea towel she was stitching together and rubbed her eyes. Not once in the time since Jack Beresford had been shot had she considered the material, other than to briefly mourn its passing, and then forget all about it.

"It didn't seem . . . important, in light of what has been happening."

"It might seem important when you're standing at the altar in your petticoat, miss!" Alice jabbed at the sheet with her needle. "I fear that you must importune either Sir Matthew or your fiancé."

Onyx sighed. "I suppose I must. The lesser of two evils will be Andrew. When he is here this Sunday, I will ask and observe him clear his throat, and hem and haw, and step about, and pose and posture, and deliver a catechism of my faults and shortcomings. Then perhaps he will come through. Altogether, Alice, it is a dismal prospect."

So dismal a prospect that she was kept awake long after Alice was snoring softly beside her, wondering how on earth she was to come by material for another wedding dress. She folded her arms across her stomach and stared at the ceiling, wondering if Jack Beresford was troubled by nightmares, wishing that her own would not chase her around and around in her head until she was clenching her jaw and entirely on edge.

She rose early in the morning. The air was heavy with mist and fog, chilly as late winter again. Onyx dressed quietly, leaving Alice to slumber, pulled her hair into a knot that perched on the top of her head, and tiptoed down the stairs.

They would hang curtains again today and pretend that the rotting sun spots did not show, and that the little rips and tears caused by the defunct vicar's defunct cat would be politely overlooked. The wallpaper was cleaner now, the shreds and tatters removed to expose the design beneath or glued firmly into place, where the strips were long enough. Lady Bagshott had sent over a terse note yesterday stating that workmen would be attacking the roof that morning.

Mrs. Sable already presided in the kitchen and seemed disinclined to talk. She nodded to Onyx and handed her a cup of tea, which she took into the piano room and drank standing by the window.

She heard Jack Beresford's step on the walk even before she saw him through the mist. He came to the front door and knocked. He did not see her as she stood back slightly and watched him through the window. He was more serious than she had ever seen him.

Onyx hurried to the door and opened it. Private Petrie stood behind him in the mist. She motioned both men into the vicarage and stood on tiptoe to take Jack Beresford's cloak from him. Without a word, he walked past her into the little parlor, where he stood before the pianoforte and ran his fingers over the wood.

Petrie remained in the hall. Onyx took him by the arm.

"Private, if you would like, Mrs. Sable has hot tea in the kitchen and probably toast directly."

I look a fright, Onyx thought as she stood in the hallway a moment and smoothed the creases in her muslin work dress. She went into the parlor and closed the door behind her. Jack turned around to face her, and her eyes widened in surprise.

She had never seen such bleakness on one face. His eyes were filled with pain, his complexion a sallow, sick shade under his Spanish tan. She wanted to reach out for him, help him to a chair, put his booted feet up on a hassock. She stood where she was, her hand still on the doorknob.

"Jack, what is the matter?" she asked finally when he did not speak.

To her horror, his eyes filled with tears, and he turned his back to her, running his hand over the piano again. He pulled up the lid and played a chord and then closed the lid again.

"I'm leaving, Onyx," he said, his voice muffled, as if he could barely control it. "My brother . . . my brother, Adrian . . . Onyx, he's dying."

She hurried to him, taking his arm to lead him to a settee, but he wrapped her in a bear hug and would not let her go. He wasn't crying, but he was so close to it that, clutched to him, she could feel the effort he made within himself to control his tears. Tentatively she reached up and gathered him close to her, her arms around him, careful not to hurt his arm.

"Tell me, Jack," she said when she could speak.

He let her lead him to the settee and they sat down together, her arm still around him. "What happened, Jack?" she asked again. "Oh, please tell me."

"A special post came late last night. Did you hear it? There was a message . . . from Sherbourn. From Emily, Adrian's wife." He paused and shook his head, taking a deep breath. "I'm not making much sense, am I?" he asked finally, sounding more like himself.

She relaxed her arm around him, and he took hold of her hand. "The other day after Lady Bagshott wrote to Sherbourn, I received some clothes and a little note from Emily. All it said was, 'Please get well soon and come quickly.'" He stood up then and paced to the window and back again, to stand directly before her. "I have long suspected Adrian was ill, but I had other concerns. The war . . ." His voice drifted off and he went to the window again, leaning against the frame. "I was . . . too busy to think much about Adrian." He gave a short laugh with no mirth in it. "And, as you know better than anyone else, I had miseries enough of my own."

Onyx rose to her feet and came to him by the window. He touched her cheek and smiled. "I dislike shoveling my problems onto your shoulders, but I know I would never feel right if I left without telling you."

"Tell me, then. What was in the letter you received last night?"

"Another note from Emily, all misspellings and tear splotches. Said for me to come quickly. Adrian was delirious and in great pain. They don't . . . the doctors don't know what it is."

"You're not well enough to travel on horseback, Jack," she said.

"I know. But I have to. I've ridden farther and felt worse before, I can assure you. Private Petrie will see that I make it. I only hope I am not too late."

"I greatly appreciate your stopping by to tell me," she said. "I'll miss you, Jack."

"And I, you. Saying good-bye hurts."

She heard Private Petrie in the hall again, so she steered Major Beresford away from the window. He went to the piano again and touched it. "What a beautiful piece of work," he said. "Do you have any music?"

"I found some in the bottom of the desk. Some folk airs, a tune by Purcell, some Mozart the mice enjoyed. None of the modern composers like Beethoven."

"Ah, yes," he replied with a ghost of his usual good humor. "Lady Bagshott's favorite musician, I believe."

"I fear that we are forever in her black book, Beethoven and I. Here, let me help you with your cloak."

He obligingly bent down a little so she could drape it around his shoulders again. He stooped over further and looked into her eyes. "I had better take another good look at your beautiful eyes," he said softly. "No telling when I will see them again." He straightened up and turned to go, then turned around again. "Onyx, will you marry me?"

Surely he was joking. Frozen by the piano, she waited for his slow wink and smile. They did not come. He was perfectly serious.

The silence between them stretched on until the air seemed to hum. Onyx knew she had to answer him. "Oh, Jack, no," she said softly. "I'm engaged."

"You can't possibly love him, Onyx, for all that I suppose he is an estimable man. Dash it all, I don't know if you love me, but I love you." He came closer and touched her under the chin. "It fills me. It may even keep me on my horse between here and Sherbourn. Marry me, dear lady."

She shook her head. "Only think what your family, your friends, your fellow officers would say. Jack Beresford wed to a penniless nonentity." Her eyes misted over. "And soon someone would recall Sir Matthew Daggett's nothing daughter, the one who . . ." Her voice faltered. ". . . who has nothing to recommend her. No, Jack. For your sake, and probably mine too."

His gaze was warm and direct. "How can you call such stubbornness nothing? You needn't hide from me, Onyx." He paused. "I knew this was not the time or the place. I meant what I said, though, and if you do not agree, can we at least be friends?"

"Oh, yes." She wished he would leave so she could run upstairs and cry.

The sun broke through the fog. Through the window, Onyx could see the line of workers heading toward the vicarage. She pointed at them. "Now there will be a roof, Jack. I shall have a dry bed."

"Small pleasure."

"The best kind."

"Not always. I had all the 'small pleasures' I wanted in Spain. Now I want big ones, magnificent ones. Maybe that's why I proposed."

She looked at him in real confusion.

"You are adorable when you are disturbed," he said. "But I can see that I'm embarrassing you now, and I wouldn't do that for the world. Well, maybe I would. I am a bit of a bully, you know."

She held out her hand. He took it and then shook his head. "A handshake won't do, Onyx B," he said, and he kissed her.

It seemed the most natural thing in the world to return his kiss, to hold him tight for the last time, to smell deeply of bay rum, and feel the warmth of him.

He let her go and pulled on his gloves. "Onyx, I might propose again sometime."

"The answer will still be no . . . but thank you, no," she replied. Her knees wanted to part company with her legs, so she sat down on the piano bench.

He blew her a kiss from the doorway. "Promise me?"

"What?" she asked, feeling cross with him all of a sudden.

"That you won't kiss any other soldiers like that, my dear." He winked. "They might get the wrong idea. My best to your estimable fiancé. I seem to have forgotten his name." He grinned wickedly. "Can you recall it?"

"Oh, go away!" she said. "But . . . be careful while you're doing it, please."

He closed the door and whistled his way down the path. She put her hands over her ears so she could not hear him ride away.

Seated at the piano in her sunny little saloon, Onyx finally had her cry.

The workmen were creating a vast distraction on the roof later that morning when there was another knock at the door. Onyx opened it, and before her stood a little man in a shiny suit, carrying a large leather satchel. He bowed elaborately. "I am Signor Sabbacini," he said, "and I have come to tune your piano."

Onyx clapped her hands and pulled the startled man into the house. Her eyes filled with tears for the second time that morning. "Oh, do come in, *signore*. I cannot express in words how welcome you are."

Sabbacini set down his valise and stalking around the piano, eyed it like a matador would a bull. He touched it, stroked the wood, and examined the hammers, making small cooings of appreciation that sounded almost like the twittering of evening birds. At last he stopped his minute perusal, took off his coat, and rolled up his sleeves.

"To work, excellent lady, to work," he said. "This will be a pleasure."

"Oh, yes," she exclaimed. "I do not know how I will ever thank Lady Bagshott. Especially after I was so rude."

He stared at her. "What has Lady Bagshott to do with this?" he demanded. "The good major, he told me about your piano. He said that he wished he could hear you play, but that he was in a hurry." Sabbacini patted his breast pocket. "He paid me in advance. I might have even cheated him. Leave me, now. I have work to do."

She left the parlor and sat down with a thump at the foot of the stairs. "Thank you, Jack," she said out loud. "Thank you from the bottom of my heart." She put her fingers to her lips, thought of his kiss, and realized that baking soda and water was a poor remedy for her discomfort.

Chapter 10

⤳

JACK BERESFORD ARRIVED AT Sherbourn a night and another day later, clinging to the pommel of his saddle while Private Petrie held the reins. For the last three hours, after he gave up the reins to Petrie, Beresford had been talking to himself, telling himself to stay in the saddle, reminding himself that soon the landscape would look familiar and they would drop down into the little valley that sheltered his home.

In a curious circumstance that he could only blame on his exhaustion, each bend in the road looked stranger than the one before. He began to ask himself if the aspect of his particular part of Yorkshire could have changed so much in only four years. "Or did I just remember things differently?" he asked his horse. "Did I dream something that could never have been so perfect?"

For the last hour, Private Petrie had been watching him closely, waiting for him to fall out of the saddle. It became a matter of pride to remain upright. Beresford sat as straight as he could and willed Sherbourn to materialize out of the rain and growing darkness.

When he realized finally that even one more mile would be beyond him, Beresford looked up and there before him was the familiar and beloved shape of Sherbourn, his birthplace and the ancestral home of many Beresford men before him who had returned from one war or another.

He needed Petrie's help to dismount, and even then it was difficult. He leaned on Petrie and stroked his horse's mane. "I should be shot for leaving you standing here in the rain," he murmured, "but I can't remedy that right now. The groom will be here soon."

Private Petrie helped him up the few shallow steps. He leaned against the stone arch that framed the entrance-way while the private knocked. Jack closed his eyes. When he had come home four years ago from London before departing for Spain, his mother had greeted him at the door, flinging it open and running down the steps, her arms outstretched. She was dead now, resting beside his father, the sixth Marquess of Sherbourn, Arthur Edmund Beresford.

This time the door opened slowly, cautiously. Chalking, the butler who had come to Sherbourn as part of the marriage settlement when Matilda Ghormley wedded Lord Arthur Beresford, stood there holding a lamp high and peering into the rain. Jack pulled himself away from the arch.

"I've come home, Chalking," he said.

Suspicion changed to wonder and amazement, and then just as quickly to an unsettling mixture of sadness and relief. The butler came forward hurriedly and took Jack by the arm, something he had never presumed to do before. He clung to Jack's arm, and with a touch of sorrow, Jack realized that Chalking was an old man now.

"Major Beresford," said the servant, retaining his grip as if fearing the major would vanish in the rain if he released him. "How glad we are to have you home!"

"No more than I am to be here, Chalking," Beresford replied. "If you will send the footman to the stable to tell the grooms to come for our horses, Private Petrie and I would count it an excellent thing. And, Chalking, find me a chair quickly."

Beresford stumbled into the entrance hall, looking around just enough to note with relief that little had changed during his years in Spain. He went immediately to one of his mother's dainty French chairs that still adorned the hallway. He sat down as Chalking relieved him of his hat and cloak, which had grown heavier with the rain.

Private Petrie stood by long enough to assure himself that the major was in competent hands and then left for the stables, promising Jack that his horse would be well dried and grained. "I will even talk to him, sir," Petrie said.

Jack managed a smile as Petrie went back out into the rain. He looked up at Chalking.

"Adrian?" he asked. "Tell me I am not too late."

Chalking sighed. "Sir, we thought this morning that he would not last the day, but he is better now. He is sleeping. The doctor only left an hour ago, but he says that Lord Sherbourn will rest through the night."

"Then where is Lady Sherbourn?"

"She is in the library."

Jack could not suppress a smile. Emily Beresford had probably never read a book in her life. "But, my dear brother, she dances divinely." Adrian's long-ago words came to him as he sat there in the entrance and tried to summon the strength to rise.

"Sir," ventured Chalking, "we were distressed to hear of your injury. I trust that the clothes I sent fit?"

"Oh, yes, indeed, and I thank you. Now, if you will help me up, I must go to Emily. Could you bring a little port wine and some bread and meat to the library?"

Chalking helped him as far as the library door. Jack knocked.

"Come in."

He walked in, straightening his shoulders, adjusting his neckcloth, and rubbing the growth of whiskers on his chin. *I don't even smell very good*, he thought. *I'll probably shock her; Adrian is so fastidious.*

Emily Beresford sat hunched over in a wing chair close to the fireplace. She did not look up when he came in, and even turned her face farther away and hunched lower in the chair. This puzzled him, but as he watched her, it dawned on him that she had the air of someone about to receive bad news who wanted to avoid it as long as possible. He watched her for a moment, and what he saw broke his heart.

The wedding of Lord Adrian Beresford, seventh Marquess of Sherbourn, to Emily Tallent, reigning London beauty, was the nuptial of the year, the crown of the 1809 Season. The wedding had taken place the last day of his leave in England. On the morning following, he had departed for Spain with his troops. On that journey, and throughout the war-ravaged Peninsula, Jack had carried somewhere in the back of his head the memory of Emily Tallent's Dresden loveliness. He had not thought of her often; he was too busy, and not so inclined. But when he did think of her, in those moments when all around him he could see only ugliness, it was to remember her startling beauty.

A different woman sat before him, gazing into the flames. As he watched her, silent, unmoving, Jack Beresford realized finally that nothing was going to be the same again.

"Emily, it's Jack."

His words took a moment to penetrate her silence. He came closer as she turned around slowly and looked up into his face. He could see that just for a second, she did not recognize him. *Have I changed so much?* he asked himself. *Oh, Emily, you have.* Then she slowly put her hands to her mouth, hands that trembled, and tears filled her eyes. "Jack? Jack?"

"Yes, Emily," he managed as he tried not to stare at her and failed utterly. "I'm home."

She rose and came toward him then. "You must have traveled straight through," she said, wonder in her voice. She held out her hand to him and he grasped it. "And look at you. Jack, are you all right?"

He didn't know what to say. He knew that as much as his arm pained him, as tired and ravenous as he was, he would soon be healed and rested and fed. As he stared into Emily's eyes, he saw only death looking back at him.

She watched his expression and drew his hand against her cheek. "Not the woman who married Adrian Beresford? Remember Emily Tallent, the silly chit who never had two idle thoughts to rub together?" Her voice broke, and she leaned against Jack's chest, shivering like a new kitten, even though the room—the whole house, in fact—was stiflingly hot.

"I am so glad . . . you are here," she said finally, when she had some mastery over her voice.

Her words chilled him. A great feeling of powerlessness settled over him like the wet cloak he had just removed. She sounded so relieved, so grateful, as if Jack Beresford could solve her problems.

"I came as fast as I could, Emily. Only tell me: How is Adrian?"

She clutched his hand still. "I will show you soon," she said, her voice a tiny whisper.

Chalking brought food and Jack ate, resting in the other chair that faced the fire. He wanted to move it back from the flames, but he was too tired.

"Tell me about Adrian."

When Emily did not answer, he looked over at her.

She was asleep, her head lolling sideways, her hands still in her lap. "Poor Emily, you're burned to the socket," he said softly. He finished eating and remained where he was, watching Emily, and waiting for her to wake up by herself. He had not the heart to disturb her.

A log crashed in the fireplace, and she was out of the chair in one leap, her hand clutching her throat. She looked over at Jack and managed a weak little laugh. "I am . . . a trifle on edge, Jack. You must forgive me."

His unease deepened. "Emily, let me see Adrian."

"Tonight?"

"Yes."

He struggled to his feet, and Emily was at his side in a moment, her hand under his elbow, steering him expertly to the door, despite her own apparent exhaustion. She controlled him like one expert in the management of invalids. Emily Tallent, who had broken more hearts in her one London Season than ten other beauties in as many years. He couldn't bear to look at her, so great was his distress.

After twenty-four hours in the saddle, stairs were quite beyond him. She summoned a footman and the two of them helped him to the second floor.

"Emily, forgive me for the trouble I am causing you," he gasped at the top of the stairs.

She shook her head. "Jack, it is not anything compared to the trouble we are going to cause you. I hate to tell you that. If you insist on seeing Adrian tonight, you must know. He doesn't . . . look like he used to. He's . . . he's . . . Oh, Jack."

The footman left him, and they paused outside the chamber that used to be his father's. Emily picked up a small bottle on the table and shook it. The smell of lavender filled the hallway. Emily pulled a handkerchief from her pocket and sprinkled the lavender on it, holding it to her nose as she took a deep breath and opened the door.

The wave of putrefaction from Adrian's room nearly

knocked Jack over as he stood in the hallway. His eyes blurred from the smell of rotting flesh, and the hair rose on his neck as he swallowed again the bread and meat that he had eaten in the library. Emily went in and he followed, breathing as shallowly as he could.

He had been in a charnel house once, a small room below the chapel in one of the monasteries in Spain or Portugal, forever nameless to him because there were so many. Spanish soldiers had come to his troop, out of breath and shouting, with the news that French soldiers were massacring the monks and throwing them down there among the long-dead religious.

They had come up on the double march in time to stop the French soldiers from their work of killing and spent the rest of the day pulling bodies from that subterranean pit of dead men's flesh and bones. Stripped to his small clothes, he had spent that whole hot afternoon in the charnel house removing the recent dead. Eventually he became used to the smell, but he knew when he climbed out of the pit that evening that if he ever smelled it again, he would remember it.

Standing at the doorway to Adrian's room, he couldn't help himself. He made gagging noises in his throat. Emily grabbed his arm and slapped the lavender-scented handkerchief over his mouth and nose. He breathed deeply of the fragrance until his head cleared and then handed it back to her.

The room was dark, lit by only one candle that flickered as it burned lower and lower. Emily put her finger to her lips. "He's asleep and I wouldn't for the world waken him. I don't know that I could, anyway. He doesn't open his eyes anymore."

He came close and looked on his brother. Adrian Beresford was an old man, with an old man's parchment skin stretched tight across his cheekbones. He was breathing through his mouth, each breath a laborious process. Every now and then he would stop breathing, and then shudder and continue the effort. His skeleton's hands rested on his distended stomach. His fingers, each one a mere thread of flesh, moved restlessly of their own accord, but he did not waken. He looked eighty instead of thirty-four.

Jack reached out and touched Adrian's hair, which used to be thick and red, and had now only the merest wisp of faded color. He touched Adrian's shoulder lightly and then his cheek. Emily's hand was on his arm again, and he followed her out of the room.

Jack sat down heavily in the chair outside the door and put his head between his knees. Emily stood beside him, her hand on his hair until he sat up. She pulled up a chair beside him and took his hand wordlessly. They sat close together until he could speak again.

"Emily, why didn't you write to me?"

She looked down at her hands. "I wanted to, Jack. I wanted to so badly, but Adrian wouldn't let me. He imagined how terrible things were in Spain. He feared that you would be unable to return here anyway and would only have the added burden of worry." She forced a smile. "You know how stubborn Adrian is."

"I know. But sometimes you just have to go around him. I wish you had, but it hardly bears dwelling on now. Who in the world is his doctor?"

Emily looked at him then. "Dr. Marchmount. He was recommended to us by friends in York. 'He is so fashionable,' they said. 'Adrian should never go to anyone else.'" Her voice was bitter. "And now poor Adrian has such sores, but the doctor says the evil humors are escaping from those wounds and to leave them alone. Oh, that cannot be right!"

"And when you take issue with him, Dr. Marchmount only gives you an arch stare and reminds you who is the doctor?" asked Jack.

"Yes! That's it! What can I do?" She began to cry again, wringing her hands in her lap. "Just when I think I cannot cry anymore, I cry again!" she sobbed. "Jack, forgive me."

He put his arm around her and held her tight until she blew her nose on her handkerchief and looked at him again.

"Dr. Marchmount gives him morphine. It is a new drug. Have you heard of it?"

He nodded.

"It deadens the pain a wondrous way, Jack, but now Adrian must have it all the time. Just two days ago Dr. Marchmount gave him too much, I think, and his breathing became so slow. That was when I wrote to you. He is better now, but who knows how long it will last? Oh, I do not know what to do anymore, Jack, and I am so tired."

"Where do you sleep, Emmy?"

She gestured toward the room again. "I sleep in the dressing room off the bedroom. That way I can hear him easily."

Jack rose to his feet. "Well, starting tomorrow, you will be moved down the hall." When she started to protest, he put his finger to her lips. "No, Emmy. I'm home now. It's my turn to help. And we'll need more help. Now, go to bed like a good girl. I'll see you in the morning."

She kissed him on the cheek and left without another word. Chalking was standing in the hallway again. He took Jack by the arm and helped him down the hall to his room, where he pulled off Jack's boots.

"Sir, when will you want breakfast?"

"Early," Jack replied as he lay down on the bed. He was asleep before the butler left the room.

Jack woke to the sound of wrens fighting outside his window. He opened his eyes. During the night, Chalking must have returned to unbutton his shirt and breeches and cover him with a blanket. He raised himself on one elbow and looked out the window.

It was the same wren house he had built twenty years before, under Adrian's supervision. He had climbed out the window and, clinging to the ivy vines, hammered it onto the window frame, lost his grip on the vine, fell, and broke his leg.

He got out of bed and opened the window. The wrens fluttered away, remonstrating with him, calling him horrible bird names. He lifted the top off the birdhouse and counted two babies inside, mouths wide open, wanting more than he could give them.

"It's going to be that way around here, Major Beresford," he told himself as he replaced the lid and crawled back in bed. "Everyone wanting more than you can give."

He raised his arms and put them behind his head, grateful that his wounded arm was only a dull ache now. He stared at the ceiling, searching out the familiar whorls in the plaster that looked like beehives and winged animals.

He wondered what Onyx Hamilton was doing, if she was awake yet, if she ever stared at the ceiling and thought about him, or if she had dismissed him as the troublesome man who had ruffled the calm sea of her life, someone she might think about occasionally, but nothing more.

He was hard put to express even in his thoughts what it was that he found so irresistible about her. Her eyes were a glory, to be sure, but when he considered the matter in the bright light of morning, they were her only majesty. She was too shapely to be stylish, and her hair was an unexceptionable shade of brown. Adrian would probably call her dull, dowdy even. Even in robust health, Onyx had not the exhausted Emily Beresford's beauty.

He looked out the window. Onyx Hamilton was more like a wren than a finch or an oriole. She was efficient and brisk, and light on her feet. He thought of her standing in the highway, pointing his pistol at the road agent. She was not afraid to defend herself. For all her small size and her shyness around people, she had oceans of courage.

"Besides, I like shapely women," he said out loud to the wrens. More than once while she was tending to him at Mrs. Millstead's, he had wanted to reach out and touch her. The only thing that had restrained him in time was the sure knowledge that he was in no condition to survive the facer she would have planted him.

She was the kind of woman, he decided, who would grow more beautiful as the years passed. She would probably always be shy around strangers, but around those she loved, her eyes would shine and she would be animated, even as she was dignified. Those dear to her would know the full, blinding force of her love and devotion. Others would only wonder what her husband saw in her.

Jack sat up. Such peregrinations of the mind were only serving to arouse him. And yet, he did not regret for a moment the warm feeling of pleasure that thinking of Onyx Hamilton was bringing him. Events of the past four years had so deadened him to even the idea of love that he could only sit there and be thankful, even as he wished Onyx were there with him.

He forced his thoughts along less unruly channels, got out of bed, and sat himself in the window ledge by the birdhouse. "Here I am, having antic thoughts, and my brother is dying just down the hall," he said. "I am amazed how life goes on."

He sat still until the wrens decided that he was a large but harmless lump and went back to feeding their babies. He looked across the dale that sheltered Sherbourn and took a deep breath of the wind that was warm on his face. He heard the tinkle of belled sheep in a distant pasture. "Dear heaven, it is so beautiful," he said in a loud voice, much to the distress of the wrens, who fluttered away.

Jack took off the riding clothes he had slept in and padded into his dressing room. He sorted through the racks of fashionable, tight-fitting jackets, pantaloons of extravagant color and more extravagant fit, the many-caped riding coats, and the evening wear, marveling to himself that he had ever actually worn such frivolous things. He dug around in the back and pulled out what Adrian always referred to as "your country-squire effects," grateful that he had hidden them away and that no one had been inclined to discard them.

When he changed shirts, he screwed up his courage and peeked under the bandage on his arm. The wound, while still red, was no longer inflamed. It had ceased weeping. He touched it and was pleased to discover that such action no longer sent little prickles down his back and legs. "I will survive," he said to himself as he buttoned on a clean shirt. When Adrian's doctor came, he could ask the man to change the dressing and put on a smaller bandage.

Shaving took a little longer than usual, but by tipping his head way over he didn't have to raise his arm so high, and it was possible. He had no patience for a cravat, so he did not bother.

The wind picked up and tossed papers around on his desk, but he did not close the window. The first odor that had assailed his nostrils upon awakening was the smell of the sickroom, and he was glad to blow it away.

The odor struck him again in the hall. He went to the end of it and opened the window, making a mental note to tell Chalking to open all the windows except Adrian's.

He went to the door of Adrian's room and leaned his head against it, listening to Adrian's stertorous breathing. Jack took a deep breath and slowly opened the door.

The room was still dark. He saw that the windows had been draped in heavy black material to keep out all light, and he wondered about that. The fire in the hearth was blazing away. He watched the flames a moment, waiting for his stomach to settle, and then sat down beside his brother.

"Adrian?" he asked, keeping his voice low.

There was no answer, but as he watched, his brother slowly moved his hand off his stomach and over to the edge of the bed. Jack put his hand over his brother's, aghast all over again at the parchment texture of his skin.

He leaned close to his brother's ear. "Adrian, I am home. I won't leave again," he said.

Again there was no reply, but the fingers moved slightly under his.

Jack remained there until he knew that one more minute would be too much for his stomach. "I'll be back later, Adrian," he whispered, patted the paper-thin hand, and left the room.

He ran down the hall to the open window and stuck his head out, taking deep breaths of air until he was light-headed. He rested his elbows on the sill, looking at nothing in particular, and thinking of baby birds with their mouths stretched open and waiting.

Emily was in the breakfast room, struggling to stay awake as she sat with her hands in her lap, nodding over the toast and tea before her. She opened her eyes as he entered the room and crossed to the sideboard, where he filled his plate with everything that looked warm and joined her at the table.

She blinked at him. "You can't possibly eat all that."

"Watch me," he said. "I'm going to eat it all, and maybe some more too."

She smiled for the first time. "I'll watch."

He ate silently, steadily. The only sound was the ticking of the clock. When he finished, he pushed his chair back, stretched his legs out in front of him, and regarded his sister-in-law.

"Well, Emmy, we need a council of war."

She nodded.

"When do you expect the doctor?"

Her eyes grew troubled again. "He has already come and gone."

"What!"

"Yes. He comes early, looks at Adrian, goes 'hmm, hmm,' gives him another draft of that medicine, tells me he will sleep, and leaves. He will probably not return for several days now. Jack, what are we to do?"

The major sat up straight again. "I've already instructed Chalking to tell the maids to open all the windows and air this house. You are going to supervise a move down the hall to another bedroom. And don't you object, Emmy. I'm bigger than you are."

"Yes, Jack," she said. Her voice was solemn, but he noticed that the dimples appeared in her cheeks again.

"I'm going to sit here while you finish your breakfast."

"I'm not hungry, Jack."

"Eat, Emmy."

She did as he said, protesting when he went to the sideboard again and brought her a baked egg and slice of ham, but eating it obediently as he sat down, crossed his legs, and stayed between her and the door until she was done.

"Now, what will you do?"

"I will look in on Adrian," she said. "The maids and I share this duty. And . . . and then I will move down the hall, Jack."

"Good. I'll be in the bookroom. I have to write a letter."

"Oh, Jack, there's something I have to tell you." Her voice sounded hesitant again, strained. "You won't like it by half. The bookroom . . . it's a . . . trifle untidy."

"What's that to anything?" he asked. "And when I'm done with that letter, I'm going to summon the bailiff for a reckoning on the estates."

"Jack, you don't precisely understand," she said slowly, carefully, as if treading on a February pond. "There's no bailiff."

"Mercy," was all he could say for a moment, considering that he was talking to Emily and not his profane troops. "Then who's . . . who's been running the estate?"

She would not look at him. Her voice was very small. "That's why the bookroom is such a mess." She raised her fine eyes to his, imploring him. "Jack, I'm dreadful with figures and columns! I am only thankful that the bailiff left after the planting and lambing. It . . . hasn't been precisely easy."

"Emily Beresford, you crazy little chit." His lips began to twitch. He tried to cover his laugh but he failed. She glared at him, showing the first real spark of life since his return. He threw back his head and laughed. "Emily! Even I know that you're a mathematical widgeon! Adrian . . . Adrian told me once that if you ever ran out of fingers and toes to count on that . . . Oh, mercy! Excuse me, dear."

Emily stared at him and then began to laugh too, until she was wiping her eyes. "Perhaps I should have paid more attention to my governess," she ventured, when she could speak. "Oh, no," she said, and laughed some more.

Finally Jack was silent. He took her hand and raised it to his lips. "Gallant, gallant, Lady Sherbourn," he said and kissed her hand.

"Welcome home, Jack," she said as she patted his shoulder and left the room.

He cleared a spot among the jumble of bills and accounts on the desk in the bookroom and spread out a sheet of paper. *Do I begin "Dear Onyx" or "My dear Miss Hamilton"?* he thought as he sharpened a pen and dipped it in the inkwell.

He wrote quickly, crossing his lines, wondering at first if he was saying the right things, and then not worrying about whether it was polished or correct. She would understand his need. He sat back with a sigh finally and sealed the letter, putting his brother's frank on it. Letter in hand, he strode down the hall in search of Chalking, whom he found leaving Adrian's room.

"Chalking, this must go the fastest way you can think of to Chalcott."

"Very well, sir."

"And when you have seen the letter safely on its way, have the stablemen prepare the chaise and four. And I want postilions. They're going to follow that letter to Chalcott."

"Indeed, sir." Chalking was much too well-bred to even raise his eyebrows as he took the letter and went downstairs.

"And, Chalking . . ."

"Yes, sir?"

"Prepare another bedroom, my mother's room, in fact. We'll soon have a guest."

"Very well, sir. And might I inquire . . . will this guest stay long?"

"Years and years, I hope, but for right now, just through the summer."

He would go in and sit with Adrian now. When Chalking or the footman or Emily relieved him, he would saddle up and look over the estate. He picked up the lavender bottle on the table and sniffed it, smiling to himself.

"Onyx Hamilton, you're about to be bullied out of your vicarage," he said out loud before he took another deep breath and entered Adrian's room.

Chapter 11

⸻

ALTHOUGH MAJOR BERESFORD had no way of knowing it, his letter arrived at the Chalcott vicarage at a most opportune time. Onyx was still smarting from the rare trimming that Andrew Littletree had given her after he had preached his sermon on "Compassion, from the Gospel According to Saint Matthew," taken his mutton with Lady Bagshott, and had his brain filled with the news of Onyx's profligacy with regard to a certain pianoforte in the vicarage.

In order to avoid the nuncheon with Lady Bagshott that followed church, Onyx had pleaded a headache and retired to the vicarage. Her head did ache. The sermon was long, and try as she might, her head had dropped and then bobbed up at several times during the service as her attention wandered and sleep began to sit on her eyelids.

She tried to stay awake. She and Lady Bagshott were seated most unfortunately right under the Reverend Littletree's gaze. To her utter dismay, she noted after she roused herself and looked back up at the pulpit that the bald spot on the top of the Reverend Littletree's head was more pronouncedly red, and that soon it would meet with the flush that was rising above his clerical collar. *"Clerical choler" would be more like it*, she thought as she put her hand to her mouth, but not quite in time to stifle a giggle. By the time the service was over, Onyx Hamilton's head did surely and truly ache.

She was not sleeping well at nights. Each change in the wind seemed to bring her sitting upright in bed. She fancied she heard Major Beresford leading his troops in a nightly charge through his nightmare. At other times she fancied his arms around her, only to wake and find that she was tangled in her blankets. She had always been a sound sleeper. Her body was betraying her now, and she longed for the simplicity of her shadowy life with Lady Daggett and Sir Matthew.

Her headache was beginning to fade when she came downstairs after a short nap to find the Reverend Littletree waiting to pounce on her in the little parlor.

He turned on her as soon as she entered the room. "Miss Hamilton, I had no idea when I affianced myself to you—no idea indeed—how inclined you were to the luxuries of the world!"

"It is but a pianoforte, Andrew," she said calmly, sitting down and wishing she could tune him out as she used to. Her head began to throb again.

To the Reverend Littletree it was more than a pianoforte; it was the great god Mammon himself, visiting a curse of greed and indolence on one who would, in a matter of weeks now, be his wife. He was having regrets of the most serious kind, he warned her. Perhaps he was a fool even to consider marriage to one whose parents were unknown and who obviously cared not a scrap for the feelings of his noble patroness, Lady Bagshott, who was already overburdened with the heavy costs of repairs to the vicarage. He looked at her as if he wished he could blame her for the leaking roof and the rotten floors, but he could not. He ceased speaking, rearranged himself along less obdurate lines, but did not unbend enough to sit down next to Onyx.

"Have you nothing to say for yourself?" he asked, glowering at her.

"No, not a thing," she replied. "You've certainly covered the subject at sufficient length."

"Lady Bagshott awaits your apology," he snapped, angry, apparently, that she would not fight.

"Then she will wait a long time, sir," Onyx replied. "I have no intention of apologizing to her. The pianoforte has never been a source of expense to her."

"No, indeed it has not! And while we are on that subject, how dare you allow Major Beresford to be stuck with its repairs?"

Jack's name pulled her to her feet as though there were strings attached to her shoulders. "It was an act of kindness, sir. I knew nothing of it until he had already left for Yorkshire!"

"I would hate to think that your wiles—those wiles that Saint Paul so vigorously warns us of in scripture— had reduced a distinguished war hero and military representative of our insane king to pudding!" he snapped back, angered into illogic.

"It would be impossible to do anything of the sort to Major Beresford. He is quite his own man," she replied quietly. "Nor would I have tried, sir. I am not a flirt."

"Who knows what you are, really?" he countered, sighing heavily, as if the burden of life with her was going to be something that only a truly sanctified man of the cloth could attempt.

His words stung and hurt and twisted around inside her, but still she refused to fight back. The silence grew heavy in the room, so heavy that she wanted to fling open the window and let some of it out. She remained where she was.

When she would not argue or defend herself, the

vicar cleared his throat and assumed another pose. "Miss Hamilton, I must leave now and return to Cambridge. I assure you that during this week I will be seriously considering if I have made a grave error in pledging to you my good name in six weeks' time!"

She looked up at him with her fine Wedgwood eyes. "And I, sir, will be doing precisely the same thing," she said.

If she had hauled out Jack's pistol and shot him, he could not have looked more surprised. He stepped forward involuntarily, ruining the effect of his "Righteously Indignant Pose," clutched at the much-maligned piano to hold him upright, and began to laugh.

"*You* don't seem to appreciate how lucky, how very lucky you are, my dear Miss Hamilton," he said through his laughter. "Do you honestly think anyone else of even the remotest consequence would ever offer for you? Your effrontery defies belief." He continued to laugh.

If she had thought his words were a firebrand placed red-hot against her bare flesh, his laughter was worse. She had been ignored and put upon many times, but no one had ever made a mockery of her. She felt sick to her stomach.

His laughter faded finally into a silly titter, and he looked at his watch. "Well, obviously we will be discussing this again in the future. Don't think that you have heard the last from me on this pianoforte, Miss Hamilton, or any other luxuries you plan to sneak into this vicarage. Good day."

The stricken look in her eyes must have pricked his conscience a little, particularly in light of his chosen sermon for the day. He touched her arm. "Have a little more countenance, Onyx!" he chided. "Is this not what they call a lovers' tiff?" He chuckled to himself over his wit, sketched a low and mocking bow to her, and left.

She was shaken beyond words. Her fingers grew cold as she clutched them together in her lap. She let out a long, shuddering breath and wished herself anywhere but where she was.

When the knock came at the door fifteen minutes later, she knew it was Andrew Littletree coming back for another swipe at her raw feelings. Again nausea stirred her stomach.

The knocking continued. "Miss Hamilton? Miss Onyx Hamilton?" she heard finally.

Daisy and Mrs. Sable were off for the afternoon, and Alice had taken herself on a walk. Onyx rose slowly and opened the door.

"The post, ma'am," said the uniformed rider at the door. She took the letter he handed her.

"I . . . I have no money to pay you for it, sir, should postage be owing," she said.

"Oh, no, no. See there? It's been franked by a lord," he explained.

She had never received such a letter. She thanked him and closed the door, wondering at the unfamiliar handwriting. It must be some mistake, but there was her name in bold, dark letters. Other than the letters that Gerald had been able to write from Spain, she had never received a letter before.

She sat down in the parlor again, removed a pin from her hair, and slit the envelope. She spread the closely written sheet on her lap and then turned to the last page and looked at the signature. She traced her finger over the name, turned the paper over, and began to read.

Dear Onyx,

I begin this letter with an apology. You have given me no leave to correspond with you, and indeed, no encouragement, but my need is desperate.

Adrian is dying. There is no other way to dress up the word. He is near to death, partly, I suspect, because of ill management at the hands of a physician I would not scruple to use on Adrian's livestock.

Since the bailiff took French leave several months ago, my sister-in-law, Lady Beresford, has been both managing the estate and trying to care for her husband. I need not waste time here describing the state of affairs at Sherbourn as I have found them, although she has done her best. Emily is in a state of complete exhaustion. If she does not get some relief from her duties, I fear I will have two invalids on my hands, plus a large estate (not to mention the other properties that I haven't even had time to think on).

As for me, I am well. My arm pains me a little, but it is healing nicely. To be honest, I haven't time to concern myself about it, and that may, in fact, be the best remedy for any ailment.

I am asking for your help. I need you here at Sherbourn to nurse my brother. To say that he is desperately ill would be to put a glow on it, I fear. To put the words before you with no bark on them, I need someone who has sure hands and a strong stomach. Someone who won't complain and who is not afraid of the hardest kind of work there is.

I can think of no one else but you. If you suspect that you are being bullied, I assure you that you are, and in the most outrageous fashion. By the time you read this letter, there will probably be a chaise and four pulling up before the gates of Chalcott to take you to Sherbourn. I am not so vain as to be confident that you will accompany them here to me, I am just desperate enough to try in the only way I know how to get you here quickly. The coachman has been given sufficient funds to enable you to make the journey easily, stopping at well-recommended lodgings.

I am certain Lady Bagshott will have many objections. To her credit, I am certain they are valid ones.

Your fiancé will certainly echo her concerns. Again, I cannot see that they would do otherwise, if they are at all involved in your welfare. I could never blame them; if you were my fiancée, I would feel precisely the same way. But I need you as badly as ever anyone needed another person. Please help me.

As to the other matter that I broached so ineptly to you on the occasion of our last meeting, I will say nothing. I assure you that I have no intention of bringing up the matter again. I overstepped my bounds, considering that your affections are already engaged elsewhere. Rest easy on that matter.

I must close this overlong letter. Forgive me for its brusqueness, but this is a subject that allows for little sensibility, I suppose. Either that, or I never was much at parlor talk anyway. I hope to see you soon.

> *Yours cordially,*
> *John H. Beresford, Major*
> *His Majesty's 45th Foot*

Onyx read the letter through once, and then she read it through again, not so much that she had not retained its contents on the first perusal, but because the letter had such a conversational tone that she could reread it and almost imagine him there in the room with her. She raised the letter to her nose. There was just the slightest fragrance of bay rum on the paper.

She had not the least doubt in her mind that she would go to Sherbourn. It remained only to pack, brave a brief audience with Lady Bagshott, and wait for the chaise to arrive. She would write to Andrew from Sherbourn. He could make of it what he wished. She could spend pages and pages of paper reminding him of Christian duty and ministries to the sick, but if he did not by now possess the insight to see this himself, there was no reason to bother.

Onyx waited impatiently for Alice's return. The first sound of her footsteps on the front walk brought Onyx shooting out of her chair and running into the entrance hall, waving the letter, which she thrust under Alice's nose.

A little smile of amusement, all that she would allow herself on the Sabbath, crossed Alice's face. She took the letter and sat herself down on the stairs. Onyx sat beside her, pleating and unpleating the folds of her best Sunday muslin while Alice read.

Finally she finished the letter, folded it, and returned it to Onyx.

"I have already packed, Alice," Onyx said. "It remains for you to do the same. I wish for you to accompany me."

"There is nothing said about me in this letter," Alice objected.

"No, but I think I understand this situation already better than Major Beresford realizes. When Papa was sick, remember how many of us were required for his care?"

"Onyx, you know that I am little use in a sickroom," Alice protested.

"I am certain there must be other tasks you can lift from Lady Beresford's shoulders," Onyx argued. "Besides which . . . oh, Alice, I need you."

"Very well. I will pack while you screw up *your* courage for an audience with Lady Bagshott," said Alice as she hurried up the stairs.

The thought of facing Lady Bagshott, particularly after her lunchtime work with the Reverend Littletree, should have unnerved Onyx, but it did not. She tied on her chipstraw bonnet and set off across the lawn. *If it were for me, I would be terrified*, she reasoned with herself. *It is not for me; it is for Jack Beresford.*

That thought made her stand stock-still in the middle of the lawn. The memory of her last meeting with Jack Beresford sent the color shooting into her cheeks. His lips were so warm, and she had felt so good with his arms around her.

Well, if he can overlook that impulsive proposal as a momentary aberration, probably a direct result of his heavy loss of blood, surely I can forget that it ever happened, she told herself. She patted her hair into place. It was a kind offer, however misguided. He had likely come to his senses by now.

There was an unfamiliar chaise drawn up to the stable entrance when she crossed the back lawn and entered by the bookroom door. The chaise had a crest on the panel, and the vehicle was covered with mud.

Jenner stood in the hallway. He looked her up and down in his usual fashion and pointed to the closed door of the bookroom. Onyx took a deep breath, patted her hair again, and knocked.

"Enter, Miss Hamilton."

She knows it is I, Onyx thought as she paused for a heartbeat with her hand on the knob. *Well, she sounds no more forbidding than I would have imagined. Courage, Onyx.*

When she entered the room, Lady Bagshott looked up from the letter in her hand. She motioned Onyx to sit down and smoothed the letter in front of her.

"I have received a brief letter from Sherbourn, Onyx. I assume you have come on the same errand?"

Onyx nodded. Lady Bagshott rose to her full height and leaned over the desk until she was almost nose to nose with Onyx. "I would advise you, Miss Hamilton, not to waste the man's time. If you hurry, you can get in several hours of travel before nightfall."

Onyx looked up at her in astonishment. Lady Bagshott stared her in the eyes and then sat down again, still regarding her.

"Well?" she challenged.

"Somehow I expected . . . I do not know what I expected," Onyx concluded lamely.

Lady Bagshott let out her short bark of laughter. "Fooled you, didn't I, Miss Baggage?" She went to the window. "Onyx, I can well imagine what you think of me, but there was a time when a letter like this from Sherbourn would have sent me packing too. There, now, I have surely surprised you!"

"I go to help, madam," Onyx replied.

"And I am sure that you will," said Lady Bagshott. Her voice was a trifle unsteady, but Onyx had the good sense not to look at her.

"Adrian Beresford is a scamp and a rascal, a cheerful kind of ne'er-do-well who has no more sense of management than the chief performer in a flea circus. He is also charming and witty and ready for any scrape. He has been a wonderful foil to Jack, who, for all his ramshackle ways, tends to be too serious. They are dear to me beyond words. I am so sorry that Adrian is dying."

It was quite the longest speech Onyx had ever heard from Lady Bagshott.

"I am glad that you are going, although I know it will be a difficult thing, Miss Hamilton," Lady Bagshott continued formally.

"Andrew will not approve, I am sure," Onyx said.

"I will make it right with him," the other woman replied. Her hands were still on the draperies as she looked across the back lawn toward the stables. She did not turn around. "If you had chosen not to go, miss, I would have abandoned all hope for you."

Onyx smiled. "I will go now, Lady Bagshott, with your leave."

"You have it," she said after a long pause. "And before you depart, stop in the kitchen. I have asked Cook to prepare a little basket with some items you might find useful."

"Thank you."

"Surprised you again, didn't I, girl?" said Lady Bagshott. "Just remember to keep your wits about you."

"I shall try," said Onyx. She rose. "Lady Bagshott," she began hesitantly, feeling her way around the words, "I want to apologize . . . for the trouble I caused over the pianoforte." She had had no intention of apologizing, but suddenly it occurred to her that she was wrong. "And I mean it," she added unnecessarily.

"Your apology—although long overdue—is accepted," said Lady Bagshott, turning around finally.

After a fresh change of horses and food for the coachman and postilions, the carriage drew up in front of the vicarage. Quickly, their few possessions were tied down. A postboy, spattered with mud like the carriage, helped Alice in while Onyx spoke to the coachman.

"Sir, I know that Major Beresford has given you leave to stop for lodging during this journey."

"Aye, he has."

"I am also certain that you are tired. But if there is any way that you see fit to drive us straight through to Sherbourn, you will get no argument from me. I am sure that you know even better than I how serious matters are."

"Happen we do," he replied. "We'll give it a go, miss." They paused that night only to change horses and eat, the coachman walking around stiff-legged while the horses were unharnessed and led away to the comforts of stall and grain. Onyx closed her eyes against the sharp edge of exhaustion in his voice as he chivvied the ostlers to put a sparkle in their steps and hurry faster. After a bite of meat and cheese and a swallow of ale, they set off again.

The coach was comfortable, but Onyx took no comfort in it, knowing how tired the coachman and postilions were. She sat upright as they bowled along, wishing there were some way she could help.

Before the sun set, Alice chuckled and pointed to Onyx's feet. "You'll get there no faster by pushing."

She smiled and stopped. "No, I won't. There seems to be little I can do."

"There is something. I suggest you try to sleep. It may be that we will be wanted immediately upon our arrival."

The sun set and the moon traveled across the sky, and still they rode on, stopping only for the barest necessities. The coachman's eyes were red from lack of sleep, but he still found a moment during the changing of horses to joke with his postilions, to jolly them into the continuation of their duties.

During one pause, Onyx approached one of the postilions, a lad scarcely beyond his first youth. He stood by the carriage, hands on the small of his spine, rocking backward and forward.

"I want to thank you for what you are doing," she said simply. "I wish I had money to pay you, even beyond what Major Beresford is paying you."

"If you had, I would'na take it, miss, meaning no disrespect, of course," he replied, his speech forthright and with the same North Country burr she detected in Jack's voice. "I did always want to do the major a favor."

"And why is that?" she asked.

"My older brother Jamie fought with the Major at Talavera."

"And where is Jamie now?"

"He died there, but Major Beresford saw to it that Jamie came home anyway. None of the other commanders ever did that for their men. Major Beresford said he didn't want his boys to take their final rest away from our dales. I am in his debt for that, miss."

"I see," she replied and could say no more.

When morning came, the sun rose on a landscape she never could have imagined. The Pennines, the spine of England, were dark hulks in the near distance. As the sun rose, she saw that their majesty was covered with the pale green of late spring. Here and there, patches of snow sprouted on the north-facing slopes of the higher crags.

In deeper green meadows that marched right down to

the road, sheep were waking. Lambs were everywhere, and everywhere Onyx saw the brisk movement of black-and-white border collies, nipping here, bullying there. To the east the land sloped in more refined fashion to the great Plain of York, and beyond that, where she could not see but could only imagine, was the North Sea.

Onyx took in what she could. Her eyes were smarting from lack of sleep, and she ached all over. Even her sagging mattress at the vicarage was preferable to the carriage, no matter how modern and well-sprung it was.

She was beginning to feel sorry for herself when she recalled her last journey and the fateful wish she had made to herself for an adventure to while away the tedium of the summer and provide her with memories for the coming years in Chalcott's vicarage. *I have certainly been dealt in large measure what I wished for*, she thought. She would have to tell Jack Beresford about her rash daydream someday. He would relish the good humor of it.

After a quick stop for porridge and tea, they continued their excruciating journey, climbing higher and higher as they left the main highway and traveled narrower roads.

And then Sherbourn was before them. She knew it was Sherbourn even before the coachman let out a halloo to put heart into his boys again and urged on the tired horses.

The manor was set in a wide valley—the postboy had called it a dale. The house was large and rambling, not built in the artificially formal style of Chalcott, with its precise lawns and careful symmetrical arrangement. There was a wildness about Sherbourn that appealed to her immediately, a comfort and welcome there that she had never felt at Chalcott. The manor was a mixture of native stone and timber and well-draped with ivy. It spoke of tradition and power, and something more.

"How odd, Alice!" she exclaimed as they drew close. "Do you feel it?"

"Feel what, Onyx?" asked Alice as she struggled to open her eyes.

"Oh, it is hard to explain. Sherbourn looks so . . . comfortable and safe. As if children have played here."

"Onyx, lack of sleep has made your brain wander," was Alice's assessment.

There were no children in the courtyard as the coachman braked to a stop in front of the manor, only another carriage, a smaller one, with a black horse tied and blanketed.

"This is early for a morning call," Alice said as she sat up. "But it is comforting, I suppose, to know that we are not the only early risers in Yorkshire."

There was a big sigh, and then a slight motion as the coachman climbed down. One of the postilions opened the door and drew out the step, helping Onyx down.

"Well, Miss Hamilton . . . ," said the coachman. He took off his hat and bowed elaborately, much to the delight and nudgings of the postboys, who grinned at him despite their exhaustion. "Here you are at Sherbourn."

Onyx shook his hand. "You are a special coachman, sir," she said. "I thank you for what you have done."

She turned to help Alice, when a low crying moan that was scarcely human came from the manor. Onyx whirled around, facing the door as it was banged open. Down the steps hurtled a fragile-looking woman.

"Jack!" she screamed. "Jack!"

Onyx ran forward and grasped the woman by the arms.

She could see that the lady was no older than herself. "Madam, may I help you?" she said.

"Jack's not with you? Oh, how could he be! He just left." She freed her hands in a sudden motion and pressed them to her forehead. "I must be going mad! Oh, please help me!"

Onyx took her hand again, this time holding the

agitated woman tighter. "I am Onyx Hamilton. Major Beresford sent for me."

"Miss Hamilton? We did not expect you so soon. I am . . ." She paused, as if for a second she could not remember her own name. "I am Emily Beresford. Please, you must help me. Dr. Marchmount will not listen, and Jack had no idea that he would be here today or he would not have left me alone. Please come."

Onyx let herself be dragged into the manor by Emily Beresford, who, for all her fragility, had the grip of an eagle's talon on her wrist. She towed Onyx across the polished stones and started up the stairs.

"He wants to bleed Adrian. Heavens! He has no blood left! How can he do this! He tells me that he is the doctor and he knows what is best for Adrian. I told him to stop, but he would not listen. He must be stopped!"

They reached the top of the stairs and Emily Beresford released her, breathing heavily. "What must you think of me?" she said in a whisper.

"I think you need help," said Onyx, stripping off her gloves and then throwing aside her bonnet. A door was open down the hall, and she ran toward it. *I shot a highwayman on the road*, she thought. *Surely I can deal with a doctor. Jack expects me to.*

Chapter 12

⌁

THE ODOR THAT ASSAILED ONYX'S nostrils made her step back involuntarily. She peered into the dark room, all her senses on edge, her stomach recoiling from what was within. She hesitated to enter, as the smells of the sickroom reminded her of the Reverend Hamilton's death ten years before. And then she saw Adrian, his body the merest ripple under the light sheet that covered him, and her courage came back.

"Wait, sir," she called to the man—it could only be the doctor—who was bending over the bed. "Please don't touch him."

The man straightened up and looked her way. He was well-dressed in black frock coat and elaborate embroidered waistcoat. In his hand he held a small metal box. Onyx looked at it and remembered such a box at her father's bedside during the final stage of his long illness. She had played with it once when no one was watching and cut her fingers for her foolishness.

"Don't bleed him," she said as she hurried to Adrian's bedside.

The doctor slammed the bleeder down on the table by

the bed. Adrian, his eyes still closed, twitched at the noise, as though his nerves were wired together. The doctor stepped toward her. He towered over Onyx, but she did not back away.

"I will not have overly nervous females telling me what is my duty," he snapped at her. "It is perfectly obvious to me that this man's black humors are about to overtake his entire system. He must be bled to release them. It is the only way. Leave me."

"I will not," said Onyx. "You will go right now before I set my postboys on you." She called to Emily, who stood in the doorway wringing her hands. "Lady Sherbourn, be so good as to summon them up here right away."

Emily darted away. Onyx turned back to the doctor, who had not retreated one step. "Lady Sherbourn tells me that Major Beresford has gone in search of a physician. Your services are no longer required here. Submit your bill, and let us not see you here again."

"You are killing this man," said the doctor.

"No, you are," she said, her voice deadly quiet. She took a step toward him, and he backed away. "If you do not leave, I will take that poker to you myself."

The doctor laughed and again Adrian twitched. "You? You?" Dr. Marchmount roared. "Is this house filled with raving females?"

"Don't try me," she replied and pressed her lips tight together to keep her voice from shaking.

The doctor stepped back from the bed, and Onyx turned to Adrian. His eyelids flickered but he did not open them. She took in his terrible emaciation and the dreadful smell that emanated from his body and raised the sheet.

His bony hips and ankles were covered with sores, raw, weeping wounds caked with his own excrement, deep holes in his already thin body. She touched one, noting how inflamed it was with filth. She raised her eyes to the physician, daring him to explain such madness to her.

"I use the body's own products to draw out the cancer, miss," he explained, his voice patronizing, cool. "As the wounds drain, he will begin to heal."

"Nonsense," she snapped and lowered the sheet again, more angry at that moment than she had ever been in her life. "These are nothing but sores! Painful, rotten sickroom sores! What medicine have you been practicing here? I say you are a charlatan and a mountebank! You should be prosecuted and relieved of whatever license, if any, you possess!"

She ran across the room and grabbed up the poker, swinging it over her head as the doctor, abandoning his air of superiority, scrambled out of the room and bumped into the coachman.

The coachman was so exhausted that he swayed on his feet, but he gathered himself together and clamped two meaty hands on the physician's arms. "You're not troubling this lady?" he asked. "After I went to such pains to get her here? Let us go below and discuss this, sir."

Onyx dropped the poker and picked up the doctor's bleeding box. She flung it at him as he ran down the stairs. "Send Major Beresford your bill, and don't ever come here again!" she shouted, pounding her fists on the banister.

The doctor turned around in the doorway only long enough to look up at her. His mouth worked but no words came out. He pointed his finger at her and then ran from the house. In another moment she heard the crack of a whip and a horse racing away. She leaned against the railing and covered her face with her hands. "What have I done?" she said out loud as the coachman lumbered back up the stairs.

"Are ye all right, miss?" he asked as he helped her to her feet.

She dusted off her dress. Her neatly drawn-back hair had come loose from its pins and was wild around her face. She smoothed it back. "Thank you, sir. Again you have been of much help to me."

"Nothing to it, miss. And now, if you think there is no one else I should eject from this house, my boys and I will tend to our horses."

She smiled at him, and he tipped his hat and bowed again.

Onyx watched as Emily Beresford trudged back up the stairs, hand-over-hand on the railing, as if she had not the strength to go another step of her own accord. She sank down on the top step and rested her forehead on her knees. Onyx sat down beside her.

"Onyx . . . Oh, may I call you Onyx? Our acquaintance is so brief "—she smiled slightly—"and somewhat precipitate."

"Surely we already know each other well enough to dispense with formalities," said Onyx.

"Onyx, when I engaged Dr. Marchmount, he told me to put Adrian entirely in his hands and do as I was told." She shook her head. "He seemed so sure of himself, so certain that he was right, that I did not question anything." She made a face. "Dr. Marchmount was recommended by the older ladies of this neighborhood and friends from York, persons whom Adrian says I must cultivate." She sighed. "It was only lately, as Adrian grew weaker and weaker, that I began to doubt. Would that I had done so sooner. Can you help me?"

"Of course. That is what I came here to do," said Onyx, feeling less sure now, but not about to share her fears with the worn-out woman beside her. "My foster father died when I was ten. I remember that he had such sores, and I recall what we did for him."

Emily brightened perceptibly. "Do you think he can be well again?"

"I do not know. We will have to wait until Jack returns with a real physician. But we can make him more comfortable."

By late afternoon Adrian Beresford was clean and

resting on a sheepskin. As she had soaked the sores with warm water and a little witch hazel, Onyx dug back in her mind to the winter of her father's final illness.

"Emily, can you get me a sheepskin?"

Lady Beresford was patting dry a sore on her husband's heel. "I am sure I can. What would that be for?" She looked away. "Forgive me if I sound suspicious, Onyx. I suppose now I am too late wary."

"That would hardly be surprising. Sheepskin is merely soft to lie upon, and there are oils in it to soothe the skin."

"I will see to it."

Albert, the footman, lifted Adrian into his arms while Onyx rapidly changed the sheets and spread out the sheepskin that Chalking had brought her. She directed Albert to lower Adrian onto his side, and she placed a pillow between his knees. "We'll have to move him often. That way the sores will have a chance to heal. I wish the light did not bother his eyes. He would so benefit from sunlight on his wounds," she whispered to Emily.

During the entire ordeal, Adrian had not opened his eyes. She could see restless movement behind his closed lids, but he made no attempt to look at them.

"Is he in pain?" she whispered again to Emily, who was busy applying the lotion that Lady Bagshott had put in the basket she had sent with Onyx.

"He is in pain when he begins to move about, and moan, and pick at his sheet," said Emily. "Then I know to give him another dose of morphine."

"You know how much?"

She nodded.

"May I suggest . . . if you agree . . . give him just slightly less than that dreadful doctor prescribed," said Onyx.

In another hour, as darkness came, Adrian began to pick at his sheet and move his head. Expertly Emily Beresford raised his head and poured a capful of morphine into his mouth, quickly closing his lips so none of it would run out. Soon he was sunk in deeper sleep.

The two women looked at each other. Emily stood up and held out her hand to Onyx, who took it and hauled herself to her feet.

"Every day is thirty-six hours long," Lady Sherbourn said.

"That will change," said Onyx. "Do you think there is anything to eat in this lovely house?" she asked.

Emily nodded. "I am sure there is. I had breakfast years ago downstairs."

Onyx smiled at Emily's little attempt at a joke. "Well, let us see. I wonder where Alice is."

She had not seen Alice since Emily Beresford came screaming down the stairs that morning. Alice was not accustomed to the sickroom, but she had vanished so completely that Onyx could only wonder.

They went downstairs, arms about each other's waists, holding each other up. Chalking met them at the foot of the stairs. "There is a small dinner ready for you." He turned to Onyx. "Your companion directed that I take her repast to the bookroom."

"The bookroom?" asked Emily, mystified.

"Indeed, Lady Beresford."

Their curiosity aroused, the women went to the bookroom and looked in. Alice was bent over the account books, reconciling the bills and expenses. She glanced up when she heard the door open, with a smile on her face that Onyx had not seen in years.

"This is too famous, Onyx!" she exclaimed, her voice alive with animation that her exhausted charge could only envy. "I have never seen such a collection of bills and statements!"

Emily grimaced. "Excuse my blushes. It is entirely my doing."

Alice clapped her hands. "Surely you will not mind

if I go over your accounts and reconcile them? I haven't had such fun since I taught Gerald his geometry, Onyx. Imagine!"

Onyx could only stare. She opened her mouth and then closed it again, feeling like a fish out of water. With an effort, she gathered her wits about her. "Alice, I am sure Lady Sherbourn will not begrudge you your fun. Only do not stay up too late over it. You'll have plenty to do for days." She closed the door and left Alice to her pleasure.

Emily stared at the closed door. "I never imagined there could be enjoyment in figures." She held out her arm to Onyx. "Pinch me. Am I dreaming this?"

"No, you're not, Lady Sherbourn," Onyx replied. "Alice Banner is a woman possessing a singular nature."

"No, no, remember? You are to call me Emily," said the marchioness. "Titles are so dreadfully stuffy. Jack calls me 'Emmy,' mainly, I think, because he knows how it rankles."

Onyx thought of her own nickname born of the clever mind of Jack Beresford but did not see fit to enlighten Lady Sherbourn. She followed Emily into the morning room, where dinner awaited them.

Emily ate but little, nodding over her food and then falling asleep like a little child kept up too late. Chalking summoned Lady Sherbourn's maid, and the woman helped her mistress to her feet and out the door.

"Chalking, if there should be any trouble with Adrian tonight, waken me, please, and not Lady Sherbourn. She is so tired."

"As you wish, Miss Hamilton."

She sat alone over dinner, automatically putting food from plate to mouth, not knowing what she was eating. She went to sleep leaning over the food and woke when the little clock chimed ten o'clock. She left the room after blowing out the candles.

The hallway was dark. She tiptoed to the bookroom

and looked in, but Alice Banner had long ago taken herself off to her bedroom, wherever that was. Chalking was nowhere in sight. Onyx went up the stairs. It seemed the height of rudeness to look in each room until she found the one with her valise, so she went instead to Adrian's room.

He slept fitfully, pulling at the covers, resting his hand on his swollen abdomen, and then lifting it off as if his spidery fingers were too heavy a weight. She pulled up a chair beside him and rested her hand on his arm.

Adrian was still then. He moved his head in her direction, but he did not open his eyes. A small frown creased the nearly transparent space between his eyes.

"You know I am not Emily," she whispered, "but you do not know who I am, do you, Lord Sherbourn?"

The frown deepened, but there was no other movement. "My name is Onyx Hamilton," she said slowly and distinctly. "Jack sent for me. Now, sleep, my lord."

The frown gradually disappeared. His breathing, although still harsh, became more regular.

She leaned back in the chair and watched him, looking for some resemblance between him and his younger brother and seeing none. Disease had so ravaged his body that he seemed to have no more substance than a pattern card. His facial features were sharp and sunken, his Adam's apple appearing absurdly large because his flesh was so wasted. The veins in his arms were elevated, huge.

"Adrian, what must you have looked like before?" she whispered and felt a great sadness settle over her. She thought then of Jack coming home after four years of terrible warfare to such misery. "Poor, poor men," she crooned to Adrian.

She woke at midnight when the clock chimed and was still awake a half hour later when she heard voices in the downstairs hall. The first thought to invade her sleep-starved mind was that the doctor had returned. She had half-risen from her chair and was looking around for the poker when she realized the improbability of that notion.

The voices were low, but as she grew more wide awake, she knew that Jack had returned. In another minute she heard him walking up the stairs, moving slowly, as if he were as tired as everyone else in this manor.

The door opened, as she had known it would, and he looked in, adjusting his eyes to the little light from the fireplace before he approached Adrian's bed. She stirred in the chair, and he stepped back quickly, as if surprised to see someone else in the room.

"Emily?" he asked.

"No. Onyx," she whispered back.

He came closer then and touched her shoulder, as if to prove to himself that she was real. When he decided that she was, he leaned over Adrian, raising the blanket higher around him. He reached for Onyx's hand then, pulling her from the chair and out into the hall. Holding her by the hand, he sat down with her on the top steps before he let go.

"We seem to have serious conversations on the stairs," he commented, turning to her in better light. "My coachman woke up long enough when I came into the stable to tell me that you were a great gun, a regular brick. And may I add, he has never been known to utter a kind word about any female. You are the first."

He shrugged himself out of his overcoat, which was wet, and draped it over the banister. "Chalking told me you were in bed."

She summoned the energy to chuckle. "Chalking abandoned me in the dining room! I fear he is forgetful. Does he generally misplace guests?"

It was Jack's turn to work up a smile. "Yes. He is too old for his post, but there is nothing Adrian dislikes more than pensioning off old servants and hiring new ones. It smacks of work, something he generally likes to avoid."

He looked sideways at her. "Chalking told me a wondrous tale about someone taking a poker and driving off a doctor twice her size. I would have put the whole thing down to advanced senility, except that I heard a similar story in the stable from the postboys, all of whom, including the coachman, as much as told me they would follow you wherever you led. Wellington would envy your command over troops."

"It wasn't that much," she protested. He was sitting so close to her, and she wished he would go away.

"It was surely that and more," he contradicted quietly. "I am deeply in your debt, Onyx B. Onyx," he amended. "When I saw the chaise in the carriage house, I was all ready to scold you for hurrying so fast, but when the coachman told me his tale, I could only be grateful you arrived in time."

"Did you locate a doctor, a real doctor?" she asked.

He nodded. "He was attending a woman in confinement and could not return with me. He will be here in the morning." Jack ran his hand through his hair, which was wet too. "What a day this has been! Harrogate is not a place I would willingly visit without serious reason."

"Why did you go there? Surely there are more doctors in York."

"Consider the logic, Onyx, my dear. When I came to the road this morning, I was on the verge of taking a coin from my pocket and flipping to decide on direction, when it occurred to me."

"What?" she asked after he yawned enormously and then seemed to forget what he was saying.

"Excuse my manners," he said. "As I sat there on my horse, it occurred to me that Harrogate was precisely the town where I should look for a doctor. Only think how many ill and infirm people drink those odious mineral waters. The place is dreadfully out of style now, but any trip I am forced to make there assures me that it is still a lodestone for the elderly. I knew I could find a doctor there."

He paused and looked more closely at her. "Do you know that the sky this morning was precisely the color of your eyes?"

She moved up against the opposite railing, and he laughed and pulled her back again.

"Onyx, you *are* a great gun! Now, what was I saying?"

"About the doctor, Major Beresford," she said, trying to sound severe and only succeeding in deepening his smile.

"Oh, yes, the doctor. I went to one of the baths and inquired of the proprietor." He stretched his long legs out in front of him on the stairs, leaning back on his elbow. "Wouldn't give me even a particle of advice until I paid for and drank some of his curative water."

She laughed. "And you are quite cured of whatever it was that troubled you, sir?" she teased.

"No, Onyx, I am not," he assured her. The twinkle came back into his tired eyes, and she knew too late she should never have asked such a question. "There is no cure for what I have."

She chose to ignore his statement, although it was difficult, sitting so close to him on the stairway. "Tell me, then. Who is the doctor?"

He seemed to recall himself to the moment. "A young fellow by the name of Waldo Hutchins. He's from over the Pennines in Lancaster. Newly out from his medical studies in Edinburgh. He has been practicing for several years in Harrogate. Each of the baths where I stopped recommended him, so it remained only to seek him out."

"And were you compelled to drink the water at each place?"

"I was. I wonder you cannot smell the sulfur on my clothes. When Adrian is feeling a little more like himself, I will not hesitate to tell him of my great sacrifice on his behalf." He looked more closely at her. "From the tiny glimpse I got tonight, you seem already to have been working miracles in that dreadful room."

"Poor Adrian," she said. "He is covered with sores of the foulest kind." Her voice hardened. "And that miserable doctor had the effrontery to tell me such things were for his own good! Horrible man. I wish I had struck him with that poker!"

Before she could stop him, Jack took her hand in his, raised it to his lips, and kissed it. "I assure you, Miss Hamilton, the redoubtable Miss Hamilton, that by the time this escapade has had the opportunity to circulate throughout this district—I give it two days—the tale will have matured until you are bending the poker over his head and wrapping it around his throat. News has a way of traveling."

She carefully extracted her hand from his grasp. "Sir, in your letter you promised me—"

He rose and pulled her to her feet. "Miss Hamilton, if you will peruse that letter again, provided you still have it, of course, I distinctly remember that I wrote, 'I have no intention,' not that 'I promise.' They are hardly the same. Correct me if I err. And I was holding onto your hand only because, well, it seemed like a noble idea, in light of your achievements this day."

"Wretch," she said, wishing the word had more force behind it, but suddenly finding herself struggling to keep her eyes open.

"And now you must go to bed. I will not have the halls of this fine old manor littered with the bodies of courageous young women who defend my hearth and home from evil physicians and then are left to languish, droop, and fade on the carpet."

"I would have gone to bed, but I did not know which room was mine."

He took her arm again, but this time to tuck it in

the crook of his. "Onyx Hamilton, you are a wonder. You have no qualms about shooting a highwayman, routing a charlatan, or nursing wounds of the worst sort, and yet you are too timid to disturb the sleep of Adrian's forgetful servants! Such a paradox."

She was too tired to remonstrate with him. She let him lead her down the hall and into a room. A fire that obviously had been laid much earlier was on the verge of going out. Jack knelt by it, stirring it with a poker and blowing on it until the flame leapt up.

"This was my mother's room. It's quite the loveliest room at Sherbourn, with the best view." He got to his feet and gestured to the little chair by the window. "Mama used to sit me there and lecture me at length on the sins of throwing rocks at robins and pushing my cousins in the pond."

She wished he would leave. All she wanted to do was rest her head on the inviting pillow and forget everything.

"But you're not even paying attention to me and my rustic stories, Onyx," she heard him saying out of the fog that waited to envelop her. "Good night, Miss Hamilton," he said. "And thank you again, from the bottom of my heart."

Chapter 13

⌒

THE DOCTOR WAS TRUE TO HIS word. He arrived the next morning in a modest tilbury, pulled by an equally modest horse. The animal assumed an apologetic air as it waited at the front entrance next to Jack Beresford's black stallion, saddled and bridled for a ride around the estate.

Dr. Hutchins would never have the command and style of the late-departed, unlamented Dr. Marchmount. He was tall and gawky, and his large hands seemed to spill out of his too-short sleeves. Onyx doubted that his hair had been combed that morning. He wore spectacles that continually drifted to the end of his long and narrow nose, and which were as continually being poked back into place.

Emily, who watched him from the first-floor landing, looked doubtful, but she said nothing as Jack ushered the doctor into the house and stood for a moment in the entrance hall chatting with him.

"He looks so . . . seedy," she whispered to Onyx. There was no denying that, but from her vantage point on the landing, Onyx noticed something about the doctor that Emily overlooked. He appeared genuinely interested in what Jack was telling him, and he seemed to give off an air of quiet capability. He looked as though he had all the time in the world. She sighed and hoped for the best.

They came up the stairs, and Dr. Hutchins held out his hand to Emily. "Lady Sherbourn, I appreciate this invitation to your lovely home."

She smiled and inclined her head toward him, but said nothing. He turned to Onyx. "And you are Major Beresford's wife?" he inquired.

Jack winked at her in that way she found so maddening but made no denials. "Oh, no, Doctor," she stammered, "I am . . . I am Onyx Hamilton, a friend . . . of the . . . family."

As Beresford motioned the doctor into Adrian's room, Onyx glared at him behind Hutchins's back. He smiled and winked again, which only ruffled her further.

Emily remained outside. "Won't you go in too, Emily?" Onyx asked. "Surely you should be there."

Emily shook her head. "I could not. No." She seemed to grow pale at the suggestion. "Onyx, I have not your courage. This is something I would rather not face just now."

"Very well, dear. Let us go downstairs into the library," said Onyx.

They remained in the library, talking in short bursts, listening in silence, waiting for the doctor to leave Adrian's room upstairs. Onyx addressed as many as a half-dozen comments to Emily that she did not seem to hear. Emily might have been watching her attentively and nodding in all the appropriate spots, but her whole heart was elsewhere.

Finally, they heard the men on the stairs. Emily's hand went to her throat. "Which do you think is better, Onyx," she asked, her voice strained, "knowing or not knowing?"

"Knowing," said Onyx immediately, thinking of the years she had wondered where Gerald was and how he had died. "Knowing is better, even if it hurts at first."

Dr. Hutchins came into the room with Jack. Emily rose to her feet, whiter than Onyx had ever seen her before. She stared at the doctor, pleading with her eyes for some sign that all would be well.

"Please sit with us, Lady Sherbourn," said the doctor, holding out his hand to her.

She would not take it and remained standing, poised for flight.

"Emily," said Jack as he walked toward her.

She backed away from him. "Onyx, I don't want to hear any of this!" she said. "Please don't make me stay."

Onyx looked to Jack for help, and he shook his head slightly. "Very well, Emily," she said, "you go upstairs and sit with Adrian. I will . . . talk to you later."

"Thank you!" Emily kissed Onyx on the cheek and fled the room.

"I'm sorry about that," Jack said to Dr. Hutchins as he sat down heavily next to Onyx.

Dr. Hutchins shrugged. "I see all kinds of reactions to such news as I have." He looked at Onyx. "It may fall your lot to tell her."

"Tell her?" repeated Onyx. "What?"

"What I'm sure she already knows. That her husband will die soon."

The words, spoken so matter-of-factly, hung in the air.

Jack stirred beside her, but she could not bring herself to look at him. Onyx spoke to the doctor. "I think we all knew. It's just . . . there's something so final about putting those thoughts into words. Forgive us if we seem remote."

The burden of his news brought Dr. Hutchins to his feet.

"You have done him a great service by nursing his sores, Miss Hamilton. That must continue, of course. He will be much more comfortable." He stuck his hands in his pockets and looked at Major Beresford. "We must lessen his addiction to morphine if he is to live much longer. As long as his dosage is so high, he won't eat."

"But with it, he does not suffer," Onyx said.

"True. Neither does he have any kind of a life in his time remaining. With your permission, Major Beresford, I would like to cut down on the dose so he can tell us himself what he would like us to do. As things are now, we don't know."

She thought of Adrian's flickering eyelids and his failed attempts to open his eyes. There was truth in what Dr. Hutchins said. Adrian had spoken to no one, not even his brother.

"How do we do this?" she asked.

"Cut back on his medicine. Wait longer between doses. You'll need nerves of iron, Miss Hamilton, when he begins to suffer." He sat down again and dangled his hands between his knees. "And yet, when the thing is done, and he is eating again, you should see some little improvement. I consider it worth the attempt. But of course," he concluded, looking at Major Beresford again, "the final say will be yours."

"No, it should be Emily's."

"I do not know that she is capable of such a decision."

Jack said nothing.

"Very well, then," said the doctor. "I must go. I will return in three days to see how things are progressing, but I will be at your command anytime. You need only send someone."

"We are grateful to you," said Jack. He walked the doctor to the door, taking his hat from Chalking and seeing him to his tilbury. He stood in the drive watching as the doctor left, and he was still just standing there when Onyx came to him.

"Jack?"

He said nothing. She came closer and touched him on the sleeve, and he flinched. "I'm sorry, Onyx," he said, not turning around. "It's just difficult."

When he turned to her, his face was composed, but the sorrow in his eyes was so intense that she wanted to put her hands over them. He waited a moment more until he could speak. "How strange this is, Onyx," he said. "People die in Spain. They die there all the time. I nearly died there. But somehow, people aren't supposed to die in England. Explain that to me, Onyx B. I'll be back."

He headed for the front entrance, where his horse waited, leaving her standing at the door. She watched him ride down the lane, forcing his horse faster and faster until it jumped a fence and trotted into the haying fields. Onyx wandered back into the house and down to the bookroom. Alice Banner had arranged the desk to her liking and was working her way down an enormous pile of unpaid bills and unentered credits. She answered Onyx only in monosyllables, so Onyx left her and went into the garden. She sat on a bench and watched the birds darting down into the shallow pan of rainwater set out for them.

Onyx knew that if she stayed at Sherbourn, there wouldn't be many times when she could come outside like this. Adrian needed constant care, and his needs would only deepen, as her foster father's had, the closer death came. Still, it was small repayment for Jack Beresford's rescue of her on the highway. *And what is the real reason that you want to stay, Onyx Hamilton?* she asked herself. *Or are you even willing to admit there is another one?*

She was still sitting in the garden an hour later when Jack returned, coming from the opposite direction and riding much slower. As he rode, he held his injured arm at the elbow. She knew it still pained him, but he did not speak of it. *Perhaps there is a lesson there for me*, she thought as she rose. Beresford rode toward her and dismounted.

"Come with me, Onyx," he said. "I have to curry my horse."

She followed without a word to the stables, walking beside him as he led his horse. He seemed disinclined to talk, but she looked at him, noting how set his expression was, how troubled his eyes.

He nodded to the stableboys, shaking his head when one of them tried to take the horse from him: "No, lad. I do my own horse. A military quirk, I suppose," he explained, addressing Onyx. "You have this uncontrollable urge to take good care of what you owe your life to." He smiled and looked at her, and she wondered if he was really thinking about his horse.

Beresford turned over a bucket and wiped it off with an old blanket. "Here, have a seat. Keep me company."

She did as he said, watching as he removed the saddle and handed it to the stableboy, whisked off the blanket, and pulled out the bit and bridle, all the while talking in conversational tones to his horse. She couldn't hear what he said, but she noticed with some delight that the horse paid close attention, his ears pricked forward.

He gave his horse a good rubdown and then picked up the currycomb.

"I am having second thoughts about your presence here," he said, his voice low. "It is hardly fair of me to ask this of you."

"I felt no hesitation in coming, Major," she said, "and your letter was quite plain."

He brushed away, his back to her. "Yes, but I did not know the complexity of this until Dr. Hutchins told me. Do you realize what agony I will be putting you through in the next few days? I've seen this sort of thing in the hospitals in Lisbon, men crying and screaming for morphine. There's nothing worse, Onyx."

"Yes, there is," she said.

He looked at her, hands on his hips. "What, tell me."

"Not ever having the chance to know your brother again before he dies."

He turned around again to his horse, brushing harder.

She knew he was crying, and her heart went out to him, even as she sat on the bucket, her hands in her lap, and did not move.

"This is worse than combat," he said finally.

"How can it be?" she asked.

"Oh, you wouldn't understand. It's something we don't talk about much because it makes us seem so uncivilized. There's a . . . a certain feeling when you rush to a fight. It's almost . . . pleasure. And if you win, oh, my, the feeling! Some men hate it, some men love it. It drives some, when the fight is over, to maim and rape." He looked at her. "I shouldn't be speaking of such things to you, but the sights I have seen . . ." He stopped brushing, his eyes far away. "As bad as combat is, there is a reward that makes it bearable."

"The reward will come here too, Jack, if we can stick it out."

"No. He will die. There's no reward."

She couldn't bear it. She jumped to her feet and put her arms around Jack Beresford, resting her head against his back. "Don't you dare give up!" she whispered fiercely. "I will not leave you to fight this one alone!"

He leaned against his horse, and she felt the tension leave his body. He dropped the currycomb and her hands, not moving, just standing there. "I couldn't do it alone," he said finally. "I couldn't. I'd leave him in his drugged state before I'd try alone. After these four years, I'm so tired."

"There's your answer, then," she said.

She let go of him, and he turned around, putting his hands on her waist. "I've complicated this issue, of course. Jack Beresford always complicates things. I love you. I don't know how you feel about me, and I'm too tired to ask right now. You're engaged to another man, and you also have some notion about 'place and birth' that I really don't understand, but I love you."

"For someone who is likely to become a marquess before the summer is out, you are remarkably thick-headed," she said with some asperity.

"Ah, your logic is special, Onyx," he said. "Being a marquess has nothing to do with intelligence. I can cite you any number of cases."

"Well, I am equivocating," she confessed. "Since you like words with no bark on them, Jack Beresford, try these: you'd be laughed out of every gentlemen's club, every polite home, every hunt club, the House of Lords, for all I know, for marrying an illegitimate woman."

She had never said the word aloud before. She waited for it to hurt, but it did not. She could see no surprise in Jack's brown eyes, no revulsion. He looked at her as she was accustomed to seeing him look at her, with warmth, interest, and a little lurking humor.

He heard her out and picked up the currycomb again.

"You left two items off your list of objections to yourself: 'She has absolutely no money and is also quite stubborn.' Onyx, you are a hard one."

"Someone has to listen to reason," she said equably, amazed at her own assurance. *I don't know why I am not crying*, she thought as he watched her. *Maybe it's because Jack Beresford is such a blockhead.*

They looked at each other. Neither would look away until Jack broke his glance and ran his hand along his horse's flank. "We are at *point non plus*, obviously."

"We are," she agreed.

"A truce?" he asked.

"Possibly."

"We'll go ahead and fight this out with Adrian, you and I. I don't think Emily can take it, and I'm going to try to bully her out of Sherbourn until we've done the thing. It *is* my decision."

"So far, I agree."

"You'll stay with me through this whole nasty summer, and I won't propose again, or tell you I love you, even though I might tease you occasionally. I'm like that, Onyx. And when it's all over, if your feelings haven't changed a bit, I'll retire from the field."

"Very well, sir," she agreed. Why does he have to smile in that maddening way? Then she thought, *At least he is able to smile.*

He turned back to his horse and finished currying the animal, while she sat back on the bucket, wondering what on earth she had gotten herself into and dreading the coming ordeal less than she would have suspected. Without Jack Beresford, she never would have agreed to stay. With him, the thing might be possible. She knew that he was thinking the same thing. "It's an unhealthy dependence," she muttered under her breath.

"Hmmm?"

"Oh, nothing. We must develop some strategy, Major," she said.

"Certainly, Miss Hamilton. To begin with, if you don't stop calling me Major, I'll drop you in the water trough."

She laughed. "Do you have any strategies, Jack?"

"I have several. You'd be amazed what I thought about on my ride." He found another bucket, turned it over, and sat next to her. "I would tell this only to you. At first I thought I would just keep riding to Liverpool and join the crew of the next ship bound for America. Then I thought I would run away and rejoin my regiment in Spain."

"Very cowardly, sir, but justified," she murmured.

He leaned sideways and touched her shoulder with his. "When you are not close by, I do feel cowardly about this whole scheme." He rubbed his hands together. "Dr. Hutchins said we could continue the overdose and Adrian would die soon. But, Onyx, I didn't stay alive for four years in Spain to come home to nothing! I want to know my brother again."

She said nothing, grateful that he was talking again, not standing silent and staring.

"And then I thought a shorter journey than America would be in order. We are going to move Adrian downstairs into the small parlor. Only think how well it will serve. No more running up and down the stairs; a room with a sunny aspect. And when Adrian does come around again—and he will—he will be in the center of the household and involved with us."

"The room is sunny," Onyx agreed, "but the light hurts his eyes. You know, if we put a mask over his eyes, we could move him quite close to the window and expose his sores to sunlight."

"Admirable," Jack said. "Do you think we can prevail upon the ever-efficient Miss Alice Banner to be Emily's guide and take her on several excursions to—oh, let us think—the York Minster, or the silk warehouses in Leeds, or perhaps some picturesque ruin or other?"

"I am certain she will oblige us."

"Then let us begin." Jack's air of enthusiasm quickly gave way to sobriety. "We will lose this war, but I want to win at least one battle." He stood up and pulled Onyx to her feet. "Let that be a warning to you. I hate to lose."

The battle began in earnest the next morning with a victory in the first skirmish. Emily Beresford, after gentle but unrelenting pressure from her brother-in-law, agreed to ride into York with Jack's measurements and direction to his tailor. "Provided he is still alive, although when last I saw him, he was healthy. I want a new hunting coat and riding breeches without holes. I am becoming a positive embarrassment to the Marquess and Marchioness of Sherbourn."

"I will discharge your errand, Jack," said Emily as she drew on her gloves and then took them off again. "Oh, should I go?"

"Yes, you should, dear Lady Sherbourn," said Jack as he put his hands on her shoulders and kissed her on the forehead. "Do you want me to disgrace the family at the fall hunt? And when was the last time you went any farther than the front drive?"

"It has been months," said Emily, pulling on her gloves again. "Please say I may select the color?" She put her hand on Jack's chest. "No one ever looked more dashing in his regimentals than you, but, brother-in-law, I do not scruple to add that you have no style when you are out of uniform."

How odd, thought Onyx as she watched Jack's graceful tableau with amusement. *Jack's shabby, unconcerned gentility is one of those things I like about him. He's so big and comfortable.* She blushed then and then turned away to admire an ugly vase on the hall table.

"Yes, yes, by all means select the color, as long as it is a red like Onyx's cheeks," agreed Jack. He put his hand on the small of Emily's back and propelled her toward the door, Alice following. "And when you have completed that assignment, I am running low on bay rum and would ask you to procure me some. It must be Jamaican bay rum, so you may have to look in several shops."

"Emily," said Onyx, "are you subscribers of a library in York?"

Emily turned blank eyes on her brother-in-law. "Are we?"

"Yes, you ignorant widgeon," he replied. "Chumming's. What is it that you wish, Onyx?"

"I would like, of all things . . . could you find *Pride and Prejudice*? It is a new book I want to read."

"What, a novel?" questioned Jack. "For one who is vicarage-bound?"

"I, sir, am not there yet," Onyx replied firmly.

"Indeed you are not," he murmured, brightened, and then pulled Emily around again. "There. That's the exact color I want for my hunting coat. That shade of blush."

"Jack, you are disgraceful," said Emily. "I do not understand why Onyx even tolerates you."

"Neither do I. If you cannot find that book at Chumming's, try Witherill's and tell them to charge it to me." He turned to Alice Banner, who waited by the door. "My dear Miss Banner, we trust that you will not permit Lady Beresford to abandon herself to dissipation on this day in York?"

Alice tittered. "Major Beresford! You ask such a thing after I have raised Onyx Hamilton!"

He bowed. "That is especially why I ask such a thing."

Onyx glared at him and Emily laughed. She stopped suddenly and put her hand over her mouth.

Jack hugged her. "There's not a minute's harm in laughter, Emily. We want to hear more of it this summer. Now, go on."

She stepped back from her brother-in-law. "Yes, I had better leave before the two of you conspirators fob off another errand on me. Before I know it, you will send me to Cornwall for smugglers' rum!" Her eyes were serious then. "I know why you are doing this, and I thank you. Only please, please, take good care of Adrian. He is all I have."

The simplicity of her plea went straight to Onyx's heart. "Emily, rest assured of that."

Emily smiled then. "I will return by late afternoon."

Jack watched the carriage leave. "She was the prettiest little lady in London," he said. "I quite lost my heart to her. We all did." He looked around at Onyx. "She dances divinely, and never once complained when I stepped all over her feet. Onyx, do you dance?"

"No. My stepmama never could see a need for lessons," she replied.

"I wish you could have seen Adrian and Emily," he said, starting up the stairs. "Albert has surely set up that bed in the parlor by now. I shall bring Adrian down."

Onyx went into the parlor, looking over the arrangement of furniture again, plumping up the pillows, smoothing back the coverlet, wondering for the thousandth time if they were doing the right thing.

Jack carried his brother into the parlor and lowered him gently to the bed. "He is so light," Jack said in a wondering tone. "Like a sack of feathers."

When Lord Sherbourn had been arranged on his side, Onyx cleaned each of the sores, noticing with satisfaction that some of them were beginning to dry out. When she finished, she folded the coverlet back and exposed him to the sunlight. Adrian twitched and groaned. She covered his eyes with a strip of black cloth.

Jack sat watching her the entire time she nursed his brother. "This is no work for a delicately nurtured female," he said at last. "My audacity at asking this of you continues to amaze me."

She regarded him, her hands on her hips. "Your audacity has always amazed me, Jack." She thought a moment. ". . . in all the three weeks I have known you."

"Three weeks? Is that all?" he asked, pulling his chair close to Adrian's head and resting his hand on his brother's skeletal shoulder.

She nodded, steeling herself as Adrian started to shake.

Without a word she went to the harpsichord by the opposite window, sat down, and rummaged through the stack of music on the instrument's lid. With a smile, she pulled out a sonata by Beethoven and began to play softly.

She was still playing four hours later when Jack finally gave Adrian his first dose of morphine for the day. Within moments, Adrian had ceased his struggles and lay still.

Onyx rose from the harpsichord, took a soft cloth, and wiped the sweat from Adrian's body as Jack sank back in his chair and let his arms go limp. When she was finished, she covered Adrian and turned him onto his back, removing the bandage over his eyes and closing the curtains until the room was in half-darkness.

After several moments of staring at nothing, Jack pulled out his watch. "We are two hours ahead of ourselves, Onyx. If he can go another four hours with only half a dose, we can count ourselves lucky."

"I wish that he would open his eyes," she said, hugging her arms around her body as she stood by the window.

"Dr. Hutchins said it might take several days. We have no way of knowing how deep Adrian was sunk in this before I came home."

She put her hand on Jack's shoulder. "Let me sit with him now."

He covered her hand with his for a moment and then patted it. "Very well. I have promised Private Petrie that I would escort him around the estate. There is time now before it grows dark."

"Jack, you should rest," she said.

"And you should not? I have my reasons. Petrie shows signs of turning into an extraordinary bailiff. He is interested in everything that goes on around this place."

"Very well."

"If you should have any trouble, only call for Albert. He will come." He looked at his watch again. "See if you can hold out until half past four. Then he should sleep through the early-evening hours when Emily is about and sitting with him." He stretched and started for the door. "It will be a long night, Onyx."

"We have been through long nights before, Jack, both of us," was her quiet reply.

She didn't know if he heard her, but he paused in the doorway and blew her a kiss.

Chapter 14

$\mathcal{T}$HE SUN WAS LEAVING SHADOWS across the lawn when the morphine began to wear off. Adrian did not open his eyes, but he tossed his head from side to side with a snapping motion that was almost hypnotic. He plucked at the parchment skin on his arm as if something was shooting fiery darts just under the surface. He spoke for the first time that Onyx could remember, but it was a strange language, low and guttural, as if he had forgotten English. The sound of it frightened her and sent little sparkles of fear up her spine, but she rubbed his arms and his back, talking to him all the while of whatever came into her mind.

Sweat poured off his body as she tried to wipe him dry. His eyes and nose began to run and gooseflesh rose on his arms and legs, even as he sweated and then yawned until she feared he would dislocate his jaw.

She fought down her own panic as she told him everything she could remember about her childhood. She rubbed his arms and legs, speaking in a low voice of Gerald and Spain. When she talked about Jack, he seemed to stop his restless movements and attempt to listen to her.

She wished she knew more about Jack, so she told him over and over about the highwaymen and Jack's rescue.

When she didn't think either of them could stand another minute, she heard Jack's footsteps in the hallway. He came into the room and looked at his watch.

"It's half past four, Onyx," he said. "You've done it." He reached for the medicine bottle, but then withdrew his hand. "Let's try for five o'clock."

She nodded, too tired to speak, and moved aside so Jack could sit in her place. He rubbed Adrian's back, speaking softly to him as he twisted from side to side, screamed suddenly, and picked at his skin.

Chalking and Albert came to the door, both of them too polite and well-trained to say anything as they glanced from Adrian to Onyx. Their concern went to her heart. She walked stiffly to the door.

"Madam, is there anything we can do?" Chalking asked in a whisper.

"Just be steadfast. Give us heart," she whispered back. "And please, please, if Lady Sherbourn should return soon, let us know immediately and do not let her in."

"We will do that, miss," said Chalking and left. Albert remained in the doorway, watching Adrian pick at his skin. He stood there a moment in silence, his lips tight together and then he spoke. "Miss Hamilton, if I am not being forward . . ."

"What is it, Albert?"

"I have some mittens. Perhaps if you put them on his hands, he would not do himself injury."

"Albert, that is capital!" she exclaimed and touched his arm. "Please hurry."

He returned moments later with the mittens and took them to the bedside, where he slipped them on Lord Sherbourn's hands and then stood back to survey the effect. Adrian still tried to pull at his skin, but he could no longer hurt himself.

Jack Beresford sat back in his chair and spoke in a careful voice that told Onyx just how close to the surface his emotions were.

"Albert," he began and took a deep breath, "have I ever told you how valuable you are to me?"

Albert permitted himself a little smile. "No, Major. I can remember any number of occasions when I put you to bed when you were a trifle bosky—pardon, Miss Hamilton—and you did not consider me particularly valuable then."

"It never ceases to amaze me what a fool I was in my younger years," Jack said simply. "If you promise to over-look my youthful folly, I promise to remember it. That will do us both good."

"As you wish, sir. If there is anything else, only call." The hands on the clock seemed not to budge after four thirty. Onyx could almost feel time perching on her shoulder, weighing her down, teasing her as the clock's hands moved slower and slower. Resolutely she looked away from the clock, ignoring it even as she listened for every tick.

"Can you play for us, Onyx?" Jack asked at last. "If you are not too tired. Perhaps Adrian will settle down."

She was too tired, but she went to the harpsichord anyway, lighting the branched candles on the instrument and the sconces on the walls between the windows. The flicker of candlelight attracted Adrian's attention for a few moments. He turned toward the candles, twisting his head around, even as his eyes remained closed.

"Jack," she whispered as she watched Adrian, "I wonder what is going on in his mind. Does he hear us, do you think?"

"I wish I knew. I only hope that cur Marchmount did not physic him beyond his powers to return. We shall know eventually."

She played Beethoven's Sonata in D, her fingers clumsy on the keys. The second time through was more polished, and by the third time, discipline took over and she was sitting up straight, curving her fingers correctly over the keys as she had been taught, concentrating on the music, forgetting for a short while the terror for Adrian that ate at her insides. She raised her hands as the final chord died away, conscious only then that her back ached and she was weary beyond words.

Jack looked at the clock. "It is five thirty, Onyx B," he said, the triumph and relief in his voice almost palpable. He took hold of the medicine bottle and measured a dose into the small silver cup, eyeing the level, pouring a little back and then adding a touch. He raised Adrian up and poured down the morphine, holding his brother in his arms until he relaxed and slept.

"Merciful heaven," said Jack. He held out his hand for Onyx, and she came to him, sitting close beside him on the little chair.

No words were spoken; there was nothing to say. Slowly Jack raised his arm and draped it over her shoulders, leaning his head against her for a moment. After several long silences, he released her and stood up, stretching and rubbing his back. He went into the hall and then looked back at her as she remained on the chair. "Well, Sergeant Hamilton, we certainly gave no quarter, did we?"

She shook her head.

He came back a few minutes later and took her by the hand, hauling her up from the chair and pulling her down to the library, where he sat her down on the divan and propped up her legs on a footstool. Albert came in with soup and cheese.

Jack rubbed his hands together. "Albert, again your excellence astounds me. Does Adrian pay you enough?"

"Certainly not, sir."

"Then I will discuss this oversight with him . . . when he returns to us."

"Will there be anything else, sir?"

Jack surveyed the tray of food. "Yes. At the risk of offending the sensibilities of my comrade in arms here, I wonder if there might be anything so common as a bottle of beer in this impeccable establishment?" He inclined his head toward Onyx. "It is harder than I realize for an old soldier to abandon all his bad habits."

She only smiled and picked up a bowl of soup. "Jack, you even have my permission to drink it out of the bottle."

His eyes widened. "I didn't know there was any other way, Miss Hamilton."

"Major Beresford, you are a dreadful actor. I wonder why they keep you around here."

Albert looked from one to the other. Small choking sounds came from his throat as he struggled to preserve his phlegmatic mien. "Madam, will there be anything else?"

"No, Albert. Except . . . thank you."

He bowed and left, returning quickly with a brown bottle, which he handed to the major. Disapproval was written all over his face, but he made no comment, only bowed again, turned precisely on his heel, and left.

Jack drank long and deep. He raised his eyebrows at Onyx in an inquiring manner.

"Don't you do it," she warned. "Even *your* credit is not that good."

He grinned, took another swig, and belched. Onyx burst into laughter. She tried to smother it but couldn't. Jack only grinned at her and took another swallow, sinking down on the divan beside her and stretching his long legs out in front of him. "Emily would never approve," he said at last.

"And you think I do?" she murmured.

"Oh, no, but you're different, Onyx." He rested the empty bottle on his stomach. "We've been through too much together, I suppose. I have only to look at you to know what you're thinking. After living four years among people to whom guile has been raised to a fine art, I find your crystal-clear emotions a regular balm of Gilead." He took another pull from the empty bottle, retrieving the last drop. "Chalking told me that he has set up a cot in the little room next to Adrian's. You have my permission to lie down on it before your face drops in that soup."

She took a few more sips and set it aside. "And what about you?"

"My dear, I will fluff up this frippery little pillow here, unbutton my pants, and stretch out on this sofa. I expect Emily at any moment, but I must grab a little sleep before the next engagement begins, and so must you. Now, get to it."

"Yes, sir," she said, amused at his audacity.

Onyx knew that she would not sleep, but her eyes closed the moment she lay down. She slept solidly until she heard the front door open and Emily and Alice came into the hall, Emily calling for Jack. She thought she would go to Emily, but her eyes closed again. She was aware that Emily and Jack came into the room where Adrian was sleeping. She heard them speaking together softly, and then it was quiet again.

She woke in the darkness to the sound of Adrian talking in his unknown foreign language again. The odd sound of it sent shivers down her spine. She lit a candle, her hand trembling as she tried to hold the sulfur next to the wick. She wrapped a blanket around herself and tip-toed into the room.

Adrian was sitting up in bed. Her heart leapt in her throat. He was so skeletal that she fancied she could see through him. The moon reflected against the whiteness of his wasted flesh, and she felt her skin crawl. His eyes were open for the first time, and his head turned as he followed her quiet entrance into the room. He said something to her, but it made no sense. She came closer, terrified of him.

Adrian stared at her. His mouth opened and closed. She inched closer and held out her hand to him, but he did not take it. She stared at him and then waved her hand back and forth in front of his face, her unease deepening when she saw that his eyes were unfocused, unseeing.

She gathered her courage about her and gently forced him to lie down. She closed his eyes and held her hand over them, feeling the orbs moving about under her touch, his eyelashes fluttering. "Adrian, please rest," she whispered in his ear. "You'll feel better in the morning."

His sigh was almost imperceptible, but at last his eyes were still and she removed her hand. She lit the branch of candles and looked about her. There on the bedside table was the book she had asked Emily to procure for her in York. She picked it up, smiling to herself.

"Oh, Adrian, it is *Pride and Prejudice*," she told him. "I especially asked Emily to find it for me." She settled herself in the chair, pulling it closer to the bed.

The book was new and smelled of leather and ink. She sniffed it. "Lord Sherbourn, I am sure there is nothing so fine as the odor of a new book. It is one of those little things I so enjoy. Jack laughs at me because I take such pleasure in little things, but it is little things I am used to."

He gave no sign that he heard her, but he was still. "Very well, then, my lord, if you have no objection, let us begin." She turned to the first chapter. "'Chapter One. It is a truth universally acknowledged, that a single man in possession of a good fortune must be in want of a wife.'"

She pulled the candle branch closer and wove the tale of the Bennet family into the night, pausing when Lord Sherbourn began to writhe and turn and pluck at his skin again. She rubbed his arms, singing softly to him, until his motions ceased. When he was quiet, she picked up where she had left off, her voice low but firm in the silence of the house.

When four hours passed, she took a deep breath and continued reading, pausing at last when Lord Sherbourn began to rest his hands on his swollen abdomen, and she knew he was truly and deeply in pain again and not merely craving the morphine. She poured his medication into the silver cup, pursed his lips, and poured it down, relaxing as he relaxed, breathing slower herself as his respirations evened out and he slept. She marked the place in the book and laid it in her lap as her head tipped forward and she slept too.

She woke an hour later to Jack's hand on her shoulder and wondered only a moment why his touch did not startle her. She was becoming familiar with it. That thought caused her a tiny distress, even as she was grateful for his presence.

"Weren't you supposed to wake me when Adrian began to stir?" he asked. "Here now, Onyx, I have slept half the night away."

"I considered," she replied, "but decided to read to Adrian instead."

He picked up the book from, her lap, turning to where she had marked. "Chapter Twenty-two! Onyx Hamilton, you are a worse widgeon than Emily!"

"No, I'm not, Jack," was her reply. "You need your rest. I am not the one who suffers from loss of blood." She turned her head to look him right in the eye. "Why do men think recuperation does not take time?"

"Because we are stupid." He touched her cheek. "You'll not object if I sit with you?"

"No, although I would prefer that you returned to the couch."

He pulled up another chair beside her, watching his brother, pulling up the coverlet, and smoothing the hair from Adrian's eyes.

"Emily?" Onyx asked.

"She had a fine time in York. I convinced her that Adrian would sleep, and she should be in bed. Luckily, she gave no objection." He laughed softly. "I think Alice Banner must have dragged her down every side street in York until she was worn down to the nub."

"Alice has never been slow in her duties. And I suspect she enjoys taking charge of Lady Sherbourn."

"Rather than her own Onyx Hamilton, who would prefer of all things not to be bullied?"

"Perhaps," was all she would say.

They sat in silence another moment. The moon's glow reminded Onyx again that summer was starting to happen outside the windows of Sherbourn. Soon all the flowers would be in bloom; the trees would lose that tentative lime green of spring and deepen into the emerald of summer. It was her favorite time of year; she wondered if she would enjoy any of it this strange summer.

She looked at Jack Beresford, who was outlined by the moonlight that flowed through the window and across Adrian's bed. She admired the serenity of Jack's face at rest, his air of complete dependability. *I always know where I stand with Jack*, she thought. *I do not think he would ever turn on me or take someone else's words for my conduct.*

She said nothing to him, even when he sensed that she was staring at him and turned toward her. She smiled at him and looked away to contemplate Adrian. Jack's gaze continued to rest on her. During the day this would have embarrassed her, but it was night now, and the moonlight softened everything. She felt safe.

Jack broke the spell finally. "Do you know, I remember a time . . ." He settled lower in his chair. "Do you mind the reminiscence of an old soldier?"

"You know I do not mind."

"I don't even recall the name of the village, but we, through, I must confess, an error of mine, found ourselves standing in deep . . . uh, water. Onyx, have the good grace to at least look away if you must laugh at me! There was no way we were going to survive the night." He chuckled at the memory. "I don't know any other time when I have been so . . . surrounded. We all accepted the fact that we were going to die."

He looked at her and touched her cheek. "You couldn't possibly imagine the feeling, Onyx. To be so sure of something so . . . final."

Adrian moved and Jack reached forward to cover his arms again. "All I wanted in the whole world was to see Adrian and my mother again and tell them I loved them. Nothing more. You see, I had never been one to say such things, not even when I bade them both good-bye after Adrian's wedding."

"What happened?"

"Well, morning came, as it always does. It may even come here tomorrow. Picton had the kindness of heart to send the Ninety-second Highlanders to rescue a foolish major and his ragtag regiment. I'm sure the Scots have a low opinion of us still." He laughed again, but it was an embarrassed laugh. "We sat there and cried like babies."

She touched his arm and he took her by the fingers, lacing his hand into hers. "I never had a chance to tell my mother I loved her. She died that spring. But Adrian—I have been given the chance and I will tell him."

Jack let go of her hand and sat forward, his hands clasped together between his knees. When Adrian grew restless, Onyx opened the book in her lap to Chapter Twenty-two. As Jack watched, and then leaned back in his chair, his feet on the bed, she touched Adrian's arm. "Hush, Adrian. Let us continue. 'The Bennets were engaged to dine with the Lucases and again during the chief of the day, was Miss Lucas so kind as to listen to Mr. Collins.'"

She woke up hours later when the book finally hit the floor. She couldn't remember the last chapter she had read, but it had been at some point when the sky was just beginning to turn pink and before the birds had caught wind of it.

Onyx looked over at Jack, feeling guilty for nodding off, but he was asleep too, his feet still on Adrian's bed, wearing socks but no shoes. His head was tipped down, and she could not see his face, but from the regular rise and fall of his shoulders, she could tell that Jack was no better at watching than she.

Her whole head was stiff from leaning so far back. She closed her eyes again and rubbed her neck. Someone cleared his throat, and she stopped her hand, holding her breath.

"Pardon me, miss, but how am I to know what happens to Eliza Bennet if you are continually nodding off?"

The voice was weak; she could hardly hear it above the racket of the grackles encroaching in the hawthorn tree outside the window. She lowered her arm slowly, as if afraid a sudden movement would disrupt the speaker.

She opened her eyes and found Adrian Beresford, Lord Sherbourn, looking back at her.

"And while we are at it, who are you?"

She could only stare at him, her mouth partly open, her eyes wide. He watched her with what she could only have described as a grimace twisting his face. When she realized he was attempting to smile, her heart went out to him and she found her voice again.

"Lord Sherbourn," she said.

"I know who I am," he agreed, "but you still have the advantage of me."

"Beg pardon," she began, "I am Onyx." She stared in fascination at his eyes, brown like his brother's, but tinged yellow where the white should be.

"Did my brother have the good sense to marry?"

"Oh, no," she said impulsively, "your brother has no sense. I'm Onyx Hamilton. We met . . . well, he saved me." Lord Sherburn's brows drew together in a frown. "It's hard to explain. Jack can tell you."

She turned to Jack, who still slept, and shook him awake. He was on his feet in seconds, looking about him in panic, and she realized she should not have startled him. She leapt to her feet and put an arm around his waist. "I'm sorry, Jack, I didn't mean . . ."

He was not attending to her. Suddenly shy and acutely aware that she was the stranger in the room, Onyx let go of him and stepped back out of the way as Jack fell to his knees and gathered his brother in a gentle embrace. He cradled him carefully in his arms.

"You have returned," Adrian said, his voice the merest whisper.

"So have you, dear brother," Jack replied.

"Perhaps . . . for a time," his brother said. He turned his head slightly in Jack's arms to take Onyx into his view again. "Could you not send that charming woman to find some food?"

Jack looked at her too. "I think she would only be too happy. And perhaps she could even wake Emily."

"Yes, that would be excellent. And how did you find Emily?"

"Burned down to the socket," Jack stated. "If I were not so glad to see you again, I would rain coals of fire on your head for not writing to me about this."

"You had enough to do. Don't scold. Is there water in that carafe?"

Onyx left the room, closing the door quietly behind her. Chalking stood just outside. He fixed her with an inquiring look, and she nodded, her eyes bright with unshed tears. "Oh, Chalking," was all she could say until she collected herself and remembered her errand. "Can you bring some gruel? And make it very thin? He is hungry. And then I think you should send someone for Dr. Hutchins."

Chalking bowed and hurried off, a spring in his step that hadn't been there before.

Onyx took the stairs two at a time and knocked at Emily's door. Emily opened it after a few moments, rubbing her eyes. She started to speak, noticed the great excitement on Onyx's face, and without a word threw on her wrap and darted down the stairs. Onyx heard the door to the parlor open and close again. She waited in the hall until she heard Chalking go into the room, leave the tray of food, and then quietly close the door behind him.

The sound of the door closing seemed to ring in her ears. "We have done the thing, Jack," she said softly to herself. Her part was over now; it remained to pack and return to the vicarage.

It was time for her to leave. The closing of the door had reminded her. She would pack and pry Alice loose from the accounts and take the next mail coach back to Chalcott.

The manor was filled with the silence of early morning. Onyx realized how exhausted she was, how desperate for sleep. She went to her room, kicked off her shoes, and sank down on the bed. She remembered covering herself with her shawl and then remembered nothing more.

Onyx woke hours later only because she knew someone was watching her. She opened her eyes and looked into Jack's eyes.

She sat up, covering her legs where her dress had wandered up to her knees. "Jack, whatever are you doing in here?" she demanded, out of sorts with him for his intrusion.

"Well," he began reasonably, "you left the door wide open and the rain was coming in the window." He shrugged. "I came in to close the window, and then I sat down on Mama's chaise. I guess I fell asleep."

He went to the window, resting his hand on the draperies, watching the rain spill down the window. "It's more . . . more than that. I guess I feel . . . lonely."

The irritation left her. While his back was turned to her, she straightened her dress and draped her shawl carefully over her stocking feet. "Jack, what have you to feel lonely about? Adrian has come back to you."

He shook his head. "No, not to me. To Emily." He sat down again in that characteristic way of his, with his hands clasped together between his knees. "I suppose nothing is ever the same again, is it, Onyx?"

"No," she agreed softly. "I don't suppose it is."

"She loves him so much. So do I, but it's different now that he is married."

Something else was troubling him. She could see it in his eyes. Funny how a tough veteran like Jack could be so exposed that way. "Jack," she asked suddenly, "do you ever play cards?"

He brightened a moment. "No! I can't keep a single secret. No one ever wants to partner me." He sighed. "Mama always said I was clear as glass. There's more, Onyx, and I don't like the way I feel about it."

She got up and sat beside him on the chaise. "What's really wrong, Jack? You should be so happy."

He waited a long minute before answering her, as if measuring her regard. "You'll think I'm terrible," he said at last. "I think I'm terrible."

"I could never think any such thing of you," she said. "Tell me what's wrong."

"I-I . . . You're the only one I can talk to about this."

"Tell me."

He took a deep breath. "Dr. Hutchins came and looked Adrian over, and congratulated us. There's more, but that subject will keep. Well, after he left, I went to the bookroom and visited with Alice." He touched her arm. "She is a wonder, Onyx. I am sure you never deserved her."

Onyx smiled. "Indeed, no." She waited for him to go on.

"She . . . she showed me the estate's books. Onyx, this place has been so badly mismanaged!" His words came rushing out in a tide of anger. "Adrian and Emily have spent money right and left. They've squandered and lived foolishly. Clothes, horses, balls, our manor in London, coaches." He leapt to his feet, unable to remain still. The room was full of him as he paced in front of the window. "And suddenly I found myself so angry with Adrian! Just furious! When I think how I starved and struggled just to stay alive for four years in the Peninsula, and all the time Adrian was back here doing a merry dance! I wanted to strangle him!" He sat down again, all the fight out of him. "What's the matter with me?" he whispered. "How can I be angry at him? Am I such a monster?"

The Reverend Littletree would have assumed a pose and spouted a sermon, but Onyx didn't know any sermons. She just pulled Jack Beresford into her arms and rested his head on her as she had done once before, crooning to him and resting her hand on his head. His arms went around her, and he clung to her.

Never in her life had she felt so needed, so complete. She rested her cheek against his head, taking a breath when he took one, totally absorbed in him. She wanted the moment to go on forever, even as at the same time she knew it should not.

"About a month after we learned of Gerald's death, I went to his room to . . . to put things away," she began, talking into Jack's hair. "All of a sudden . . . Oh, it's so hard to talk about, even now—even to you. I was so angry with him for leaving me alone. I'd lost my great companion, my buffer against the slights that were dealt us. It hurt." She loosened Jack's grip on her and pulled away so she could look at him. "I don't pretend to understand why love has to hurt so much." She gazed into Jack's eyes. "Gerald had let me down, but it wasn't a thing of his doing. I don't understand why anger has to be part of grief, but it does." She looked away then, shy again. "I don't pretend to understand it."

Jack sat back and contemplated his hands for a moment and then went to the window again. He shoved his hands deep into his pockets. "Adrian always was a spendthrift," he admitted, "a care-for-nobody. I've spent half my life following behind him and shoveling up the residue. Why should it bother me now? Maybe I've turned him into something he isn't. People have a way of looking better and better from a distance, especially when one's own circumstances are far from sanguine."

She could only agree, thinking how in moments of stress she longed to be back in Sir Matthew Daggett's house, where no heroic efforts were ever expected of her.

Like the summer rainstorm, Jack Beresford's moment of anguish passed. He managed a lopsided smile. "If I'm a wise man, I will appreciate what I have," he said, almost to himself. "Perhaps I'll learn to polish my pianoforte, even if it is never tuned."

She nodded. He turned to look at her. "Just don't . . . don't leave me right now. Coming home is harder than I thought. I know you have to return to Chalcott, but not now, please."

"No, not now," she agreed. "Not now."

Chapter 15

ꝏ

NOT NOW" BECAME "NEXT WEEK," and then the week after. As early summer flowered and deepened, no week was the right week to leave.

Alice Banner left, following a note from Lady Daggett, reminding her that she was to return to Bramby Swale and help prepare Amethyst for the coming London Season.

"I do not wish to go, Onyx," she said as she packed. She straightened up from her task and looked at her charge. "Although I do not think that you need me anymore, my dear."

Onyx thought a moment and then nodded. It was true.

She made her own decisions and kept her own counsel now. She might have been nearly twenty-three and on the shelf, but at last she knew she was a woman, and Alice Banner's work was done. Onyx also knew that she would miss her companion. Even more than that, she knew Emily would suffer the loss of Alice Banner.

The thought was unspoken, but Alice understood. "When I am gone, if Lady Sherbourn should require my services, please tell her she only needs to write to me and I'll come."

The two women embraced. "I'll tell her, Alice. Have a safe journey," Onyx said and left so Alice would not see her tears.

There was no time to mourn the loss of Alice Banner. Almost before Onyx was aware of it, Sherbourn reached out and enfolded her in its generous embrace. Each night after she said her prayers and lay down to sleep, Onyx thought about her growing attachment to the place and the people. She would tell herself that in the morning she would have to remind them all that everyone was managing well and did not strictly need her anymore.

But every morning as she hurried down to breakfast, there would be Jack Beresford, sitting as he always did, his long legs stretched out in front of him, his body relaxed, his mind busy with things for her to do. She could not tell him no. She was not sure that he would have listened to her if she had reminded him that her marriage was only weeks away.

Dr. Hutchins's assessment of Adrian Beresford was on the mark. Lord Beresford would never be released from his addiction to morphine, even though he was alert now and eating again. His system craved the morphine, and as the days passed and the pain increased, it was his solace. After each visit, Dr. Hutchins would walk in the gardens with Jack and Onyx, listening to them, reminding them of what was to come.

"I do not believe Lady Sherbourn hears me," he said as they walked slowly among the blooming sweet peas.

"She does not," replied Jack. "She sees that he is alert and eating, and truly looking less wasted, and she . . . thinks what she will."

"It is entirely natural, but then the burden falls on you two," the doctor replied.

"We can bear it," Jack said.

Yes, we can, Onyx thought. *We could not bear it alone, however. I cannot leave Jack. Not yet.*

"And how, sir, are you?" Dr. Hutchins asked.

"I don't sleep on that arm yet, but I am much better," Jack replied.

Only someone who sees him occasionally would even have asked, Onyx thought. She derived a secret satisfaction watching Jack Beresford eat his steady way through every meal the serving maid set before him. The starving man with the gaunt cheekbones who had saved her life—or at least her virtue—on the highway had disappeared under the weight of several well-placed pounds and ounces.

He was outdoors every day, usually on horseback, overlooking the labor of the men of Adrian's estate. Emily was aghast the afternoon he came into Adrian's room with his clothing soaked and smelling of sheep dip, but Onyx only laughed and tossed him a towel from Adrian's closet. Lord Sherbourn went so far as to comment, "Some of us truly throw ourselves into our work."

As he dried his hair off and put the towel around his neck, Jack had looked at them and flashed his famous smile, the one they saw more and more frequently. "I can't help it, dear brother. Being bailiff seems to suit me right down to the ground."

"To each his pleasure," Adrian had replied and then laughed in that hissing way of his, the way he laughed to keep from hurting himself, when Jack flicked him with the towel.

Onyx knew that Jack was stronger the morning he came up behind her in the hall, grabbed her about the waist, tucked her under his good arm, and ran with her to the curving driveway, where his horse was waiting. She shrieked and laughed the length of the hallway and was still laughing when he set her down by the door.

"I just wanted to see if I could do it, Onyx B," he explained. "You're in serious danger now." He swung into the saddle, blew her a kiss, and jumped his horse over the fence into the haying field. She stared after him while Albert forgot his training and laughed out loud, and Chalking looked on, his lips twitching.

"Albert, laughing only encourages him," Chalking said when he was under complete control again himself. "Remember when he was a child?" He paused a moment to reflect. "Of course you do not—you were a child then too."

Onyx picked up her hairpins from the floor and tucked them back into her disheveled chignon. "Chalking, it's good to have laughter around here." Adrian was calling for her, demanding to know what was going on. She hurried to tell him.

"Not now" is going to turn into forever if I don't leave right now, she told herself that night in bed. Her dreams were restless ones, wild ones, dreams that made her blush, and Jack Beresford figured in all of them. She filled herself with resolve, but it vanished every morning over breakfast with Jack Beresford. All he had to do was look at her, smile, and say, "Onyx. I have a little task for you today. But only if you have time . . ."

She rescued kittens from the stable, climbing the rickety ladder while the coachman held it steady and looked the other way when she came down with her dress full of mewing babies. And then it became her task to feed the poor motherless things, sitting cross-legged on the floor by Adrian's bed and then transferring the kittens to his lap, where they purred and slept.

When the kittens graduated to pabulum and Emily took over, there was the matter of hiring a cook that fell to her. "I can't do that, Onyx," Jack told her over breakfast of burned toast and overbaked egg. "I wouldn't know how to go about it. And Emily? Onyx, really. Do this little thing for me."

And Onyx did; her reward was Jack's sigh of pleasure after the evening meal and Adrian's better coloring.

"You are a woman of considerable competence," Jack said one evening.

She looked up from the letter she was writing to Andrew Littletree. It was a letter long overdue, considering that he wrote to her every week without fail, adjuring her to follow Christian principles and then reminding her what they were, as if she had never gone to church or cracked open a Bible in her life.

"What?" she asked, eyeing him suspiciously. He burst into laughter, holding up both hands to ward off her irritation. "No, no, I mean it! And I mean nothing by it!"

She put down the pen. "Jack Beresford, you are a great rascal, and you know it."

"Hear, hear," said Adrian faintly.

"I merely said that you are a woman of great competence," said Jack again in an aggrieved tone.

"And that has always been the prelude to another request," she responded, wondering what evil demon was nudging her on. It was guilt, pure and simple. She never dreamed about Andrew Littletree. "Is it kittens this time? Another cook? New wallpaper in the parlor? Are the underhousemaids quarreling?"

"My, we are testy," Jack said. He smiled at her in that maddening way of his that only became another source of irritation to her.

She felt a spark of real anger then, and the unexpected emotion almost took her breath away. She felt helpless and foolish. *How can I lash out at this dear man?* she thought. *What is the matter with me?*

"I'm sorry," she said and folded her hands across the writing desk. She had been feeling out of sorts for days now, berating herself because she did not have the spirit to leave this place, angry with herself for turning her dreams over to Jack Beresford each night.

It wasn't something she could tell anyone. How could she explain to these people that she was dreading her return to Chalcott and marriage to the Reverend Littletree? In the spring, before Jack Beresford had thrown his pistol to her and she had shot the highwayman, the whole idea had been possible. She had known that there would never be a better offer than that awarded her by the condescending vicar. In ways both overt and subtle, lest there be any mistaking the message, Lady Daggett had let her know that someone of her background could look no higher.

And now Andrew Littletree had taken up where her mother had left off, digging and jabbing, reminding her, admonishing her, scolding her. Onyx was beginning to dread the arrival of the postboy with the mail. And she did not know how to tell anyone how she felt. No one had ever been interested in her feelings before. She was tired of "gratitude" and "duty." Maybe she was just tired.

Onyx covered her face with her hands for a moment and then rose quickly to her feet. "I'm sorry," she said again and fled the room.

She wanted to be alone, to try to make some sense out of the strange restlessness she felt, the curious wantings that made marriage to Andrew Littletree seem a pale shadow indeed. No one at Sherbourn could possibly understand how she felt—most assuredly not Jack Beresford. In a mysterious way that she still resolutely refused to consider, he was the author of her misery.

Onyx walked to the bench at the edge of the formal garden and plunked herself down. She wanted to indulge in a cleansing bout of noisy tears. She had no idea what she wanted.

She knew Jack would follow her, and she bitterly regretted her hasty exit from Adrian's room. She rested her chin on her hands. Lady Daggett would never know her. She had changed from a pliable ghost who did what she was told, into . . . What? *I don't even know who I am anymore*, she thought.

224

"May I join you for a moment?"

She didn't move or even look up, but Jack sat down beside her.

"What's troubling you, Onyx?" he asked at last.

"I don't think it's anything I want to talk about."

He moved closer to her but made no attempt to put his arm around her. She could still savor the spicy fragrance of bay rum about him, even though it had been hours and hours since he had shaved and ridden out on his daily supervision of the estate. *How tired he must be,* she thought, with another pang of guilt. *There is Adrian to worry about, and Sherbourn, and now I am a trouble.*

"If it is something you wish to talk about sometime, only ask me, Onyx," he said finally.

Before she realized what he was doing, he turned toward her and clasped her face carefully between his hands, looking into her eyes, searching them. "I know you are a believer in small pleasures, but at some point you may have to fling open your arms and grasp something greater. I only hope your courage won't fail you."

She wanted him to kiss her. She wished he would, but he did not. He only touched his cheek to hers for the smallest moment and went back into the house.

Onyx sat on the bench and watched the lights in the house wink out one by one. The candles in Adrian's parlor burned the longest. Jack was probably sitting with him, waiting for the dose of morphine to glaze his brother's eyes and then staying a few minutes longer.

Emily's light was out quickly, and then Jack's. Onyx got up and went in the house, closing and locking the front door. The stairs were familiar to her in the dark. She had been up and down them many times to check on Adrian.

The lamp by her bed had been lit, and the covers turned down. Onyx smiled to herself. Emily was such a dear. She undressed quickly and pulled on her nightgown. There on the pillow, in the edge of the shadows, was a note. The handwriting was the bold scrawl she remembered from an earlier letter. Her fingers trembled as she picked it up.

> *Forgive me. I would like to say more, but for now, just forgive me.*
> *Jack*

She clutched the note to her and hopped into bed, pulling the covers over her head. The tears came then; they were not the noisy, gusty kind she used to cry, but the silent tears that slid down her face and did nothing to ease the pain.

Onyx slept toward morning and woke later than usual, the note still tight in her hand. She read it again and put it under her pillow. She dressed hurriedly and ran down the stairs and into the breakfast room.

The room was empty except for Albert, who was clearing off the table. He looked up when she made her precipitate entrance, blandly ignoring her expression of deep dismay when she saw that Jack Beresford was not in attendance.

"Onyx, there you are!"

Emily came into the room, pulling on her gloves. "You must come with me." She accepted the cup of tea that Onyx handed her, took a sip, and put it down. "Jack told me something this morning over breakfast that he had forgotten to tell us last night. One of the crofters' wives has a new baby. Imagine! Jack said that he came upon the happy event yesterday when he stopped for a drink of water. Jack told me quite solemnly over tea and toast this morning that I needed to remember my role as Lady Sherbourn and take something to the family. Cook has prepared a basket. Do say that you will come with me."

"I should not, Emily," she protested. "Who will watch Adrian?"

"Adrian sleeps now, and Chalking is with him," Lady Beresford replied as she took Onyx by the arm. "Jack told me that you could come. He said you need to get out more yourself."

"I suppose he is right," Onyx said. Her eyes burned from lack of sleep. "I will come. Let me get my shawl."

An hour later, she had to agree that Jack was right. The day was beautiful, the wind teasing and light, the sky that particular shade of cobalt that she was coming to call "Yorkshire blue" in her mind. The lambs in the pastures on both sides of the road had outgrown their stiff-gaited, lopsided air and frisked about with complete assurance that they would not fall. Onyx sniffed the air appreciatively. The fragrance of drying timothy grass from the hay fields was everywhere. In fact, the road was cushioned by dried timothy that had fallen off the hay wains.

Emily drove the gig, sitting upright, her hands held high and light. Onyx admired her skill and told her so.

"Adrian taught me to drive," she replied. "He is . . . was such a whip. You only had to promenade on Rotten Row at five of the clock on any afternoon and see what an admiring crowd he could collect when he was handling the ribbons of his phaeton."

"You must have been an excellent pupil," Onyx said. She wanted to curl up under a tree and sleep. The training derived from boring hour after boring hour at Lady Daggett's whist table came to her rescue, and she stayed awake and managed to maintain an alert expression.

The baby was properly cooed over by Emily, who flitted about on light feet, patted each towheaded child on the head, and distributed jellies and fresh fruits from the Beresford succession houses. She shook her head at holding the baby, however. "Dear me, no," she said in her soft way when the woman in bed held the infant up to her. "I would not know what to do!"

Onyx took the infant and cuddled her, admiring the fine way her lashes curled and the way she rooted toward Onyx's finger when she touched her cheek.

"Onyx, you are good with babies," said Emily. "Think what an unexceptional mother you will make."

"Lady Sherbourn, how you run on," Onyx teased in turn. She handed back the baby, watching with a smile on her face as the mother began to nurse the baby.

Onyx looked about the room. It had been newly plastered. Outside, the workmen were putting the final touch on the thatching.

"Major Beresford has seen to it," the crofter's wife explained. "He has been riding all about, so my man tells me, seeing to what needs doing."

Emily was quiet. She went to the doorway and stood looking out, as if propelled there by the woman's words.

After another smile at the baby, Onyx collected the empty basket, said good-bye, and left the cottage. Emily was already in the gig. She was silent for much of the ride home. As Sherbourn came in view, she sighed and slowed the gig, her hands expert on the reins.

"Adrian should have seen to all that," she said.

"Oh, Emmy," said Onyx, unconsciously copying Jack's pet name. "You know that he could not! He has been so ill."

"He could have . . . before." She sighed. "I fear Jack was right when he exclaimed about our improvidence."

"He said nothing of the sort," Onyx said.

"Well, it is true. There are things I would do over, if the chance should come. Onyx, do you think it will? Tell me truthfully, please."

Onyx was silent a long moment. "No, I do not," she said quietly. "Emmy dear, you already know that. You just need to face it now."

There was nothing more to say. Emily's back was still straight and her hands properly fixed on the reins, but her eyes were bright with unshed tears. When they reached the drive, she handed the reins to the waiting groom and went directly inside. Onyx heard the door to the parlor close quietly behind her.

Onyx followed slowly. The day had been so beautiful. She did not wish to go indoors again. She stood on the bottom step, hesitating, when Albert appeared in the doorway, his face as white as paper. She stared at him as her heart leapt in her throat and stayed there.

"Albert! Is it Adrian?"

He shook his head.

"What, then?" she asked in alarm as she hurried up the steps and into the hall.

"Miss Hamilton, perhaps I speak out of turn . . ."

"Albert, what?"

"It is Major Beresford, Miss Hamilton. A letter came."

"Albert, please!" she said as she removed her bonnet. "Where is he?"

"The library. I do not know that you should go in there, Miss Hamilton," Albert admonished. "The letter was from the Reverend Andrew Littletree. I don't know what it was that set Major Beresford off, but, miss—"

She was already running down the hall before he finished his sentence. The library door was closed. She knocked on it. "Jack?" she called. And then, louder, "Jack?"

There was no answer. She opened the door. Jack sat in the wing chair by the unlighted fireplace. He sat as ramrod stiff as Emily Beresford in the gig. There was nothing about him that looked familiar except for the hunted look she had dreaded in their early association.

The room reeked of brandy. She put her hand to her nose and looked at the opposite wall. The wallpaper was soaking with brandy, the floor puddled and littered with shards of broken glass.

He looked at her then, his eyes expressionless with that inward-turning pain she had hoped never to see again.

Her eyes questioned his. Although he gave her no permission, she came into the room and shut the door behind her. She nearly sat down in the little French chair by the door, but thought better of it. *If I sit there, he will know I am afraid of him. And then how will he feel?* She came into the library and sat down in the chair opposite him.

He regarded her as he poured out another drink, looked at it, swirled the brandy around in the glass, and then threw it with great force against the wall. She flinched but made no sound.

The letter lay in his lap. It had been crumpled and then smoothed out and then torn in half.

"Jack, please," she said as he poured another glass. He set down the bottle with a thump.

"I told myself when I left Spain that I would never drink another drop," he told her. "And I will not."

She got up and took the bottle from him, corking it and putting it back on the sideboard. She sat down again and looked at the letter in his lap. The silence seemed to stretch on for hours.

"It was my turn for a letter from Andrew Littletree," he said finally and threw the glass of brandy in his hand against the wall. He spoke slowly, enunciating his words carefully, as if every muscle in his body was just then involved in speech. He yanked the letter off his lap and crumpled it again, throwing it against the wall to join the tide of brandy and broken glass.

"He prosed on and on about my 'condescension.'" He spat the word out as Onyx winced. "My condescension in allowing you to serve such Christian duty in my home. My home . . . I can quote it . . . 'surely one of the most illustrious seats of peerage in the kingdom'! How the man rattles on!"

Jack leapt to his feet, his agitation bubbling over. "He hoped that you were deporting yourself in proper fashion, doing nothing to call attention to yourself, remembering your station." He wheeled around and knelt in front of her chair, his hands on her legs. "Does he write to you like that every week?"

She nodded, afraid to speak.

He bowed his head in her lap. "And you take that, week after week? No wonder you were out of sorts the other night."

"Andrew can be . . . kind." She faltered. She wanted to put her hands on Jack's head, to touch him, but she was afraid.

"Kind!" he roared, animated again and on his feet. "I'll tell you how kind he was in that letter! Do you know what he had the nerve to write?"

Onyx shook her head. Her heart was thumping so loud she could hear it all over the room.

"He thanked me for saving your virtue on the highway, and then . . ." He went to his target wall and scooped up the letter again, opening it. ". . . and then in a perfectly chatty tone he informed me that if, by chance, I had not got there in time, he would have had no recourse but to . . . to, here it is: 'deny to wed and turn you back to the mercies of your foster parents'! How it galls me!" He read on. "'Surely such a deflowered woman, although blameless in the eyes of God, would scarce be the proper vessel for a man of the clergy.' Good enough for God but not for him! And you're going to marry this bag of hypocrisy?" He knelt by her again and gripped her tight around the waist. "Well, have a care you do not break your leg, Onyx Hamilton. He'll probably shoot you!"

"A woman must marry," she said in a low voice. "And I can do no better, given my circumstances."

"Your circumstances!" he roared. "I tease and flirt, and propose, and you have not heard a word I have said because you are being so blasted noble!"

She shook off his hands and rose to her feet. "You dare not marry someone like me!"

"Sit down," he commanded. "I am not done."

"Oh, yes you are!" she flung at him. She was shaking so badly that she had to hold her hands together.

"No, I'm not," he raged and pushed her back in the chair. "The people around you have been so careful to remind you day after day, year after year, of the circumstances of your illegitimate birth. Did they never once give a thought to the sweetness of your spirit, your unfathomable courage, the tender care you take of others? I could go on, but why? When are you going to wake up? Are you going to wish for something better when it's too late?"

"Oh, stop!" she said, trying to rise. "I don't have to listen to this!"

"Yes, you do. Sit down." His voice was calmer then. "I would do anything for you, but the only person who can convince you of your own worth is Onyx Hamilton."

He sat down again, exhausted. "And that is why I am angry." His voice was uncertain, clouded over with emotion. "And that, dear lady, is a lie too. I am afraid. If Andrew Littletree were to walk through that door, I would tear him apart with my bare hands." He managed a shuddering laugh but would not look at her. "You were in some danger when you came through that door a few minutes ago."

"No, no," she whispered.

"I have done it before." He stared at his hands. "Sometimes they still look red." He closed his eyes. "I had thought that the war was over for me. I could return to Sherbourn and put it out of my mind. But all it takes is one priggish letter from your future husband, and I would become the murderer I was before, because that is what we were in the 45th. I might as well be back in Spain."

He got up again, and before she could stop him, he threw the entire bottle of brandy against the wall, where it shattered like an explosion. "When is this war going to end?" he shouted.

"Perhaps when I leave," Onyx said. "I am going to pack."

"No." His voice was steady again. "I am going." He noticed her horrified expression and managed a faint smile. "Only as far as Leeds. I have to get away for a few days. I've turned this household on its side this afternoon. Shame on me for doing that."

"Jack, no. None of us . . . understood."

"You did," he said, calm once more. He went to the wall and stood there staring at the destruction he had caused. "I've heard you outside my room on those nights when I summon my boys for that final assault on the walls at Badajoz. Or maybe it is Ciudad Rodrigo, or La Albuera, or Salamanca. There are so many that I cannot remember them, each one more bloody than the one before. Onyx, I dream in red."

He passed a shaking hand across his eyes. "You understood. But then I got myself so busy making myself useful, making everyone comfortable, going about the estate like an Eager Edgar, being all things to all people. 'Oh, look at Major Beresford. He's going to save this estate from the folly of his brother.'"

He looked at her, fixing her with a stare that left her shaken. "I'm still so angry at him. How dare he die and leave me with this mess when I'm in worse shape than he is? And no one understands but you, and now I've scared you. Forgive me, if you can."

With a cry, Onyx threw her arms around him, pulling him as close to her as she could, her hands pressing hard against his back. He did not raise his arms to embrace her, but he bowed his head against her shoulder.

"Adrian is dying, and so am I," he murmured. "The only difference I can discern is that I have to keep hauling my body around for another forty or fifty years."

He freed himself from her grasp and left the room. Onyx stayed where she was. The house was absolutely silent. No one moved except Jack. She heard him mount the stairs two at a time, slam around in his room, and then run down the stairs again and out the door. Soon she heard his horse's hooves on the gravel drive.

Onyx wasn't sure that she could even put one foot in front of the other and get herself out of that awful room. She shook all over. Like an old woman, she hobbled into the corridor and down to Adrian's parlor. She entered without knocking, sank down on the floor by Adrian's bed, and rested her head close to his hand.

Slowly Adrian raised his hand and placed it on her head.

Emily sat on his other side in dumbfounded silence.

"He's going to Leeds," Onyx said at last when she was able to connect thoughts to words again. "Should I go after him? I will, you know. What's in Leeds?"

"No, Onyx, m'dear, don't go after him. Let him be." Adrian's voice was drowsy. "Jack always comes about."

"You don't perfectly understand, Adrian," she began.

"I . . . understand enough. I claim the attention around here because I am so visibly dying. Hush, Emily, you know it is true. Have a little countenance. Jack's troubles are not so visible." His hand slipped off her head. "War must be a devilish business," he said, his words a jumbled muddle as the pain let go and the morphine took over. "Must be even harder than . . . finding good boot-blacking." He rolled his eyes toward Onyx. "Oh, haven't I led a decision-filled life?" He looked at Emily then, and his eyes filled with tears. "And when will it end? For me? For him?"

Chapter 16

❧

THE NEXT FOUR DAYS WERE END-less. Onyx knew that whatever came after this time spent waiting would hold no candle to the anxiety she felt each night as she closed her eyes and worried about Jack Beresford. Each morning she woke and worried about him. As she conversed each day with the cook and supervised the work of the grooms and maids, Jack was never more than a thought away.

Her concern took her into his room one quiet afternoon when Adrian drifted in and out of consciousness and Emily sat and knitted at his bedside, her face set and drawn.

Onyx went into Jack's room quietly, somehow half-expecting to see him lying there. His presence was almost palpable. She smiled to herself. *Jack, you're so untidy*, she thought as she gathered up towels and grimy clothes into a pile by the door, wondering why the servants hadn't tidied the room, and at the same time, grateful they had not. It gave her something to do for him.

Humming to herself, she cleaned out his shaving brush, wiping the soap spots off his mirror, curious that his toothbrush was stuck, handle down, in the soil of a potted plant. If ever a man needed a valet, it was Jack Beresford. Or a wife.

She picked up a towel off the washbasin, raising it to her face to smell the bay rum, and then wiping her eyes with it when she cried.

"This will not do, Onyx B," she told herself. The window was open. She went over to close it and looked down at the birdhouse. She lifted off the roof, and two baby wrens stared back at her and then opened their beaks to the point of dislocation.

Obviously this was a second family. Jack had told her about the first clutch of eggs he had seen there in early summer. She rested her elbows on the windowsill, noticing that the babies did not seem afraid of her. Jack had obviously made them his pets.

She wished she had something to feed them. Tipped on the sill was a small box of dirt. Her eyes alive with laughter, Onyx dug around gingerly until her fingers encountered a worm. She lifted it out and into the mouth of the first wren, found a second worm, and then a third.

"Jack, you must have been a dreadful trial to your mother," she said as she concluded the meal and put the roof back on the birdhouse. *Only think how much fun you will be with your own children*, she thought, not brave enough to say such things aloud.

She looked around for something to wipe off her fingers and picked up a small piece of material by Jack's pillow. She looked closer. It was a tiny scrap of her wedding-dress silk. He had kept it all these weeks. She put it back on the pillow and left the room.

Dr. Hutchins came every day now. He was angry to find Jack gone, but his irritation lessened after Onyx walked with him around the garden, talking to him, appealing to him.

"I've never been to war, Miss Hamilton," he said

finally as she stood with him. "I have seen wounds of war, though. Several recuperating soldiers came to Harrogate for the waters. It's really no talent to cleanse and splice the body back together. The mind is another matter."

He touched her shoulder. "But until Major Beresford returns, it falls on you, Miss Hamilton. Adrian hasn't long. I'm amazed how quickly he has gone downhill just since my last visit. I am not sure I understand why, entirely."

She did not enlighten him. That was a matter between her and Adrian Beresford, Lord Sherbourn.

Lord Sherbourn had brought the issue to her attention the day after Jack left. Emily was out of the room when he motioned to Onyx to come closer. She did, kneeling on the floor by his bed.

He was a long time in speaking. His skin was now quite yellow, his eyes even more vividly so. His ghastly deterioration had ceased to frighten her. She tended to his sores and kept him clean with no word of complaint, but she knew, as she knelt by his bed and rested her cheek on the edge of the mattress, that he had something important to tell her.

"I have lived a pretty frippery life, m'dear Onyx," he said at last, "but it has been fun."

She waited through the long pause as he gathered his scattered thoughts into one cohesive unit. "Never gave much thought to Jack. He always did what I asked. Nothing was too hard, no request, however odd, too out of range. He was always so easy to use."

She thought that he had gone to sleep and raised her head. He was looking at her and moving his mouth, but no sound came out. She touched his arm and he closed his eyes, pulling each thought together again.

"It is time . . . I did a good turn for Jack."

"And what will that be, dear Adrian?" she asked. "Can I get you something?"

"Put the morphine where I can reach it. I'm going

to peg out." He calmly watched the look of anguish cross her face. "For Jack. It's time his needs were . . . tended to. Mine have gone on long enough, wouldn't you agree?"

He had not said so much in a week, and the effort clearly exhausted him. He was waiting for an answer.

She shook her head. "I won't do it, Adrian. Think how it would devastate Emily. And Jack." She rose up on her knees and kissed him, resting her head lightly on his chest. "But I love you for what you have just said."

"Maybe there is hope for such a frivolous fellow?"

"Oh, yes."

"But it is time that I gave up."

She could not disagree with him.

When Dr. Hutchins returned the next morning, Emily joined him and Onyx for the walk around the garden. "What are we to reasonably expect, Doctor?" Lady Sherbourn asked, her voice clear and her head high, as if she were behind the reins of her husband's phaeton.

Dr. Hutchins eyed her and then tucked her arm in his.

"Lady Sherbourn, his kidneys are failing. His liver is gone. He cannot eat anymore. Liquids form his only sustenance. Have you noticed his cough? His lungs are filling with fluid. In a week he will probably drift into a coma. He will be out of pain then, but he will also be out of reach. I can offer you no more consolation than that."

"It is enough, Dr. Hutchins," Emily replied calmly. "Pray God we can bear it."

She sent for her sisters, Lady Blanding and Mrs. Towerby, and they arrived the next day, quiet women each as beautiful as she was. Emily introduced them to Onyx.

"Onyx Hamilton," said Lady Blanding. "Such a singular name. Wherever have I heard it before?"

At the beginning of this long summer, Onyx would have blushed and drifted into the shadows. But no longer. She did not mince her words. "Lady Blanding, I am the foster daughter of the Reverend Peter Hamilton, who is the late husband of Lady Marjorie Daggett. The family estate is at Bramby Swale."

"Ah, yes," said Mrs. Towerby, "it seems that I remember the story. You were . . ." She paused.

"Found in a basket on the church steps near Bath. My twin brother, Gerald, and I. Gerald died for king and country in Spain, for all that he was as illegitimate as I am. If there is anything more you choose to know, just ask. I am not shy about these things any longer."

"Indeed you are not," murmured Emily's elder sister. They managed, by careful organization, to avoid association with each other.

And then Jack returned. Lady Blanding and Mrs. Towerby—they must have had Christian names, but after Onyx's bit of plain speaking, they had never chosen to enlarge their acquaintance—had convinced their little sister to ride in their barouche around the estate. Onyx had finished cleaning up Lord Sherbourn and was moving him back onto the sheepskin when Jack's arms reached around her. "Let me help you."

His face was right next to hers. He kissed her on the cheek. "I'll do it, Onyx," he said. "Sit down a minute. You look like a ghost."

She did as he said, watching him, holding her breath. "Jack?"

"Yes, brother. I'm here. Sorry to be away so long. I had some rather serious business to attend to, but I think things are arranged to my liking now."

Onyx could only stare at him. He looked so good, so changed from the desperate man in the library.

He glanced around at her. "Over there by the door, Onyx. There's a parcel. Bring it here and sit on the bed so Adrian can watch too."

She did his bidding without question. The parcel was wrapped in ordinary, brown paper. She brought it to

Adrian's bed. "Is it for Adrian?" she asked. "Should I open it for him?"

"It is for you, Onyx. A little token from some grateful brothers. I should have done this weeks ago, and goodness knows we owe you something for all your help."

Mystified, she tore off the brown paper. It was yards and yards of silk, beautiful silk, silk worth hundreds of pounds more than the material she had mourned on the highway. She held her breath and traced her fingers over the design of butterflies.

"I found it in Leeds in the silk warehouse."

She looked at Jack, who was sitting quite close to her, and then at Adrian. "You shouldn't have." She smiled. "But I'm glad you did. It's certainly something to remember you by."

"The proper answer, Onyx B," Jack said. "Be careful, now. There's something cushioned inside the silk."

She looked down at the silk in her hands again and lifted off the layers until she came to a hard object. She pulled aside the last of the silk to expose to view a vase.

It was Wedgwood, a lovely lavender-blue vase that would admit no more than a few narrow stems of the daintiest flowers. From its fluted opening to the perfectly formed base, it fit in the palm of her hand.

Jack took it from her hand and held it next to her eyes. He smiled and she found his smile intensely disturbing, even though it lifted her heart to see it again after the famine of the last four days.

"An exact match," he murmured. "Don't you agree, Adrian?"

Adrian stretched his lips across his teeth in a smile.

"I never dreamed of anything so lovely," said Onyx as she reached out to touch the vase.

"Nor I," Jack replied as he watched her. He put the vase in her hand again, curling her fingers one at a time around it. "The shopkeeper told me something interesting about Wedgwood. He said it's a strong pottery, for all its delicate appearance. It lasts and lasts and never goes out of style. I . . . I think there is a lesson in that."

She struggled to keep back the tears. Jack put his hand on her lips. "Don't you dare cry," he warned. "If you do, I'll have to kiss you." He leaned over to Adrian. "That will make her so mad she'll have to stop crying."

Onyx burst into tears.

"If ever I saw an invitation," murmured Adrian as his eyes closed.

Jack put his hands around her neck and drew her closer.

"Here's something else to remember me by." She closed her eyes as he kissed her. Her heart that had been in her throat dropped to her stomach and glowed there.

"That's enough of that," said Adrian, opening one eye.

Jack stopped. He winked at her.

She got up from Adrian's bed, wondering why there were little light sparkles around the edge of her vision and wishing there were some way to get to the door without having to walk there. She was sure she would stumble over every piece of furniture in the room. Her legs had turned to rubber.

"Onyx, give that silk to Emily. You probably don't know this about her, but that charming widgeon is a case-hardened seamstress."

"N-no, I . . . I . . . didn't," she stuttered.

"Onyx, don't stammer," Jack said. "You sound like I did."

Emily began the dress the next morning, unfolding it on the floor of Adrian's parlor, walking around it, shears in hand, eyeing it from every angle like an artist with brush in hand.

"I think little puffed sleeves would be best and fairly low-cut across the chest." She regarded Onyx in a thoughtful manner. "You could wear something like that well, and you won't catch cold in summer."

Onyx was only glad that Jack was off riding the estate and did not hear that remark.

"I think . . . a generous flounce that comes up to your knees would be quite the thing. It will give the silk such motion. Here I go, Onyx. Hand me the pins when I ask for them."

They were basting the dress together when Jack returned late that evening. Onyx could hardly bring herself to look at him. She had replayed that kiss over and over in her mind, and she knew that he would only have to look at her and know what unruly tumult she was thinking.

He had the good grace to spend the little time Adrian was conscious visiting with his brother. They did nothing more than sit together, Adrian's hand in Jack's, while Emily chattered to her sisters, who also sewed, and Onyx kept her head bent over the fabric.

Jack nodded to Onyx before he left the room and spoke to Emily. "Emmy dear, if you need me in the next few days, just send one of the stableboys. Private Petrie and I are fair caught up in the first harvest."

"Certainly, brother." Emily held up the wedding dress. "It is exquisite!"

He was looking at Onyx when he replied. "Yes. So I always thought."

Adrian harbored his strength in the next two days. Albert raised him up with several pillows so he could watch as Emily handed Onyx up onto a table and fitted the dress to her. She turned around obediently as Emily pinned and tucked, stood back, ripped out a seam here, supplemented one there, and pinned and hemmed. Her mind was busy with the dress, and Onyx was grateful. She blessed Jack Beresford for giving his sister-in-law something to do while her husband lay dying.

When Jack came in early that afternoon on the advice of Albert, the dress was finished. Emily had spread it out on the bed so he could see it. "And I have promised to lend Onyx my wedding veil," she said.

"Will you be married out of Chalcott?" Jack asked.

"Yes," she replied quietly. "I received a letter from Andrew this morning. The date is set for Wednesday next."

If he was surprised, he did not show it. "We'll miss you," he said.

Somehow that should have relieved her, but it did not.

He rose to go back to the fields.

"What . . . doing?" asked Adrian.

Jack bent close to his brother again. "This afternoon? The barley. Adrian, it is a wonderful crop. So is the wheat."

"Tonight?"

"Yes, I'll be back for dinner."

Jack went to the door. He looked back at Onyx and then held out his hand to her. "Come with me for a while, Onyx. You need to get out."

She followed him into the hall. "We can take the gig. Emily's sisters have left it in the front. If you don't mind a walk back to Sherbourn, I want to show you the harvest before I go on."

They drove in absolute silence. Onyx could think of nothing to say, and Jack kept his own counsel. He spoke to the horse, and they stopped at the top of a ridge overlooking Sherbourn. He helped her out, careful not to hold her too close.

"Over here. I just want you to see the view. And I have something to say to you. Something I think you'll be glad to hear."

She sat down on a rock and he sat beside her, leaning forward with his arms on his knees. "After the Battle of Badajoz, we were bivouacked in a little town near the

Portuguese border. It was Holy Week, and there was a *feria* going on, a little fair."

He looked over his shoulder at her. "You wonder where this is going? Be patient, Onyx, and quit squirming. There was a man at the fair, a *curandero*. I suppose we would call him a doctor—with all due apologies to the estimable Waldo Hutchins.

"There was such a crowd around him that I had to see what was going on. I went closer. An old man with the oddest growth over his eye lay there with his head in the *curandero*'s lap. The *curandero* took a knife, and before I had time to brace myself, he whisked that blade across the man's eye and lifted away that whole lump. It still makes me shudder."

"What on earth?"

"It was amazing. The old man sat up and felt his face, and then he said, '*Yo veo*! I can see!' Oh, there was blood everywhere, but he just kept dabbing at it and exclaiming that he could see again."

Jack stood up and put his hands in his pockets, looking out across the vast expanse toward the dale below. The wind ruffled his hair. "I feel that way, and I wanted you to know that you were absolutely right."

"About . . . what?" she managed.

"About those little things you were forever rambling over when I met you. The little joys you get. That used to irritate me about you. I wanted you to stretch for bigger things. But in the final assessment, you were right."

He turned back to her. "I just had a hard time seeing it, rather like that *viejo* in the *curandero*'s lap. My senses have been so sharpened in these last few days as I watch Adrian die, and I can only give you the credit. I'm grateful for every tiny moment with him. When he opens his eyes and tries to smile, I feel so good. When Emily laughs about something, I want to shout. The wind feels good; the rain feels good. When I lie down to sleep and the pillow is cool, I feel good. This was going to be the worst summer of my life. It has become the best." He laughed. "You must think I'm even crazier than I was before."

"No." She smiled back.

He came to her then and took her in his arms. "I love you, and I always will, and nothing would make me happier than to marry you. You don't have to answer me right now. Walk back to Sherbourn and think about it." He kissed her, and she clung to him, kissing him back with all the fervor in her heart.

He finally let go of her and held her at arm's length. He reached out his hand and touched her cheek.

She blushed and turned away.

"Better start running, Onyx. We're much too alone up here. I'll talk to you tonight."

She blew him a kiss and started down the hill toward Sherbourn. The air was cool with the coming of autumn. She whirled around, her arms out, and ran home.

The house was quiet when she walked in through the back entrance and stood still a moment to catch her breath. She heard voices in the library. She almost opened the door before she realized that the elder Tallent sisters were talking about her.

"Surely Major Beresford could not be contemplating what I think he is thinking," said one.

"Well, that would be a mistake if ever I saw one," said the other. "Can you imagine such a scandal? He would be laughed out of the House of Lords, if ever he tries to take up his seat."

"Emily is quite taken with her," said the first.

"Emily is without a brain," said the other. "It's not our place to speak, but let us hope that Onyx Hamilton is not so dead to duty that she ruins someone's life."

"And only think how the neighbors would regard their children!"

"Mongrels."

"Curs."

"I'm glad our husbands are so unexceptional, even if Mr. Towerby does fall asleep each night over his cards. May the Almighty deliver respectable men from encroaching females."

It was as if a *curandero* had cut out her heart, squeezed every drop of blood from it, and then stuffed it back in her chest. She felt her whole body sag as she leaned against the wall and closed her eyes. *I am going to die right here in the hall*, she thought.

The women began to talk of other things. Onyx tiptoed back to the door and found the servants stairway, moving silently to her room—Jack's mother's room—where she sat on the bed, holding herself together with her arms.

The beautiful wedding dress hung on the wardrobe door. She got up and took it down, folding it carefully, but leaving Emily's veil. She packed quickly, taking only a dress or two and her nightgown, knowing that Emily could be relied upon to send the rest of her clothing. In yesterday's letter, Andrew had enclosed enough money for her to return on the mail coach.

She went to Jack's bedroom, fed another worm to the birds, took a deep breath of Jack's bay rum on his pillow, and then closed the door behind her. She could hear Emily in her room, talking to her maid, but she did not pause there. She would write.

Down the stairs she went, knowing which ones squeaked and which ones didn't. Chalking watched her, the expression on his face betraying his mastery of the nonexistent butler's art. He shook his head, but she put her finger to her lips and he remained silent, even as he watched her.

She peeked in Adrian's parlor. His eyes were closed, sunken deep in his head, but she approached the bed and knelt beside it, taking his hand and holding it until his eyelids fluttered and he woke. She rested her cheek on his hand.

"I'm leaving, Adrian."

"No. Jack told me . . ."

"It's best. I know it is."

He tried to raise himself, but could not. "Come closer," he said. He made an extraordinary effort to speak. "I wish . . . you would think about yourself. I have for years. Great fun."

"Adrian, I can't. Jack would suffer far more if I married him."

"That is a great hum," he said. "Promise, nothing foolish. How is he to heal without you?"

She smiled. "It's already begun, Adrian. You'll see. Trust me." She kissed him. "Oh, I do love you, Adrian. And Emily. You have meant so much to me."

"No good-byes."

"No." She kissed him again and left the room, hurrying out the front door and onto the lawn. Chalking hurried after her. "But, Miss Hamilton, it is a long walk!"

"No, Chalking. There are hay wains driving by all the time. I won't have long to wait and will be at the crossing in time for the mail coach. Please give my best to Albert and the coachman. Oh, and the postboys too, and . . ." Her eyes filled with tears. "And you, Chalking. How I respect you."

Chalking bowed but said nothing. He was the last person she saw from Sherbourn as she started walking down the lane, her eyes wide open, on her way to the mail coach.

Chapter 17

ＯNYX HAMILTON ARRIVED AT THE vicarage on Sunday evening in a drizzle. She had wrapped the wedding dress deep inside her valise, where she hoped it would remain dry. The little Wedgwood vase was tucked in the folds of the dress. There was a place for it on the mantelpiece in the vicarage.

She knocked on the door, and Daisy opened it, shrieked, and called for the Reverend Littletree. He came hurrying out of the parlor, pulling on his frock coat, his eyes wide.

"Onyx! Miss Hamilton!" he said, too surprised to strike any kind of pose.

"I have returned," she said unnecessarily. "May I come in, Andrew?"

"Well, as to that, Miss Hamilton, I have taken up residence here. Step inside the front parlor, and I will get the umbrella."

She went into the little parlor, her eyes searching for the pianoforte immediately. It was gone. Where it had been planted in all its carved splendor was a small table covered with books and papers. Onyx could only stare at the spot as her valise dropped from her hand.

"Oh, that," Andrew said. "I could not imagine that you would have any time for such a bagatelle when we were married." He smirked at her. "I fully intend to keep you quite, quite busy, my dear Miss Hamilton."

"Oh." Dear Miss Hamilton could think of nothing to do justice to the occasion. She felt herself sliding toward the hole that she had so recently climbed out of.

He rummaged in the closet and found the umbrella.

"Here, let us cross the lawn to Chalcott, and I will outline some of the pleasures you have in store here."

"Yes." She was reduced to monosyllables after less than five minutes in the Reverend Littletree's company.

By the time they reached the bookroom door to Chalcott, Onyx Hamilton had learned that the morning after her wedding she would be busy organizing the shire's first missionary society to the millions of heathens of India. "Oh, they are in such need of salvation, Miss Hamilton. And only think, it will be your responsibility!"

She also learned that it would be her happy task to transcribe all of the Reverend Littletree's notes from a summer of homiletics into a good round hand for future reference. "I took copious notes, Miss Hamilton. Never has my interest been so captured. You will have the pleasure of learning as you write. Think of it."

She thought of it and wished herself with the heathens of India.

If Lady Bagshott was surprised to see her, she did not show it beyond a flicker of an eye and a slight drawing together of her eyebrows.

"You are dripping all over my carpet," she scolded. "And you look cold. Littletree, that will be quite enough. You can take yourself off. I will summon a maid. Goodness knows they have little enough to do here and, as it is, eat me out of whatever fortune Lord Bagshott left me. Leave us, sir."

Before a maid came to escort her into the upper reaches of the house, Lady Bagshott took her by the arm. "What of Adrian Beresford?"

"He is probably only a day or two from death, Lady Bagshott."

"And you could not see it through to the end?"

"No," Onyx replied simply. "I could not. Moreover, there are things that happened that I will not tell you, madam. They are all I have."

"Very well, minx, if that's what you choose. Go along, now, and come to me when you have something to say."

She had nothing to say on Monday but sat by the window watching the rain, wondering if it were truly possible to die from a broken heart. Knowing that it was not brought her no consolation. She hung the wedding dress in the back of the wardrobe, out of sight.

Tuesday the sky was clear, a washed-out blue that was a pale cousin to the brilliance of Yorkshire's summer glory. She took up her post by the window, situating herself so that she was positioned in a northwesterly direction. *If I look this way, I can pretend that I see him. When things become so bad in the vicarage, I can stand at the window and play my wishing game.*

But she knew there would be no more wishing game. That had died with Gerald. She would have to face that fact now.

Onyx was still at the window Tuesday afternoon when there was a knock.

"Come in," she said. She should have opened the door, but she felt disinclined to move.

Lady Bagshott came into the room. Her face was a study in composure. She held out a letter, and Onyx's heart that had been wrung of blood plummeted to the floor. Jack's handwriting was on the envelope.

"Adrian died yesterday," said Lady Bagshott. She looked at the letter. "He had sunk into a coma from which he never recovered. He was in no pain at the end."

Good, Onyx thought. *Good that one of us should be in no pain. I'm glad it was Adrian.*

"Have you absolutely nothing to say, girl?" said Lady Bagshott, her voice rising.

Onyx shook her head and then covered her face with her hands and leaned against the windowpane, crying deep, gasping sobs. Her body felt as though it would turn itself inside out as she struggled to breathe.

Lady Bagshott was across the room in a few steps. She sat beside Onyx in the window seat and held her until she was through crying. She said nothing and made no motion to caress her in any way, but she held her tight and would not let her go until there wasn't a tear left in Onyx's body.

Onyx wiped her face with her handkerchief. "Is there . . . was there a message for me?"

Lady Bagshott looked at the letter. "I don't know. Jack starts to wander at the bottom of the letter. I imagine he is under a great strain."

Oh, you have no idea, Lady Bagshott, Onyx thought.

"What does he say?"

"It's curious. Something about *curanderos* and eyes. I don't understand it. Well, I will go now. Blow your nose, and I will send up my abigail with some cucumbers for your eyes. Won't do to have bags under them for your wedding tomorrow. Won't do at all. Oh, the funeral is tomorrow too, and then Jack writes that Emily is leaving immediately with her sisters for her ancestral home."

Onyx's wedding day was as beautiful as a bride could wish for. She sat in her bathwater until it was quite cold and then dried off and pulled on everything except her wedding dress. Lady Bagshott had sent her maid to arrange her hair, plus a little necklace of sapphires. "Something old and borrowed and blue," said the abigail. "You know how Lady Bagshott loves to economize."

The maid helped her with her wedding gown and then went downstairs to dress Lady Bagshott. Onyx sat on her bed. She picked up the little bouquet and smelled it. It reminded her of Yorkshire and her last day in the meadow with Jack, so she put it aside. She went to the window and stood looking toward Sherbourn, shading her eyes and wishing for one miraculous glimpse.

And then she knew she could not go through with her marriage to Andrew Littletree. The feeling seemed to come from nowhere, and it covered her like a little shower. No matter that the Daggetts were just now driving up in their coach to the front entrance. They had spent the night at a nearby inn. No amount of persuasion had convinced Sir Matthew to sleep under his older sister's roof, even when Amethyst pouted and stormed and declared that her dress would be wrinkled past remedy.

Onyx had never done anything so disobedient in her life. She unbuttoned her dress, reaching around to the back until she was free of it and could step out.

Someone knocked at the door. "Who is it, please?" she asked, hoping that her voice did not tremble.

"It is I, Lady Bagshott."

"Then come in, madam."

Lady Bagshott swept into the room, resplendent from her purple turban to her purple sandals. She watched Onyx Hamilton remove the dress and her eyes grew wider as her color grew darker.

"What are you doing, Miss Hamilton?"

"I am taking off this dress, Lady Bagshott, and when I am done, it goes back to the wardrobe. I will put on another dress, and if I cannot escape from this place by the doors, I will climb down the vines outside this window. I will not marry Andrew Littletree. Not. Not. Not."

She stood there defiantly in her petticoat and chemise.

Her hands trembled and shook. She remained in that pose until Lady Bagshott began to rumble deep in her throat. It was the sound of volcanoes, of stage-coaches all hurtling toward the same inn, of thunder over the Yorkshire fells. Onyx stared in total amazement as it finally dawned on her that the woman was laughing.

Lady Bagshott sat on the bed and rocked herself back and forth. She held up a hand, as if to stop herself, but the wave of humor was remorseless as a tide. She abandoned herself to her mirth as Onyx watched in slack-jawed wonder.

Lady Bagshott finally gathered her wits about her and said in a strangled voice, "Oh, he was so right!"

"*Whom* are you talking about?" Onyx demanded. "I am through with this silliness. I don't have to marry that nonsensical man. I have learned enough of the sickroom this summer to command a princely wage in Bath or Tunbridge Wells, tending to the elderly and infirm."

That information set Lady Bagshott off again. She whooped and gasped until the moment faded. "I rather think you should hurry to Yorkshire and marry Jack Beresford," she said when she was able.

"Oh, no," she protested. "Think of my circumstances. How can someone who doesn't even know who her father is consider marriage to a marquess? You must be all about in your head, Lady Bagshott. I know I was thinking of such a thing, but I'm quite over it now."

"Quite?"

"Quite, quite."

"Well, let me tell you, my frippery miss. So you don't know who your parents were? What is that to anything? I know who mine were, and it is no consolation, believe me!" She patted the bed. "Sit down. I have something to tell you before you totally destroy the happiness of a perfectly decent, if somewhat ramshackle, man. And yours too, I suspect. Mercy, but you are stubborn! I wonder where you get that from?"

Onyx sat down on the bed.

Lady Bagshott cleared her throat in the best imitation of the Reverend Littletree. "You will not like this by half," Lady Bagshott said, "but how can I make amends for that? Besides, you have changed over this summer. Perhaps it will not seem so odd for someone who shoots highwaymen."

"Indeed," Onyx murmured. "How can anything ever seem odd again? Fire away, Lady Bagshott. I begin to feel somewhat diverted already."

"Diverted indeed! I hope you are sitting completely down, miss."

"Completely."

"Twenty-three, goodness, almost twenty-four years ago, my father engaged an Italian dancing master one summer to teach me the steps before I was to go down to London for my first Season." Her face softened for a moment, and then she fixed Onyx with her level stare. "His name was Geraldo Onicci. Twins ran in his family, he told me one afternoon when we really should have been dancing."

Onyx stared at her as her mouth slowly opened.

"You see, my dear, dear girl, I named you and your brother after my lovely dancing master."

"Geraldo Onicci?" Onyx repeated. "Gerald and Onyx."

"He was a handsome man with numerous remarkable attributes, not the least of which were his beautiful jet-black hair and eyes of quite an extraordinary shade of blue. Don't think you didn't give me a real start at the beginning of this summer!"

"Indeed," Onyx repeated.

"Can you say nothing but 'indeed' and fix me with that simple-minded stare?" demanded Lady Bagshott.

"Probably not," Onyx replied. "This is a bit of a surprise, you must agree."

"I was surprised twenty-three years ago, miss! You are merely astonished!" Her voice became softer then. "And what could I do? The scandal would have been breathtaking." She laughed to herself. "All my friends thought I was spending a year on the Grand Tour. Little did *they* know!"

"What did you do, madam?" Onyx asked.

"Papa dismissed my dancing master, and I spent a prodigious time indoors, miss! When the time came . . . I knew that the Reverend Hamilton was a good man. When you were born, I named you and pinned your names to the blanket. My maid carried you two in one basket to the steps of the church. No one outside the family ever knew."

Onyx put her hand in Lady Bagshott's.

"I have had my regrets, of course, but these I must live with. Lord Bagshott and I were never able to have children. I have thought of you many times over the years. And when Gerald died . . . oh, Onyx, how it hurt."

Onyx tightened her grip on Lady Bagshott. "I own we were surprised to see you at the memorial service."

"I could never have stayed away," Lady Bagshott said simply. She sat another moment and then let go of Onyx. "And now there will be no wedding?"

"I have already told you that I will not marry Andrew."

Onyx stood up and took her wedding dress from the back of the wardrobe, folding it carefully and replacing the Wedgwood vase within it. "The Reverend Littletree is about to be jilted at the altar. That is the only way, of course. This perfidy will allow him the opportunity to blame it on my misplaced ancestry and entitle him to the sympathy of the world. As for me, I care not."

"Bravo, my dear, as your father used to say. Of course, I cannot acknowledge you. Such things are not done."

Onyx only smiled. "It doesn't matter. I thought it did once, but I was wrong."

"I can serve you best in other ways, if you should chance to consider an alliance with Jack Beresford. I expect to make many future trips to Sherbourn. I imagine there will be many christenings to attend there. Mercy, child, how you can blush! Jack probably even finds that endearing."

Lady Bagshott went to the window, looking down on the people assembled on the front lawn, waiting for Onyx and Lady Bagshott to come out. "When the polite world sees how regularly the very proper Lady Bagshott visits the new Lord Sherbourn and his romp of a wife, there will be some revision of opinion among the better families. The rest you need hardly concern yourself with."

"And the Reverend Littletree?"

"My dear girl, he does not know it yet—and indeed, neither does the governing board of King's College—but Andrew Littletree is going to receive a letter informing him of his new position as professor of homiletics. Andrew Littletree will bore an entire generation of student clergymen but will, I am thankful to say, have no direct effect on the tender lives of any parish. I suspect this could earn me some heavenly credit. Here, let me help you button that! You must hurry."

She turned Onyx around and did up the buttons. "And when I have finally stuck my spoon in the wall, my dear, you will be gratified to receive a generous settlement. The estate, I fear, is entailed away to a relative of Lord Bagshott's, but what is that to anything? You'll already be long husbanded by a peer of the realm and quite the wealthiest man in Yorkshire."

"If he will have me," said Onyx as she crammed the rest of her belongings back in the valise and fastened it shut.

"He will have you. Make no mistake."

Onyx turned to look at her, almost spoke, but changed her mind. She put on her shoes. "Lady Bagshott, you'll have to advance me the loan of the fare on the mail coach."

"With pleasure. If we sneak down the back stairs, I

am sure that we will find a gig waiting to take you to the highway."

"Lady Bagshott, you had every intention—"

"I did. You know how I hate to waste anything. Especially you and all those grandchildren I am already anticipating."

"Lady Bagshott, I must know something."

"Make it fast, girl! Those people won't wait forever!" The thought made Lady Bagshott laugh.

"Why did you not say something to me sooner? And indeed, madam, you must admit that toward me you have been a perfect Gorgon."

"Yes, I have, haven't I?" agreed the Gorgon. "I suppose I wanted to see what you were made of before I spilled my budget."

She coughed, and Onyx was wise enough to look away for a moment. "You'll do, miss, you'll do!'

"Lady Bagshott, I—"

"No tears, no tears. Give me a hug. That's a girl. Now, hurry up!"

Onyx was deposited at the crossing by Sherbourn the next morning. She was stiff from sitting upright all night beside a farmer and his wife who both smelled of onions and quarreled until nearly dawn. Her head ached, and the old doubts were starting to chase themselves around in her head.

She started walking across the haying field. The valise was light and she did not mind carrying it. She craned her neck for her first glimpse of Sherbourn. The air was cool, and autumn was in the breeze. Soon there would be snow and long days indoors before the fire.

She stood still. *What if he does not want me? What if Lady Bagshott and I both have windmills in our heads?*

Onyx could not be sure, but she thought she saw Jack Beresford riding across lots toward the crofters, who were forking the last load of timothy grass onto the wain. She hurried closer and hoped it was he. Soon she was running across the field and waving her arms, taking her chances, living deep, as Jack Beresford had told her to do. She called to him, and he stopped and slowly dismounted, as if he were an old man.

He was dressed in black, and the sight of it brought tears to her eyes. *Oh, Jack*, she thought. *And you had to go through that without me.*

She waved to him, jumping up and down, and then he started walking toward her. Soon he was running, with his arms open wide.

He grabbed her and threw her in the air, catching her in a froth of petticoats and silk stockings she had saved for her wedding but hadn't taken the time to change. He was crying and laughing at the same time, and when he kissed her, there was nothing gentle about him.

"Did Lady Bagshott change your mind?" he asked when he let her up for air.

"No, I had changed my mind earlier, only she . . ." Onyx stopped. "What do you mean, Lady Bagshott? Oh, I sense a great plot here, you scurvy man."

"I did indeed go to Leeds during those four days, Onyx almost-Beresford. I also went to Chalcott for a little consolation and plain speaking from that magnificent harridan. I was treated to a most diverting tale of Italian dancing masters and twins." He let go of her long enough to bow before her. "Will you marry me, Onyx Onicci?"

"I should not, of course," she began and then couldn't say any more until he stopped kissing her. "I should rather take up a career tending the sick."

"I'm sure there will be plenty of croup and chicken pox and cuts and bruises around here to tend, my beloved," he said. "I know that motherhood must sound dreadfully tame to you after the events of this summer, but if I were the father, would that sweeten the pill just a little?"

"I wouldn't have it any other way."

He kissed her again, holding her so close that she began to wonder what the men in the haying fields were thinking.

"As I see it, we have two choices," he said. His voice sounded quite unsteady, and that seemed ample repayment for her own rubbery legs. "We can wait six months until the deepest period of mourning is over around here. You can return to Chalcott for this time. I will remain here. Or—and this is the alternative I suggest—we can go to Sherbourn Crossing immediately and be married at once, and blast the neighbors."

His hands were around her waist. "I prefer the second choice, Jack. But surely you have no license," she reminded him, and she brushed his hands down, another mistake.

He patted his pocket. "Oh, it's at home. In my riding coat is a special license. I was busy that day in Leeds."

"You were, sir. I love you."

"And I love you. Before he was swallowed whole by that coma, Adrian told me to hang on, and I did just that."

Her eyes brightened with tears as she kissed him and steered her beloved Major Jack Beresford in the general direction of Sherbourn, one campaign over, a better one beginning.

About the Author

Photo by Marie Bryner-Bowles, Bryner Photography

There are many things that Carla Kelly enjoys, but few of them are as rewarding as writing. From her short stories about the frontier army in 1977, she's been on a path that has turned her into a novelist, a ranger in the National Park Service, a newspaper writer, a contract historical researcher, a hospital/hospice PR writer, and an adjunct university professor.

Things might be simpler if she only liked to write one thing, but Carla, trained as a historian, has found historical fiction her way to explain many lives of the past.

An early interest in the Napoleonic Wars sparked the writing of Regency romances, the genre that she is perhaps best known for. "It was always the war, and not the romance, that interested me," she admits. Her agent suggested she put the two together, and she's been in demand writing stories of people during that generation of war ending with the Battle of Waterloo in 1815.

Within the narrow confines of George IV's Regency, she's focused on the Royal Navy and the British Army, which fought Napoleon on land and sea. While most Regency romance writers emphasize lords and ladies, Carla prefers ordinary people. In fact, this has become her niche in the Regency world.

In 1983, Carla began her "novel" adventures with a story in the royal colony of New Mexico in 1680. She has recently returned to New Mexico with a series set in the eighteenth century. "I moved ahead a hundred years," she says. "That's progress, for a historian."

She has also found satisfaction in exploring another personal interest: LDS-themed novels, set in diverse times and places, from turn-of-the-century cattle ranching in Wyoming, to Mexico at war in 1912, to a coal camp in Carbon County.

Along the way, Carla has received two RITA Awards from Romance Writers of America for Best Regency of the Year; two Spurs from Western Writers of America for short stories; and two Whitney Awards from LDStorymakers, plus a Lifetime Achievement Award from Romantic Times. She is read in at least fourteen languages and writes for several publishers.

Carla and her husband, Martin, a retired professor of academic theatre, live in Idaho Falls and are the parents of five children, plus grandchildren. You may contact her at www.carlakellyauthor.com or mrskellysnovels@gmail.com.